Two detectives stood back a few paces from the scene

The shorter, light-haired man acknowledged Natalie with a polite nod, while the other—

The other detective was tall and broad shouldered, dressed in a sports jacket that had seen better days and denim pants that had been washed enough times to mold his long, muscular legs just a little too keenly. His thick, wavy hair needed to be cut, his light eyes were deeply shadowed under brows as dark as his hair, he needed a shave and he was scowling at her as if she were the enemy.

As if reading her mind, the detective raked her up and down with a look so intimately insulting that she could feel the heat rise to her cheeks.

She realized that he was prepared to dislike her.

Fine. Because she didn't like the looks of him, either.

USA TODAY BESTSELLING AUTHOR

ELAINE
BARBIERI

SILENT AWAKENING

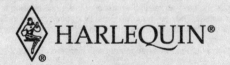

HARLEQUIN®

TORONTO • NEW YORK • LONDON
AMSTERDAM • PARIS • SYDNEY • HAMBURG
STOCKHOLM • ATHENS • TOKYO • MILAN • MADRID
PRAGUE • WARSAW • BUDAPEST • AUCKLAND

This story is derived from an actual criminal case history. The cancer-inducing drug referred to on the following pages, used on rats for research purposes, is untraceable in the human body. It remains unidentified to the general public for obvious reasons. The way this unnamed drug was utilized for revenge by a spurned lover is factual. The characters, plot and the name of the drug are fictional.

ISBN 0-373-22873-2

SILENT AWAKENING

ABOUT THE AUTHOR

Elaine Barbieri was born in a historic New Jersey city. She has written forty-two novels and has been published by Berkley/Jove, Leisure, Harlequin, Harper, Avon and Zebra Books. Her titles have hit *USA TODAY* and major bestseller lists across the country, and are published worldwide. Ms. Barbieri has received many awards for her work, including Storyteller of the Year, Awards of Excellence and Best Saga Awards from *Romantic Times* magazine. Her novels have been Doubleday and Rhapsody Book Club selections, and her book *More Precious Than Gold* was a launch novel for Romance Alive Audio. Ms. Barbieri lives in West Milford, New Jersey, with her husband and family.

CAST OF CHARACTERS

Natalie Patterson—The CDC lab tech couldn't let justice go undone. But exposing a brilliant murderer puts her on the killer's most-wanted list.

Detective Brady Tomasini—The tough homicide cop and the classy lab tech are like oil and water. So why is serving and protecting Natalie becoming the most important duty of his career?

Dr. Wilson Gregory—He's very eager to have Natalie stay at his family apartment and continue to advise the police staff.

Dr. George Minter—Natalie's boss is very proud of her. Has his pride become her death warrant?

Dr. Hadden Moore—The genius psycho's hatred of Natalie is matched by his admiration of her smarts. Which will win out?

Charles Randolph—Natalie's colleague thought he had a claim on Natalie that no one could break—until Detective Tomasini stepped into the picture.

Detective Joe Stanksy—He knows something's getting to Brady. Will his prediction that his partner's bachelor days are over come to pass?

Mattie Winslow—She invited her family to dinner—and unwittingly, to death.

Prologue

The stench of charred, human flesh had long since dissipated from the unidentifiable, skeletal remains lying partially concealed in a snowbank. Obvious to the heavily bundled, uniformed officers carefully searching the frozen undergrowth of the upstate New York Adirondack wilderness, however, was the bullet hole in the back of the weathered skull, indicating that the victim's death was neither natural nor accidental.

The determined officers continued their investigation, snow crunching under their boots as certain truths became evident.

The first was that if not for the hunter who had stumbled on the scene, the remains might never have been found.

The second was that the crime scene had been so thoroughly compromised by weather, the passage of time and wild animals inhabiting the area that the search for clues was virtually pointless.

The third was that the story of the hunter's grisly discovery would be news for a few days, but if the remains could not be identified and leads failed to develop, which appeared the most likely probability at that point, the public would lose interest in the stymied investigation.

Remaining was the most difficult truth of all—the fact that the unidentified victim would then become just another John Doe.

Chapter One

"You're wasting your time."

Natalie Patterson looked up from her microscope as Chuck Randolph spoke. Wearing wire-rimmed glasses, his sport shirt covered by a white lab coat identical to hers, he was standing beside her workstation, closer than was necessary, and he was making her uncomfortable.

Natalie frowned. Chuck was a nice guy. He was good-looking, too, if she chose to discount the way he stared at her with his sober brown eyes, and concentrated instead on his pleasant features and slender, athletic build—unusual for a man who spent the greater part of the day either peering through a microscope or writing reports. But she didn't discount it. Nor did she choose to consider that he was single and only a few years older than her twenty-four years, also unusual in her line of work at the Centers for Disease Control and Prevention. Most of the men there were either years older than she, married, or not interested in a serious-minded brunette who was dedicated to her work—or worse, were married *and* interested.

Actually, she liked Chuck. She had gone out on a few casual dates with him. He was intelligent, resourceful and had a dry sense of humor that she enjoyed. They had a lot in common, but *like* was the operative word. She had taken a step back when it seemed his feelings were beginning to run deeper.

It appeared that she hadn't stepped back far enough.

Chuck continued, "Just about everybody in the lab has already checked out those specimens with negative results, Natalie. I know New York is frustrated by the case, but we don't have an answer for them."

Chuck's tone was casual, but he was still looking at her in a way that said his feelings for her didn't match his tone, and Natalie did not immediately respond.

At her silence, Chuck frowned and prompted, "Why? Have you come up with something?"

"No, but—"

"But?"

"I don't know…something about these specimens bothers me."

"You can't be more explicit than that?"

"No, and I guess that's the problem."

Chuck said flatly, "Give it up, Natalie. Those specimens have gone the whole established route, from the New York City Police Department, to the health department and sentinel labs, and now to us. We've conducted every possible test on them here, including a PCR test for the presence of DNA unique to disease agents, just in case. It bothered every one of us when we came up empty, but we've all accepted that we've done everything possible to determine the cause of the deaths."

"I know, but—"

"That isn't what I came here to talk about, anyway." Chuck moved closer. She noted the line of discomfort between his brows as his expression softened and he said, "I thought you might like to go to lunch today. George is out of the office and we can take a little extra time."

Dr. George Minter, their gray-haired, stoop-shouldered supervisor who suffered from a severe case of myopia, had been like a father to her since she'd arrived at the CDC. She knew that even if he were in the building, he would look the other way and pretend he didn't notice if she took an extended lunch hour. But that wasn't the point. Chuck was too nice. She didn't want to lead him on.

She replied as gently as she could, "Not today, Chuck. I have to finish up here."

"Maybe tonight, then. Dinner."

"Maybe."

Encouraged by her response, he replied, "There's a restaurant on Ponce de Leone Avenue that I think you'll like. You favor Italian food and I figured that you—" He halted at her uncertain expression, then continued more softly, "It's just dinner, Natalie. No commitment involved. Give it a chance. You have to eat, and you might end up enjoying yourself." He added, "Think it over. I'll talk to you later."

Later.

Natalie sighed and turned again to her microscope as the lab door closed. She really liked Chuck. She enjoyed his friendship, but she wasn't sure how to handle the situation so they could remain friends. Despite her age, her experience with men was limited. Aunt Charlene hadn't been much help in that department. Incredibly dear but a confirmed spinster, her aunt had raised her after she was orphaned by a rare virus that struck her parents when she was eight years old. Her first serious love affair in college with a jock named Billy Martindale hadn't afforded much additional insight. It was a disaster. In retrospect, she realized that Billy never saw past the present or the physical. He didn't understand her dedication to her studies or her dreams for the future.

The sad truth was that for a while, she actually started believing Billy's incessant mantra that she was too serious, she was wasting her youth, she'd regret not taking advantage of all he had to offer her—until she learned the hard way that he had used that line too often on too many other girls. After that experience, she had sworn that she'd never let anyone get her that much off course again.

She had then turned even more firmly toward her books. She had devoted all her energy to her renewed desire to emulate her heroes, the researchers who had identified the virus that had killed her parents just in time to save her life. She'd graduated with honors and dated casually afterward. Being hired by the CDC a few years previously had been the realization of her dream.

Natalie glanced around the lab, noting for the first time that with Chuck gone and everyone else out to lunch, she was alone in the state-of-the-art facility, but she had no desire to stop to eat. The unusual appearance of the liver specimens nagged at her.

Natalie adjusted the microscope focus as she reviewed the specimens' background again in her mind.

A young woman named Mattie Winslow, living in Queens, New York, had invited her family to her house for an outdoor barbecue. By the end of the day, many of the guests had gotten sick and died, including Mattie and her husband, Gus. It was a tragic circumstance, but not entirely unusual on a hot day when the possibility of food contamination was at its highest. The only problem was that local public health officials had found the food from the party to be uncontaminated. Nor had they found contamination in the water, soil, or air at the Winslow residence. Every other possible substance was tested, including insects, plants, and pollen gathered in the vicinity. All came up negative, but even the few guests who survived the sickness suffered extensive, permanent damage to the liver that was incapacitating.

A mystery.

Yet the appearance of the liver specimens was tauntingly familiar to her.

Natalie looked at the specimen under her microscope more closely. The erosion of the surface, the peculiar deterioration—she was certain she had seen it before.

Frustrated beyond measure, Natalie drew back from the microscope. Her jaw was set when she walked out into the hallway toward the medical library.

Hardly aware that hours had passed, she was filing through yet another shelf of medical journals when she found an issue that was excitingly familiar. She leafed through it, her hands shaking with anticipation as she scanned the article she had read shortly after arriving at the CDC a few years earlier.

A British facility conducting cancer research had developed a drug called Candoxine, which their scientists used to induce cancer in laboratory rats. The lab reported progress against a particularly virulent strain of cancer. While investigating the death of one of their researchers, they had determined that Candoxine caused sudden death to humans. It then broke down and became totally untraceable except by use of a process they subsequently developed specifically for that purpose.

Natalie turned the page and gasped. Included in the article was a photo of a liver attacked by Candoxine. The pebbled surface and the degeneration were exactly the same as the specimens presently under her microscope.

Natalie stared at the article, trembling at the magnitude of her discovery.

The similarity in the deterioration of the livers was indisputable—which made only one explanation plausible in view of the negative results of tests conducted on the specimens.

The deaths at the Winslow family barbecue could not have been accidents.

They could only have been…murder.

"THAT'S CRAZY! WHO IS this woman, anyway? I don't intend to run around in circles, chasing a murderer who doesn't exist just because a four-eyed, middle-aged, lab-coated nerd at the CDC can't find a point of *natural* contamination in the liver samples and claims those people at the Winslow barbecue were poisoned. I've got *real* cases to work on."

NYC Homicide Detective Captain John "Bulldog" Wilthauer glared at his detective and growled, "Take it easy, will you, Tomasini?"

Brady Tomasini, with six years on the squad under his belt, was thirty years old, tall, dark and handsome—a point rabidly contradicted by some fellow officers who resented their wives' reaction to him—but he was definitely a man who had seen it all. Wilthauer's glare was impressive, considering the broad shoulders, expanding waistline and sagging jowls for which he was so aptly nicknamed, but Brady did not back down. He was tired and irritable. He'd been up most of the night with his dog, Sarah, a twelve-year-old shepherd-Labrador mix he had picked up as a pup somewhere on the street when he was a rookie. The canine had rewarded him with unconditional love in the time since, and he had dropped her off at the vet's office at seven that morning with instructions to do whatever was necessary, short of euthanasia, to make the old girl feel good again. He had arrived at his desk to face his heavy workload weary, unshaven, and depressed at the thought of what might be waiting for him when he returned to the vet's office that evening. He had been hoping for a few minutes to gather his thoughts on the brutal homicide that had been plaguing his partner and him for the past week, but he had known he was in for trouble the second Wilthauer left his office and turned toward him with a file in his hand. He had remained silent when Wilthauer threw the file down on his desk and started to talk. He was only too keenly aware that with every word Wilthauer spoke, a few more detectives at surrounding desks in the crowded squad room had quietly vacated the premises.

For good reason. He was pissed.

Brady glanced at his partner, Joe Stansky. True to form, Joe had reacted to Wilthauer's discourse by leaning back in his desk chair and listening in silence.

Brady met Wilthauer's glare with one of his own. He knew what this was all about. The media had given a lot of play to the Winslow barbecue incident and the city's failure to make progress on the cause of the deaths. Receiving notification from the CDC in Atlanta that the deaths were suspected homicides was a nightmare for the squad, and for Wilthauer in particular, who had had the case dumped in his lap. Wilthauer had explained that the findings of the CDC lab were being contested, and he was turning the file over to Brady just in case the findings were verified.

Just in case.

He'd heard that before.

Brady glanced again at his partner. Joe maintained his silence, clasped his hands behind his head and leaned farther back in his desk chair. He should have expected as much. His own outspoken manner and Joe's laid-back personality were as different as night and day, so much so that they were referred to in the department as the odd couple—a joking reference no one dared make to Brady's face.

Brady silently acknowledged that the dark hair, strong features, and powerful stature he had inherited from his father contrasted sharply with Joe's light coloring and slight build. He also knew that his reputation as a ladies' man—whether deserved or not—was as great a contrast with Joe's successful twelve-year marriage as their personalities. What a casual observer would not take into consideration, however, was that the thoroughness and determination with which both men tackled every case was mutual, and that although their differences in style and personality were strong, their commonsense method of deduction and the core values that were the greatest influence on their stability as partners were in perfect step, making them the most formidable homicide team in the squad.

Unfortunately, Wilthauer was not the "casual observer." A twenty-year veteran of the force, he knew how to make the best use of the talent under his command.

Aware that he was wasting his time, Brady protested, "Take it easy? You're not fooling me, Captain. This Winslow case is a hot potato, and you're dumping it in our laps like it was dumped in yours."

"It's not a homicide case, yet. The reports we've heard might turn out to be nothing more than smoke and mirrors."

"Meaning?"

"Like I told you, the CDC in Atlanta notified the British lab that developed Candoxine of their suspicions. The British lab said the claim was preposterous, because the use of Candoxine was confined exclusively to research purposes in their lab. The Brits readily supplied the testing equipment that was supposed to prove Candoxine *wasn't* involved in the deaths. When the test came up positive at the CDC with the use of the Brits' equipment, the Brits protested again and demanded that the specimens be retested at one of our labs and by one of our technicians here in the city."

"So?"

"So the specimens are going to be retested in the NYC Health Department lab, and the CDC in Atlanta is sending its expert here to observe."

"The CDC *expert*? And who might that be?"

"The lab tech at the CDC who identified Candoxine in the specimens."

"Right. That should go over big at our lab here."

"But if the test turns out negative this time—"

"Sure. You know as well as I do what the chances are of that happening, especially if the CDC has any say in it."

"Whatever happens, the case is all yours and Joe's."

"You know how heavy our caseload is, Captain."

"So?"

Silent for a few moments, Brady said abruptly, "When's this testing supposed to take place?"

"The CDC expert arrived in the city this morning. The test is set for sometime after lunch."

"Great."

"It might be a good idea if you and Stansky went to the lab to watch."

"No, thanks."

"You'd be doing yourself a favor. You could save yourself some time by finding out more about this Candoxine drug from an expert."

Brady looked at him coldly. "Which will be totally unnecessary if the test for the presence of the drug turns out negative."

"Right."

"But there's not a chance in hell of that happening, is there, Captain?"

"What happens, happens, Tomasini. Just make sure you or Joe keep me informed so I can keep the media happy."

"Thanks."

"Needless to say, everything else goes on the back burner if the test turns out positive. The Candoxine case would be first priority."

"Thanks again."

Wilthauer shrugged his beefy shoulders and snickered as he turned back toward his office, but Brady wasn't laughing. Instead he looked at his partner as Wilthauer's office door closed, shook his head, and said, "We're screwed."

NATALIE WALKED DOWN the hallway of the NYC Public Health Department, her briefcase in hand. It seemed to her that the hallways of all public institutions looked alike: paint of a nondescript color; marks on the walls and floors that were reminders of the steady traffic filing through the corridors daily; occasional chairs and end tables sporting tattered magazines in welcome areas that weren't welcoming and in waiting areas that provided little help in passing the time. Yet the familiarity of the scene did little to settle her discomfort.

Natalie adjusted the jacket of her dark linen suit and raised a self-conscious hand to her tightly bound hair. She had arrived in the city early that morning and had barely had time to settle herself in her hotel room before she had to gather her paperwork and start out for the lab. She had purposely donned an ancient pair of reading glasses that she now used only to boost her confidence. Her shower had been rushed, and the steamy New York heat that had frizzed her determined curls had defeated her efforts to appear the consummate professional by melting off her makeup and by turning her sedate, linen suit into a mass of wrinkles.

Natalie's lips tightened into an anxious line. Being a little less than average in height and with a slight build, shiny brown hair, big gray eyes and a damned dimple in her cheek that she could not seem to conceal made it difficult in her profession. She was intelligent, observant, competent, well-educated and experienced in her field. She reserved expressing her opinions until she was satisfied with her conclusions, but defended her conclusions adamantly and intellectually once they had been reached. Yet she had trouble being taken seriously because of her appearance. She had battled being called "kid" or "darlin'" and even "honey" all her life, and she was only too aware that she was now taking those problems with her into hostile territory.

Natalie silently groaned as she glanced down at the ID tag

that had been pinned on her at the entrance of the building. She was an outside professional dispatched to oversee local professionals as they did their work—a situation she would heartily resent if she were the technician who was testing the Candoxine sample here. She had done her best to avoid the situation, but George had insisted. She hadn't intended that her discovery in the medical journal and the subsequent research she had done on Candoxine out of professional curiosity would make George dub her the U.S. expert on the drug. Yet for all intents and purposes, she supposed she was, and George was proud of her.

So here she was. George was also equally resolved that no determinations would be made during the ensuing testing in NYC to negate her accomplishments or the accomplishments of the CDC lab. Besides being a point of professional pride with George, it was also a matter of funding—a double whammy.

Politics. George's pride in her did not negate the fact that she was presently a pawn in the game, but she realized only too clearly that she was a necessary pawn who needed to uphold the credibility of the CDC. She was also beholden to George for his confidence in her and his support. He deserved hers in return.

Besides, George had made it clear in his own, sweet way that her future at the CDC depended on it.

Aware that she could do nothing more about the circumstances of her visit than she could about the NYC humidity, Natalie paused at the doorway of the lab, pushed it open, then stood hesitantly in the opening as a smiling, middle-aged, female technician in a lab coat approached.

"Miss Patterson?" And at Natalie's nod, "How do you do? My name is Mildred Connors. We've been waiting for you."

Waiting. Damn.

Natalie said apologetically, "It took me longer than I

thought it would to get here from my hotel. I hope I haven't messed up anybody's schedule. I realize how important lab time is and I—"

Natalie's apology came to an abrupt halt when she turned the corner of the corridor and saw the sober-faced group awaiting her. She stiffened her back determinedly.

Mildred Connors said formally, "Miss Patterson, I'd like you to meet Dr. Wilson Gregory, Dr. Philip Truesdale, and Dr. Phyllis Ruberg. Dr. Gregory will be conducting the test. The rest of us will be observing, including these two gentlemen, Detective Joe Stansky and Detective Brady Tomasini, who are here at the request of the New York City Police Department."

Natalie acknowledged the introductions with quick, assessing glances. Dr. Wilson Gregory was trim, middle-aged, balding. He wore wire-rimmed glasses, a spotless lab coat, and surgical gloves. Dr. Philip Truesdale, sporting a well-trimmed beard, glasses, and the traditional lab coat, appeared younger and more intense than Dr. Gregory. Dr. Phyllis Ruberg, a slender, gray-haired, female contemporary of the other two, did not pretend to smile.

Natalie's gaze halted abruptly on the two detectives standing back a few paces from the scene. The smaller, light-haired fellow acknowledged her with a polite nod, while the other—

The other detective was tall and broad-shouldered, dressed in a sports jacket that had seen better days and denim trousers that had been washed enough times to mold his long, muscular legs just a little too keenly. His thick, wavy hair needed to be cut, his light eyes were deeply shadowed under brows as dark as his hair, he needed a shave and he was scowling at her as if she were the enemy. She realized abruptly that he was prepared to dislike her. That was all right, because she didn't like the looks of him, either.

As if reading her mind, the detective raked her up and down with a look so intimately insulting that she could feel the heat rising to her cheeks. She turned back toward Mildred Connors when the older woman said, "Shall we begin?"

Annoyed to have been even momentarily distracted, Natalie watched as Dr. Gregory snipped off a piece of the affected liver tissue and prepared to start.

Immediately engrossed in the procedure, Natalie observed in silence. Surprised when Dr. Gregory questioned her off-handedly throughout the test about the properties of Candoxine, the purpose it served in the British lab and the procedures used in handling it, she responded knowledgeably and succinctly. She watched him intently and cautioned him without hesitation at different points in the testing when he appeared to rush a step, explaining that the peculiarities of the drug sometimes demanded a longer response time if a more thorough and precise result was to be obtained.

Natalie took a relieved breath when the testing drew to a close. The lab became somehow stifling, a condition she was annoyed to admit no doubt resulted from the realization that she was again the focus of the Detective Tomasini's insolent gaze. Doing her best to ignore him, she turned her attention to Dr. Gregory when he said, "We'll have to wait until tomorrow for the final results, but I'd say the tests prove pretty conclusively that Candoxine is present in these samples, and that the liver deterioration of all those affected at the Winslow barbecue was caused by Candoxine poisoning. I applaud you, Miss Patterson."

"I think it might be best to hold off on the congratulations, Dr. Gregory." Detective Tomasini spoke up for the first time, his deeply voiced caution falling like a pall over the smiling group as he continued gruffly, "These results are too important for anybody to rush to premature conclusions and, like you said, the tests won't be complete until tomorrow."

Frowning, Dr. Gregory responded, "I suppose you're right. We should wait for the tests to be formally concluded, but anyone with lab experience would assume the results would turn out positive. He'd also agree that Miss Patterson was exceptionally astute in identifying the source of the contamination by recalling an obscure article in a medical journal that was years old, and that she deserves congratulations and credit for her accomplishment."

"Sure, fine, but I'd rather wait until tomorrow." Turning unexpectedly toward Natalie, Tomasini addressed her condescendingly by saying, "If that's all right with you, *Miss* Patterson."

Miss Patterson.

Natalie forced a cold smile. Detective Tomasini had left no doubt in anyone's mind what he intended to stress by his emphasis on the word *Miss*. He was putting her in her place—making sure she remembered that, with the exception of Mildred Connors, she was the only professional there who didn't have a Ph.D., an M.D. or any other laudable initials of that status after her name.

Natalie responded, "You're the homicide expert, Detective, but I think we can trust Dr. Gregory's judgment in this case where he's the expert."

"Oh? I thought *you* were the expert. Isn't that why you're here supervising him?"

"I'm not supervising Dr. Gregory or anyone else." Natalie's face flamed. "I'm simply representing the CDC to validate the accuracy of these tests."

"I guess you'll have to show up here again tomorrow, then—when the tests are completed."

"She'll be here, of course." Dr. Gregory interrupted opportunely, "There are some papers Miss Patterson will have to sign tomorrow when a formal conclusion is reached. I assume we can expect to see you and Detective Stansky tomorrow, too, Detective Tomasini." Not waiting for his response, Dr.

Gregory extended his hand toward the two detectives in informal dismissal and said, "And thank you for your concern."

Accepting his hand, Tomasini replied, "You're welcome." He nodded at Natalie briefly, his gaze almost palpable before he turned to his partner and said, "Let's get out of here."

Unable to bear the awkward conversation sure to follow the detectives' departure, Natalie said, "If you don't mind, I'll leave, too." She paused to add, "I just want to be sure you understand that my presence as an observer doesn't indicate the CDC's lack of confidence in anyone's ability here. As Detective Tomasini pointed out so clearly, Dr. Gregory, your experience and expertise far outrank mine, and it isn't my intention to pretend otherwise. If that was the impression I gave, I apologize."

"My dear…" Responding with a smile that was truly generous, Dr. Ruberg spoke up for the first time, saying, "I think I speak for all of us when I say that we understand your position and the importance of the findings here. Don't concern yourself. Everything is fine."

Back in the hallway later, Natalie approached the exit, overwhelmed by the generosity of the treatment she'd received from the professional staff at the facility but seething at the obnoxious Detective Tomasini's obvious objection to the necessity of her presence during the tests.

She didn't like it.

She didn't understand it.

She was presently helpless against it.

Damn! What had George gotten her into?

THE LAB SCENE behind them was still on Brady's mind as he slid his car into Drive and took off from the curb, cutting off a silver Honda without looking back. The image of angry gray eyes remained with him, displacing the responsive blast of the Honda's horn as he advanced through the traffic. It occurred to him in retrospect that Felicia, his very vocal former girlfriend, would say he had acted like a jerk back there at the lab.

He figured he had acted like an ass.

Brady shook his head. He supposed lack of sleep was partially to blame for his reaction to the CDC "expert," but he knew that wasn't entirely true. For some reason, Natalie Patterson had ticked him off. Maybe it was because he never had appreciated the just-graduated-from-college, know-it-all type she represented—the kind who thought everybody had to listen when she started talking. She had probably graduated from college with the idea that the world was waiting for her talents. Being hailed the U.S. expert on an unknown drug by an agency as renowned as the CDC had obviously given her an inflated sense of importance, if he were to judge from the way she watched the test and took every opportunity to caution a seasoned Ph.D. as if he were a novice.

Besides, he didn't like the way she had tried to put him in his place.

Brady huffed. Good luck on that.

Brady screeched the car to a halt at the light, giving Joe the opportunity to say, "What was that all about, Brady?"

"What are you talking about?"

"You were pretty rough on that girl back there."

"Rough on who?" Brady replied caustically, "The U.S. *expert*?"

"That's what she looked like to me."

"Not to me. She's probably right out of school, and she's already an expert on a drug that nobody else in the U.S. knew existed?" He shook his head. "I don't think so."

"What's eating you?"

"Come on, you're happily married, but you're not dead. She's a babe!"

"You're saying good looks and brains are mutually exclusive?"

"She did her best to hide her looks, like she was trying to impress somebody with her brains."

"What's wrong with that?"

"Why the need to *try* to impress somebody?"

"What's your point? Are you mad because she isn't quite the four-eyed, middle-aged, lab-coated nerd you expected her to be?"

"She did her best to look like one."

"You're losing me, pal."

"The last thing we need on this case is a pain-in-the-butt expert who's trying to prove herself by sticking her nose into our investigation."

"You're crazy, you know that?" Joe paused, then said, "You look like hell, you know. How much sleep did you get last night?"

"Enough."

Joe stared at him. "Look, I don't know what's got into you, but I'd say laying off that CDC girl would be a good idea. She'll probably be back in Atlanta by the end of the week, anyway, and that'll be the last we see of her."

"Not soon enough, if you ask me." Relenting in the face of his partner's obvious disapproval, Brady said, "Look, none of this makes sense, Joe. Candoxine? Who ever heard of it? If it was confined exclusively to research purposes in a lab in England, how did it make its way out of that lab and here to this country? And what possible reason could somebody have for poisoning a family in Queens with it?"

Joe raised his brow speculatively. "I guess you're assuming the test will come out positive tomorrow, then."

"Everybody seemed to think so."

"Then why the big speech about not jumping to conclusions?"

"I told you. That Natalie Patterson pissed me off."

"Really? You usually don't have that reaction to a hot little number like her."

"Janie would like to hear you say that."

"Come on! I'm just repeating what you said."

"She didn't look that good to me."

"Sure."

Ignoring his partner's response, Brady said, "We've got a day's reprieve before we can do anything on the case, anyway. I say we get something to eat and then try to clear up what we can on our desks. I need to get home on time tonight."

"What for?"

"I've got things to do."

"Oh? What's her name? No, don't tell me." Stansky shook his head. "Just tell her to let you get some sleep for a change."

Yeah, sure. He forgot. He was supposed to be a stud.

Brady slipped the car into Drive and took off from the light with a screech of his wheels that set Joe to cursing.

Chapter Two

"The results are conclusive. The liver specimens test positive for Candoxine."

Natalie glanced around the lab at the gathering of smiling faces as Dr. Gregory made his pronouncement. She had awakened in her hotel room that morning and had dressed conservatively in a sober brown suit that she believed made her appear older and, she hoped, more credible, yet doubts had assailed her. What if she had made a mistake when testing the liver specimens at the CDC? What if by some chance the results proved negative after all? What if Doctors Gregory, Truesdale and Ruberg decided the tests were inconclusive and challenged the results, thereby ultimately challenging the findings of the CDC?

What if…what if…?

But her doubts had proved groundless and, to her relief, everyone present appeared as pleased as she was to have the results confirmed.

Natalie glanced at the tall figure standing silently beside a lab table a few yards away. She altered that last thought. Everyone in the room appeared pleased that the results of the test had confirmed her report…with the exception of Detective Brady Tomasini.

Natalie struggled to present a composed demeanor. She had become intensely aware of the arrogant detective's presence the moment she walked into the room that morning; but then, how could she not? It wasn't only that she couldn't miss him, considering that Tomasini easily dwarfed the other occupants of the lab with his height and stretch of shoulders, or that she knew he might be considered good-looking by some women—if they were the kind to appreciate his type. Neither was it the fact that he seemed more rested, making the intensity of his surprisingly light eyes keener as they seemed to linger on her longer than necessary, or that the more conventional sports jacket, crisp shirt, tie and freshly pressed slacks he wore did nothing to tone down his intimidating demeanor. She had done her best to ignore him as his stare had bored into her back while the results of the tests were thoroughly examined and rechecked, yet she had been unable to miss his subtle, negative reaction when the results were confirmed.

Natalie's lips tightened almost imperceptibly. The man had a way of putting her immediately on the defensive, which she didn't appreciate. She had worked too hard to eliminate negativity from her life to allow it to seep back in now.

To be succinct, she didn't like him—apparently no more than he liked her.

Intensely aware that the detective had walked forward to join their group, Natalie smiled and accepted the hand Dr. Ruberg offered her. She shook it warmly as the older woman said, "I want to be the first to congratulate you, Natalie. You've done us all proud. You've proved the true professional that you are by identifying a source of contamination that we couldn't find. However ghastly the thought that the people in the Winslow party may have been deliberately poisoned, it's a relief for us here to know that there isn't a virulent, as yet unidentifiable virus out there somewhere, just awaiting the right set of circumstances to burst into an epidemic."

"I'm glad to see somebody's happy about the results."

Detective Tomasini's interjection turned the attention of all in his direction. He pinned Natalie with his penetrating stare as he continued, "I suppose congratulations are in order, Miss Patterson, but since you were so adept at identifying the Candoxine, maybe you can tell me how such a carefully controlled substance managed to make its way out of a British lab to the U.S."

Openly annoyed by the question, Dr. Gregory replied in Natalie's stead, "I think we're all agreed that Natalie's done her job and done it well, Detective, so I guess it's time for you to answer that question by doing *your* job."

"Actually, I'd like to respond, Doctor." Refusing to back down from the detective's challenge, Natalie replied with a cold smile, "In my opinion, there's only one way the Candoxine could have found its way out of the British lab, Detective Tomasini. It had to be smuggled out."

"Oh, I didn't realize you're a conspiracy theorist."

"I don't like labels, Detective. I find them inaccurate and limiting, and you've just done me the favor of proving my point. No, I'm not a conspiracy theorist, but I have spoken several times to the Director of Manderling Pharmaceuticals, the British lab working with Candoxine and, as you probably read in my report, I'm satisfied that all the necessary precautions were taken to isolate the drug. There's no way it could've been removed from the lab by accident."

"Since you're the U.S. expert on Candoxine, I suppose I have to take your word for it."

"Drug development is a risky, painstaking and expensive business," Natalie said even more coldly. "Hundreds of millions of dollars are spent with no guarantee of success, making protection of the developmental process an integral component in the successful approval of any drug, Detective, but you can check out Manderling Pharmaceuticals' procedures yourself if you doubt me."

"Oh, I believe you. I wouldn't expect that someone like you wouldn't have done your homework."

Blood rushed to Natalie's face. "Someone like me?"

"Right...an *expert*." Tomasini continued, "It just seems to me that you don't fully comprehend the complexities of the scenario you've created."

"*I've* created? I had no part in creating this scenario. The only part I played was in uncovering it."

"Oh, right again. I did fail to give you credit there, didn't I?"

"I'm not looking for credit, Detective. I've only done my job."

"I suppose."

Natalie said flatly, "Whatever. As far as I'm concerned, it's a moot point. As Dr. Gregory said, the rest is up to you."

Deliberately dismissing the detective with a turn of her back, Natalie smiled at Dr. Gregory and said, "Please let me know if I can do anything to facilitate the formalities. I won't be flying back to Atlanta until tomorrow and I'd be pleased to help."

"That's very generous of you, Natalie." Natalie noted that Dr. Gregory's smile dropped a notch in intensity when he turned to Tomasini, offering his hand as he said, "I'll send a report to your office as soon as possible, Detective. Other than that, I suppose we're finished here. I'm sorry your partner couldn't be here today. I know you both must be anxious to begin your investigation. I wish you luck."

Appearing unaffected by the hostility he had created, Tomasini shook the hands offered him and replied, "It's not goodbye, doc. I have a feeling you'll all be seeing a lot more of me around here before we're finished with this case."

Dr. Ruberg watched as the detective left, closing the door behind him. She slipped her arm through Natalie's and turned her toward the office door as the other doctors took up behind them. She leaned toward Natalie to comment softly, "That detective looks like a sharp individual to me, even if he is a little hostile. Damned sexy, too. I have to admit, if I were a few years younger, I might do my best to make him feel welcome when he returned."

Momentarily speechless, Natalie stared at Dr. Ruberg. Stunned at the unexpected twinkle in the woman's eye, she gasped, "You can't mean that. The man's a Neanderthal!"

Dr. Ruberg's only reply was an amused twist of her lips as she drew Natalie toward the door.

"WHAT DO YOU MEAN, you want me to stay in NYC for a while, George?"

The pride in her supervisor's familiar voice rang brightly over the telephone line, twisting Natalie's stomach into knots as he continued, "I don't know what you said or how you conducted yourself during the testing, dear, but it appears everyone you dealt with was very impressed with you. Dr. Gregory informs me that he's expecting some pressure from the media as the result of your findings, and he freely admits that neither he nor his colleagues are familiar enough with Candoxine to competently handle questions. He's asked if I could lend you to them for an indefinite period to function as the U.S. expert on the drug."

Natalie silently groaned. It was just past 6:00 p.m. A few minutes earlier, she had been sitting slumped on the edge of the bed in her hotel room, consoling herself that within two days she had accomplished everything she had come to the city for and that the worst was over. She was acutely aware that the worst included her introduction to the exasperating Detective Tomasini. She was somehow embarrassed to admit even to herself that the obnoxious detective had played a large part in her having been anxious when she had entered the lab for the final test results that morning, and that his infuriating attitude had almost forced her to lose control. She had been relieved to be going home, but it now appeared that wasn't going to happen.

Natalie protested, "My being the U.S. expert on Candoxine is a misconception, George, and you know it. I discovered its presence in those liver samples simply by chance."

"You're too modest, Natalie."

Ignoring George's response, Natalie continued, "I'll concede that I've been in contact with the British lab that developed Candoxine, and have since done some research on its properties, but—"

"Which means you know more about the drug than anybody else in the States does."

"Yes, but—"

"It's only a temporary assignment, dear, and it's a feather in our cap to have your assistance requested."

"George…"

"Dr. Gregory is expecting that they'll be asked to cooperate with the investigation when needed and he'd like you to be the liaison with the police department."

Natalie went still. "You mean I'd be involved in the investigation?"

"As an observer…on an as-needed basis…yes. It's an excellent opportunity for you."

"I'd be working with the detectives assigned to the case?"

"You'd be working primarily with the detective who is the principal on the case."

Oh, no! With her luck, it would be the Neanderthal.

"As I said, it's only temporary, until the lab is comfortable with the situation."

"What if *I'm* not comfortable with the situation, George?"

Natalie could almost see George smile as he said, "I've already granted Dr. Gregory your assistance, dear."

Silence.

"You know we'll all miss you here, but I'm extremely proud of everything you've accomplished, and it gives me great pleasure to see the caliber of CDC personnel recognized."

Natalie silently groaned. George was proud of her. There was nothing more to say.

"WHAT'S THIS all about?"

Leaving his morning cup of coffee steaming on his desk, Brady strode into Captain Wilthauer's office and slapped the newspaper down in front of him. The headline glared up at them:

Mysterious Winslow Deaths Suspected Homicides

Captain Wilthauer's bloodshot eyes rose slowly toward Brady as he replied, "So?"

"Who leaked this to the press? You know damned well we're not sure about any aspect of this case yet. The poisoning might've been accidental."

"You know what the chances of that are."

Brady did not respond.

"Look, we've sent the food specimens from the Winslow picnic to the lab for testing. As soon as we find out how the Candoxine was ingested by the victims, you and Stansky are on your own. But until then, the public is demanding an answer here, and the Commissioner is determined to give them one."

"The Commissioner, huh? This is a mistake, and you know it. If there is a killer out there, he's just been put on guard."

"We're going to have to take that chance, Tomasini. The Commissioner has the last word."

"That's where you're wrong. The lab has the last word, and you can bet your tail that I'm hoping the lab turns up accidental poisoning."

"We'll see, won't we?" Wilthauer smiled. "Whatever happens, we're going to eliminate a lot of speculation because the CDC has agreed to allow its expert to remain in the city to do all the testing for as long as we need her."

"Her?" Brady felt the knot that tightened in his gut. He repeated, *"Her?"*

"Meaning Natalie Patterson, of course." Wilthauer stared at him confusedly. "You ought to be glad. She'll get the media off your back by answering most of their questions. Hell, there's nobody who can contradict her here, either, considering the situation."

"Right." Brady gave a harsh laugh. "Have you seen this expert?"

"No." Wilthauer shrugged. "So what?"

"She's a babe, Captain, even if she tries damn hard to disguise it, and she's young. She's got a hell of a lot less experience on the job than those doctors at the Health Department who couldn't figure any of this out, and she's got the look of somebody who's trying to convince herself and everybody else that she knows what she's talking about." Brady leaned forward as he said adamantly, "Unless I miss my guess, those reporters will tear her apart."

Wilthauer looked up at him for a moment, then replied, "What's got into you about this Patterson woman, Tomasini?"

Brady drew back as if he had been singed.

"What happened? Doesn't she like you?" Wilthauer shook his head. "Look, Romeo, take my advice and keep away from her. If she falls flat on her face, I don't want any of my detectives going down with her."

Romeo.

"Tomasini, did you hear me?"

"I heard you. Did you hear me?"

Wilthauer's expression grew frigid. "Should I have?"

"How do you expect Stansky and me to conduct an investigation if we can't depend on the information we're getting?"

"She hasn't been wrong so far."

"That's no guarantee."

"All right, show me where Natalie Patterson doesn't have the background for this investigation, and I'll get her off the case. Put up or shut up, Tomasini. Now get out. I've got work to do."

Brady walked back out into the squad room and signaled Stansky to his feet.

As they reached the door, Stansky asked, "So, how did it go?"

"I told you," Brady replied coldly. "We're screwed."

STUNNED, DR. HADDEN MOORE stared with disbelief at the headline on the newspaper lying on the table in front of him. No, it couldn't be true! Candoxine was untraceable in the human body. There was no way an autopsy could have revealed that it had caused the Winslow deaths!

He read the article. Frustrated, he slammed the newspaper back down on the table. He had executed the perfect crime and had achieved the perfect revenge on the woman who had led him on and betrayed him—only to be foiled by yet another woman!

Mattie Winslow appeared before Hadden's mind's eye as she had looked the first time he saw her, and he seethed with a familiar rage. He had been representing Manderling Pharmaceuticals at a reception given by Parkerhouse Pharmaceuticals, the major U.S. drug company contracted to handle production of the British lab's breakthrough cancer drug when it was approved for sale in the U.S. She had been wearing a black cocktail dress that hugged her slim, faultless figure. Her eyes were the same color as her lovely hair, her perfect features bright with laughter, and her beautiful legs so long and slender that his heart had started racing the moment he saw her. She had been the most desirable woman he had ever seen.

By far the most brilliant scientist on the staff at Manderling, he was also the most extroverted in a field where introverted types abounded. Brilliant and handsome, with blond hair, blue eyes, patrician features and a carefully tended physique, he had always stood head and shoulders above the average man, both literally and figuratively. He had been a prodigy from the moment his progress was measurable as a child. He had graduated university at the age of seventeen and had earned his doctorate at the age of twenty. He was also fluent in five languages, which he spoke with no discernable accent, adding to his suitability as temporary liaison in a country as diverse as the U.S. He had been the perfect choice on many levels to represent Manderling at Parkerhouse when a meeting between the two labs had been deemed necessary.

Yes, there had been no one who could match him at the party the night he met Mattie, and he'd had the world at his feet.

He recalled the event, his heart pounding. Mattie had entered the room on the arm of a researcher from Parkerhouse whom she was dating. It was love at first sight for him, and he was determined to have her. The common fellow she was dating was no challenge at all, and in the weeks that followed, he wined, dined and charmed her. He would have given her the world if—

Fury again flooded his face with color. He had been so sure of Mattie's love, so certain that no woman, most especially the magnificent creature who had stolen his heart, would be foolish enough to refuse him when he offered her his ring. Yet she had actually had the gall to pretend to be surprised when he did, and to explain that although she was fond of him, she didn't love him the same way he loved her. Even after she had rebuffed him, he could not make himself believe she had simply led him on.

Whore!

He finally had come to the realization that Mattie was lying, that her rejection was simply more of the same type of thing he had experienced all his life—jealousy of his superior intelligence and achievements. When it came down to the wire, Mattie had known she would always stand in his shadow while standing at his side, and she had been too vain to accept that fate.

But he had loved her and had been prepared to forgive her and overlook that flaw in her character. He was certain he could make her see that she had made a mistake in passing up the opportunity to rise with him as he met his destiny.

Mattie had said she thought it would be best if they stopped seeing each other, but he'd been persistent. He'd called her until she had her number changed and unlisted. He sent her flowers and precious gifts, hoping to win her back, but she refused to accept them. Desperate to talk to her, he approached her on the street, but she would not speak to him.

He began watching her apartment day and night, hoping to catch her with the new man who he then became certain had taken his place. Neglecting his work in order to keep up his constant surveillance, he'd finally returned to his temporary office at Parkerhouse Pharmaceuticals only to be served with the restraining order Mattie had signed against him.

Humiliated, he had been unable to restrain his rage when he was served, and an appalling scene had ensued.

His fury took a quieter tack, however, when his work visa was unexpectedly revoked and he was forced to return to England without Mattie.

He was a different man after that. With Mattie dominating his thoughts and his heart broken, he became quiet and morose. Yet hope remained…until the day he learned Mattie had married another man.

It was at that moment when he awakened to the true depth of Mattie's betrayal, and his hatred for her then flowed through his veins with molten rage, encompassing his every thought.

His fury was too overwhelming for his common contemporaries at Manderling to comprehend, and they began avoiding him. His "problem" was finally brought to the attention of the board of directors, who worked within the legal system to assert that he'd had a breakdown and needed temporary confinement and treatment in a mental institution. Yet he knew that wasn't true. He knew the members of the board had simply taken the opportunity to serve their concealed jealousy and the fear that he would one day replace them.

But he didn't blame them. It was all Mattie's fault, after all.

Aware that he was powerless against the courts, but too smart to allow them a control he did not sanction, he decided to play along. He told the doctors at the institution exactly what they wanted to hear, and allowed only enough time to elapse between phases of his "recovery" for his act to be convincing.

He was released within six months.

He then began planning his revenge in earnest.

Manderling Pharmaceuticals so *generously* restored him to his former position after his release. He had access to the Candoxine once more, but that did not surprise him. The drug had been his brainchild, after all, and he was the man with the greatest knowledge of its intricacies.

He was so careful. He removed Candoxine from Manderling's stores in small amounts that would not be missed, uncaring of the time it took to accumulate the quantity needed.

It amused him to realize that, although everyone was exceedingly kind when he returned from his "breakdown," they were relieved to see him leave when he finally served his notice.

Back in the U.S., he headed straight for the little house in Queens where research had revealed that Mattie and her new husband had taken up residence. He watched for several days as Mattie and the common fellow came and went in the daily routine that had been denied him.

Deceitful witch!

He had been determined to make her pay for the misery she had caused him.

It wasn't difficult at all to ascertain the perfect moment to pick the lock and slip into the house unseen. Placing Candoxine in the lemonade Mattie had prepared for the barbecue the next day had been inspired. He knew Mattie would choose that drink over any alcoholic beverage that was being served. He also knew Candoxine was untraceable, that it deteriorated in the human body and would not be discernible under normal laboratory procedures in the remnants of the lemonade.

Then he had sat back and waited for the "natural, inexplicable catastrophe" that followed.

Mattie and her husband…dead.

The parents who had given birth to Mattie…dead.

Relatives who had doted on her…either dead or so impaired that they wished for that sweet release.

He had not been concerned by the furor that followed as public health officials conducted autopsies and tests, failing again and again to ascertain the source of the deadly contaminant. It was the perfect crime, revenge was sweet and he was free to return to his former profession in England whenever he desired.

Hadden looked down again at the unexpected headline in the newspaper. It screamed out at him in the silence of the room, and his fury heightened.

Mysterious Winslow Deaths Suspected Homicides

His perfect crime unearthed by a lowly, inauspicious laboratory technician who was being feted at his expense.

No, he would not allow it!

He would see to it that this woman did not profit from the blow she had dealt him. He was good at that.

He searched the article again, his gaze finally coming to rest on the technician's name.

Oh, yes.

Her name was Natalie Patterson.

Chapter Three

"I don't believe it."

Brady sat at his desk in a squad room functioning at full tilt around him. He was deaf to the shuffle of handcuffed prisoners being moved across the room with mumbled protests, the loud conversation at the desk behind him, the droning hum of fans intended to circulate air that never seemed cool enough on a hot summer day and the burst of laughter from the doorway at a joke not meant for tender ears. Unbuttoning his shirt collar and loosening his tie, he stared down at the report faxed to him that morning. He repeated, "I don't believe it."

Stansky looked up from the paperwork on his desk, which abutted Brady's. He said, "Okay, I'll bite. What don't you believe?"

"Did you read this fax that came in this morning from Manderling Pharmaceuticals?"

"Did it have my name on it?"

"No."

"Then I didn't read it."

"It's in reply to the fax I sent them about the Winslow case."

Stansky's fair face twisted and he groaned. "Dammit, Brady, that Winslow case is all I've heard about for the past week. We do have other cases, you know."

"Yeah, sure, but only this one has Wilthauer breathing down our necks."

Stansky opened his mouth as if to reply but then shut it abruptly, and Brady's gaze narrowed.

"Say it."

Stansky shook his head. "Say what?"

"What you were going to say."

"I wasn't going to say anything."

"Say it, Joe. You know you will, sooner or later."

Stansky paused a moment longer, then leaned across his desk to reply in a softer voice, "Look, I know Wilthauer is on our backs about this one, but I never saw you so wrapped up in a case before." He paused again, then added, "That little CDC chick wouldn't have anything to do with it, would she?"

"Little CDC chick?" Brady forced a surprised expression that he was sure wouldn't fool anyone, especially Joe Stansky. The truth was, that "little chick" had a lot to do with his interest in the Winslow case. After his conversation with Captain Wilthauer, he'd called in a favor from an old buddy in the Atlanta PD. What he'd learned hadn't confirmed his thinking.

In the first place, Miss Natalie Patterson wasn't a "fresh from the university know-it-all" as he had thought. She was actually twenty-four years old. She'd had a brush with the radical scene in college, but she had graduated with honors and seemed to have put the past behind her. She had several years' experience in the field, making her qualifications quite adequate for her job at the CDC. Her work at the CDC was more than adequate, too, if he were to believe the evaluations written by her supervisor, Dr. George Minter, a tough old cookie who seemed to have taken a "special interest" in her. It did not escape his notice, however, that Minter was the same man who'd named her the U.S. expert on Candoxine and recommended she be sent to NYC to supervise the testing of the liver samples.

He didn't know why learning about her personal association with a fellow worker at the CDC, Charles Randolph, bothered him. Randolph was highly regarded at that agency. It was rumored he had a thing for her and wasn't the type to give up. That was understandable, Brady supposed.

He'd had to face the fact that there was nothing negative in Miss Natalie Patterson's background. The only question that remained was if she was really an expert on Candoxine. As far as he could see, the answer was that she was the best the CDC had to offer.

And…it was damned hard to admit that he had been wrong.

Stansky interrupted Brady's thoughts to say, "That's right, that CDC chick. You know damned well who I'm talking about."

"Oh, you mean the CDC woman you agreed was a 'hot little number?'"

Stansky sneered. "Right. That one. You know, the same woman who tested the Winslow barbecue food this week and discovered traces of Candoxine in the lemonade."

"After both our lab and the Health Department lab tests failed to reveal any contaminants."

"So she found Candoxine when our labs couldn't. So what?"

"So you should've been at the Health Department lab the day the specimens were confirmed. You would've thought she'd won the Nobel Prize the way those doctors acted."

Stansky retorted, "Your reaction to Natalie Patterson is unreasonable, Brady, and you know it. I don't know why she strikes a sour note in your mind, but did it ever occur to you why those doctors may have made such a fuss over her discovery? Dr. Gregory wanted her to be temporarily assigned to his lab so the heat would be off them when the press came calling, and he didn't want her objecting. That was pretty smart of him, if you ask me."

Brady did not respond and Stansky said, "Just forget it, will you? What does that fax say?"

"Nothing—except that Natalie Patterson probably solved the case for us, too."

"Give me that fax!"

Stansky read the fax, then looked up. "Maybe this Patterson cookie does deserve the Nobel Prize. I'd say this is pretty cut-and-dried. This guy Dr. Hadden Moore met Mattie Winslow in the States when he was sent here by Manderling. If everything this fax reports is true, it all went south from there. He stalked her to the extent that she signed a restraining order against him." Stansky took a breath, then added, "You're right. Natalie Patterson did just about solve the case for us. All we have to do now is find out if this Moore guy is still in the country. If he is, we'll find him and Wilthauer will be happy, the Commissioner will be ecstatic and this case will be history."

"Yeah."

"What's wrong now?"

"Wilthauer wants us to keep 'the babe' informed on our progress in the case."

"Us?"

Brady stared at him.

"Who's the principal on this case?"

"Me."

"So—the job's all yours."

"Maybe not." Brady stood up abruptly. "Let's go talk to Wilthauer."

NATALIE WALKED ALONG the crowded New York street, weaving between loitering office workers determined to soak up as many rays as possible during a limited noon break on a sunny summer day. She avoided collision with determined street vendors selling all manner of wares—hot dogs and pretzels, knockoff jewelry and handbags, "rare" and used books, "original works of art" or anything else a wandering tourist or a willing New Yorker might buy.

She was neither a New Yorker nor a wandering tourist, but she should've known better than to expect to make time when traffic was at its height and taxis were unobtainable. She had finally caught a bus and had ridden as far as she could before getting off to walk the rest of the way to the police precinct assigned to the Winslow case.

She also should have known better than to wear shoes that weren't completely broken in.

Natalie grimaced as she continued walking. It was only a few more blocks, but she was sweltering in her sober brown suit, she was hungry and every corner where crowds converged to await the signal to cross a street added to her irritation.

Chuck had called her the previous evening to say he missed her and that the days dragged without her. She had been miserable in her lonely hotel room where the droning of the TV was the only sound that broke the silence. Talking to him had lifted her spirits to the point where she sincerely began questioning her former feelings. Chuck was such a great guy. When she was new and uncertain at the CDC, he had been gracious and willing to help her with every problem. There had never been a hint of condescension in his voice or mockery in his gaze—unlike her brief encounters with the obnoxious Detective Tomasini.

Natalie stared at the flashing street signal, then finally admitted to herself the true source of her irritation. George had committed her to completing all the lab work connected with the Winslow case and she had spent the past week conducting tests on samples of the Winslow barbecue food. She had known what to expect, yet the discovery of Candoxine residue in the lemonade had made her flesh crawl. With that grisly finding behind her, she had spent her spare time at the

Health Department lab occupying herself with studies regarding the ongoing West Nile virus problem in NYC and its environs. She was enjoying her participation in that important project. The work was intriguing. It took her mind off the Winslow case, and she was pleased with Dr. Gregory's reaction to her initial efforts; yet as far as she was concerned, she wanted nothing more than to get as far away from the rapidly developing murder investigation as possible.

Also, if she were totally honest, she would have to admit that she was dreading another session with the odious detective in charge of the Winslow case.

Natalie waited impatiently for the signal to change as swiftly moving street traffic roared past and the crowd built up on the corner behind her. The image of Detective Tomasini's mocking expression returned to mind, and her irritation swelled. Captain Wilthauer had insisted that her presence was necessary at this meeting so she could be brought up to date on the most recent information received on the case. He had also explained that he needed her help in alerting all his detectives to specific information regarding the properties of Candoxine that were essential at this point in the case. The call was a testament to her credibility—yet her discomfort did not abate.

Dr. Ruberg's reaction to Detective Tomasini still mystified her. She simply could not fathom how such an intelligent woman could find a man like him appealing. Tomasini was—

Natalie gasped as whispered words and a lightning fast thrust in the middle of her back sent her lurching forward into the street.

Her horrified scream was simultaneous with the screech of an approaching limo's brakes and the sharp, breathtaking burst of pain that sent her spiraling into darkness.

"A CONCUSSION…needs to rest…needs to be careful for the next week, at least…"

Mumbling and disjointed phrases in soft tones roused Natalie to wakefulness. She attempted to open her eyes, but the light hurt, and she squeezed her eyes shut again.

Finally peering out from between slitted eyelids, she saw an attractive woman in a lab coat move into her line of vision. The woman questioned, "How do you feel, Natalie? My name is Dr. Weiss. I've been taking care of you since your accident."

Accident? No. It wasn't an accident. She knew that because—

The pounding in her head started again and she couldn't remember.

The doctor cautioned, "Lie still, please. You have a concussion. Bystanders pulled you out of the path of an oncoming car just in time when you fell into the street, but you struck your head on the curb. Headaches, scraped knees and a general soreness notwithstanding, you should be all right in a few days. You were lucky. The accident could have been fatal."

"Not an accident…"

The doctor turned to a shadowed figure near the doorway that mumbled something in response. Natalie strained to see the person, but her vision blurred and she closed her eyes.

"What did you say, Natalie?" The doctor's voice again. "I couldn't understand you."

Her eyes still closed, Natalie replied with a touch of breathlessness, "Not an accident…someone pushed me."

The doctor shook her head sympathetically. "I'm sorry. Such careless behavior is unforgivable, but unfortunately all too common in a crowded city."

"Not an accident," Natalie repeated. She raised her hand to her head as a vague memory nagged. A pain stabbed sharply and she rasped, "Somebody shoved me. I felt it."

The doctor turned back briefly toward the doorway, then replied, "We can discuss this later, Natalie. You're in no condition to talk now."

Her stomach suddenly queasy, Natalie insisted faintly, "It wasn't an accident…" before surrendering to the encroaching darkness.

"WHAT DID she say?" Brady stood near the entrance to Natalie's hospital room. He frowned as Dr. Weiss approached, awaiting her response.

"She said the accident wasn't an accident. Somebody pushed her." Dr. Weiss glanced at his left hand with a look that was slightly less than professional. She smiled at the absence of a ring as she continued, "I wouldn't take what she said too seriously, though, Detective. It's quite normal to be confused after a head injury. Somebody at the back of the crowd might have pushed a little too hard and caused her to fall into the street, but I doubt it. It's been my experience that she probably won't even remember what she said when she wakes up again."

Brady shook his head. "Somehow I don't think so, Doctor. She's a very precise woman. She doesn't make haphazard statements."

Drawing Brady into the busy hospital corridor, Dr. Weiss asked, "Is that why you're here, in an official capacity because she claims she was pushed?"

"No, I'm here because—" Brady paused. Yes, why was he here? Wilthauer had called for a squad meeting with Natalie Patterson because of the fax he'd received from Manderling. They had waited impatiently for her to arrive, only to receive a phone call from Dr. Gregory when she was already an hour late, informing them that Natalie had had an accident, that she had been taken to the hospital unconscious and that he was on his way there. Dr. Gregory had said he'd let them know more about her condition as soon as the information became available.

Brady hadn't been inclined to wait.

Dr. Gregory and he arrived at the hospital within minutes

of each other to find Natalie still unconscious. Satisfied that her injury wasn't life-threatening, Dr. Gregory had gone back to his office. Not quite certain of the reason, Brady had stayed.

It had occurred to Brady as he watched Natalie lying in the hospital bed, a bruised patch on her forehead where she had received several stitches and raw, scraped palms the only visible signs of her injuries, that she looked far different from the self-possessed academic that she had sought to appear to be when they had previously met. Instead, she looked young, innocent, and so damned helpless and alone that it twisted him up inside. He wasn't sure if what he felt was guilt for the way he had acted toward her or if—

Dr. Weiss asked at his continued hesitation, "Is Natalie a friend of yours?"

"We're working together on a case." Brady considered his response further, noting the spark of interest in the striking doctor's eyes and the bare finger on her left hand, which still bore the mark of a ring. The doctor was obviously recently divorced and making certain he knew she was available. Under other circumstances, he might've been flattered enough to accept the doctor's unspoken invitation. Instead, he heard himself add, "But she's a...special friend."

"Oh. She's luckier than I thought." Dr. Weiss added with a shrug of her shoulders, "Stay as long as you like, Detective. She should wake up soon."

"Right."

Brady watched the sway of Dr. Weiss's hips as she strode down the hallway. Interesting. Dr. Weiss obviously had plenty to offer, and he had just turned it all down. For the life of him, he didn't know why.

Brady glanced into Natalie's room.

Not an accident. Somebody pushed me. I felt it.

Brady walked back inside, pulled the armchair closer to the bed, and sat down.

CONSCIOUSNESS CAME slowly and painfully. The throbbing in her head had not subsided, but the semidarkness of the room was a relief when Natalie opened her eyes and attempted to get her bearings.

Memory nagged again and fear stabbed her gut. She had been standing on a street corner waiting for the light to change when someone had deliberately pushed her into the path of an oncoming car.

Accident…accident…

Natalie closed her eyes, unable to hold back the tear that slipped out the corner of her eye as the pounding in her head increased. She gasped when a calloused hand smoothed it away and a deep voice said, "Are you all right, Natalie?"

She recognized that voice.

Natalie opened her eyes to the image that had haunted her angry thoughts for the past week. She said in a croaking voice, "What are *you* doing here?"

Detective Brady Tomasini smiled as he responded, "It's nice to know you're glad to see me." It took Natalie a moment to realize she'd never seen him smile before. The transformation was startling.

He sobered as he asked, "How do you feel, Natalie? Do you want me to call the doctor?"

"Natalie?" she continued hoarsely, "When did we get on a first-name basis?"

"When they brought you into the hospital unconscious." He asked again, "Do you want me to call the doctor?"

"No. I'm not ready for her yet."

"The nurse?"

"No."

"Your supper came while you were sleeping—a liquid diet, I think. Do you want anything?"

Natalie shuddered. "No."

"Some water?"

Natalie eyed him cautiously, "Why are you being so nice?"

"All I did was ask if you wanted some water."

Natalie swallowed with difficulty, then said, "Yes."

She was uncertain how to react when Tomasini held the cup close to her lips and tilted the straw into her mouth, but she swallowed thankfully.

A sudden thought occurred to her and she asked abruptly, "Am I dying?"

Amused, Tomasini replied, "Not that I know of."

"Then why—?"

"You were late for the meeting at the precinct, and Dr. Gregory called and said you'd had an accident."

"It wasn't an accident."

All sign of levity disappeared from Tomasini's expression. "That's what you told the doctor this afternoon when you woke up the first time."

"It wasn't an accident." Natalie closed her eyes again as the pounding in her head increased. She persisted with her eyes closed, "Somebody pushed me. I felt his hands."

Natalie opened her eyes slowly. Tomasini wasn't laughing.

"Dr. Weiss said the sensation of being pushed was probably just a result of your concussion."

"She doesn't know what she's talking about."

He looked amused again. "That's what I thought you'd say."

Natalie took a deep breath, winced at the effort, and said, "Why would somebody push me, Detective?"

"Brady."

"What?"

"My first name is Brady. In answer to your question, I

don't know." He added, "I'm not even completely sure I can believe what you're telling me now. You might wake up to-morrow and forget everything you just said."

"Somebody pushed me!"

"All right, don't get angry. They'll throw me out of here if I upset you."

The sound of footsteps turned them both toward the door as a gray-haired nurse entered. Her cheerful voice reverber-ated in the silence of the room as she said, "So you're awake at last. Good for you! Maybe this fellow will go home, now that he sees you're all right." She smiled as she turned back toward the door. "Dr. Weiss is still on call. I'll bring her back to take a look at you. I'll only be a minute."

Natalie looked at Brady as the nurse left the room. She said, "You've been here all day?"

"No, only since they put you in here."

"You know what I mean."

"Have I been sitting here, waiting for you to wake up? Yes. Why? Because when you first opened your eyes, you claimed someone deliberately pushed you into the street. For some reason, I believed you and I wondered why somebody would want to kill you."

"Kill me…" A chill ran down Natalie's spine. "Somehow I didn't think of it that way."

"What did you think?"

"I don't know."

Natalie saw him frown as he searched her face. She noted the concern that knit his dark brows and she wondered what he saw. A slowly escalating fear gained control as she asked, "Who would want to kill me?"

"That's what I was going to ask you. It could've been a random act—some psychopath with a grudge against some-thing or other. Unfortunately, that kind of thing does happen occasionally."

"No…I don't think so. It was—" Memory nudged again and Natalie shuddered. Her breathing grew agitated as the memory cleared and she gasped, "It wasn't random."

"How do you know that?" Brady moved closer. He gripped her hand as she started to shake. He said tensely, "Natalie?"

"I know because—" Natalie's breath quivered on her lips. Her eyes widened as she managed to choke out the words, "Because…he said my name."

BRADY INSTINCTIVELY moved closer. He held her hand tighter, but she was suddenly trembling so badly that her teeth were chattering. Leaning closer, he whispered against her cheek, "Don't be afraid, Natalie. You're safe now."

Natalie mumbled with growing incoherence, "How did this happen? I don't understand. He said my name…my name…"

She moaned and twisted in bed. A wave of panic overwhelmed Brady and he pressed the call button. Where the hell was everybody? He turned as Dr. Weiss ordered sharply from behind him, "Step back, Detective. Move out of the way, please."

Brady drew back to the far wall and watched as Dr. Weiss talked softly, responding to Natalie's increasingly confused mumblings. He saw her speak to the nurse, then accept the syringe the nurse handed her a few minutes later. After injecting it into the IV, Dr. Weiss turned toward him to say, "Perhaps you'd better leave for a little while, Detective. There are some things I'll need to take care of here that'll take me a half hour or so. Don't worry. Natalie will be fine while you're gone."

Nodding, Brady started toward the door. He had reached the hallway when he heard Dr. Weiss call out, "Wait a minute, please." Drawing him outside the room a few moments later, Dr. Weiss said, "I heard what Natalie told you, Detective, but you have to understand that situations like this are quite common with head trauma. Natalie may even come up with more alarming delusions before this is over. She's confused…frightened. She's had a terrible experience and her mind is trying to make sense out of it. In my opinion, it wouldn't be wise to put too much credence into what she says for another day, at least until she's completely coherent."

"You could be right, Doctor." Refusing to add that she could also be wrong—*dead wrong*—Brady said, "You said you'd be busy here for a while?"

"About half an hour, at least. Natalie needs to be made more comfortable before she's settled in for the night." She hesitated. "Why don't you go down to the cafeteria and get yourself a cup of coffee? I'll make sure somebody stays with her until you return, if that's what's concerning you." She patted his arm. "She'll be much better tomorrow. You'll see."

Brady walked rapidly down the hospital corridor, his expression tense. He didn't like this. Dr. Weiss could be right, of course. Everything Natalie had said could be a result of her injury, but he didn't buy it.

Brady scrutinized the surrounding rooms as he passed. He had half an hour. Visiting hours were in effect, making it difficult as he searched the faces of the crowd moving down the hallway, but he also knew there was safety in numbers. With Dr. Weiss and the nurse in Natalie's room, and with steady traffic moving past, Natalie would be safe enough for a while—at least long enough for him to get outside so he could use his cell phone to call the precinct and to make a quick call to the veterinary hospital.

Sarah was going to miss his nightly visit.

Wilthauer would have a fit when he called.

Stansky would be sure he'd gone crazy.

Hell, maybe he had.

Brady rang the elevator and waited anxiously. Actually, no

one was more surprised than he was at the range of emotions Natalie—a virtual stranger—had raised in him. A few hours earlier, he had been gritting his teeth at the thought of seeing her at that precinct meeting; yet the moment he saw her lying in that hospital bed, battered, bruised and so damned helpless—

Brady felt an inexplicable heat rise to his face. He'd find the animal who'd pushed Natalie into the street and make sure the bastard never tried anything like that again.

He had half an hour.

The elevator doors opened and Brady stepped inside. He automatically scanned the hallway again as the elevator doors closed.

DR. HADDEN MOORE strode down the hospital hallway at a modest pace. It was almost nine o'clock and daylight was fading on the busy streets outside. Inside the hospital, the hallways had cleared of visitors and the nurses were busy dispensing meds before the patients were settled down for the night.

He wasn't concerned by the late hour. Visiting hours didn't apply to him. Dressed as he was in a white lab coat he had removed from the hospital linen closet, and with a stethoscope around his neck that he had found lying nearby, no one gave him a second look. The nurses' station was vacant when he strolled past and he picked up a chart without challenge. Yet it didn't really matter if he were challenged. He had a Ph.D. and he was completely confident that he was capable of carrying off his disguise in a convincing manner.

Hadden halted and leaned down toward the water fountain, frowning as Dr. Rita Weiss strode toward the elevator. Dr. Weiss was late leaving the hospital. His short visit to the emergency room earlier that day had been very informative. Natalie Patterson had been brought in and her injuries treated.

She had been admitted and her care turned over to the recently divorced, efficient Dr. Weiss, whom a chatty clerk had helpfully pointed out to him. He had then gone to the cafeteria to pass the time until Natalie was situated in her room, the location of which the clerk had also cheerfully provided.

He had waited patiently until a later hour when he knew he could make his entrance virtually without being noticed.

His smile faltered as he approached Natalie's room. Aware of the merits of well-planned strategy, he had resumed his surveillance of Natalie's daily routine since she'd been assigned to the city, but she had emerged from her hotel later than usual that morning, surprising him. He had followed her covertly and had watched as she walked to the corner, failing again and again to hail a cab before finally boarding a bus in frustration.

He'd boarded the bus behind her, but she did not even look his way.

Disembarking from the rear door of the bus at the same stop as Natalie, he had then followed her cautiously as she continued on through the heavy pedestrian traffic.

He saw her irritation when she stopped at the last street corner and waited for the light to change. The crowd behind her swelled in size as she stood on the curb, alternating on obviously aching feet, and it was then that he realized he had been presented with an opportunity too irresistible for him to turn down.

No one paid attention to him as he slipped up behind Natalie in the crowd. Nor did anyone notice when, in a flash of movement too quick to perceive, he pressed the flat of his hands into the curve of her back and shoved her into the street.

He had been euphoric. Yet his euphoria came to an abrupt end only seconds later when two fellows managed to jerk her out of the limo's path. She struck her head on the curb as they did.

He supposed that was why neither of the men had waited around after the ambulance arrived. But by that time the situation had slipped beyond his control. He'd had no recourse but to follow the ambulance in a cab in order to find out the result of his effort.

And now here he was…determined to finish what he had started.

Hadden neared Natalie's hospital room, his heart pounding. He was about to step inside when the unexpected sight of Detective Tomasini of the NYPD dozing in a chair beside her bed halted him.

Damn the man! What was he doing here?

Hadden pulled back without being seen, then stared at Natalie lying so still in the hospital bed. Her long, dark hair was stretched across the pillow in sharp contrast with the stark white of the bed linens and the bandage she wore on her forehead. She was petite, silent, her small features delicately composed, the long, black fans of her eyelashes lying like lush crescent moons against her pale cheeks. Surrounded in immaculate white, the pale beam of light shining down on her in the semidarkness forming a gleaming halo around her head, she looked like a celestial being—innocent and so completely pure that she stole his breath.

He paused at that thought.

But Natalie Patterson wasn't pure, and she wasn't celestial. She was the lab technician who had foiled his perfect revenge and because of her, the entire NYPD would soon be out searching for him.

Hatred surged hotly through him as Hadden turned abruptly and started back down the hallway.

He'd be back.

Chapter Four

The sound of morning activity in the hospital corridor beyond Natalie's door woke Brady abruptly. Angry with himself for having dozed, he glanced at the bed a few feet away where Natalie slept, breathing easily. Her color had improved and her features were relaxed. Her sleep appeared to be natural and presently devoid of the nightmares that had awakened her several times during the night.

Brady rubbed his palm across his stubbled jaw, then ran a hand through his hair in an attempt to restore a sense of order to his disheveled appearance as he pushed himself upright in the chair. He recalled Natalie's incoherent mumblings jarring him from his semisleep during the night and the sudden panic that had snapped her eyes open. He had moved to her side spontaneously. He had comforted her, telling her she didn't need to be afraid, that he was there and he'd protect her. He had whispered reassuringly until her breathing became normal, and he had suffered a sense of helplessness when she awoke again, tortured by the same frightening torments. The experience had been bittersweet as she turned to him in her terror; yet as confusing as his feelings had become, he was certain of one thing—he would protect her with his life.

His attitude toward her had changed drastically. He couldn't be sure if guilt at his misjudgment of Natalie was responsible; if having misjudged her once, he was anxious not to repeat the same mistake, especially when the stakes were so high. Or if his reaction to her utter helplessness was what had kept him sitting at her bedside, holding her hand until she fell back to sleep again.

It annoyed him that he'd been unable to remain awake all night, but he had consoled himself that he had been immediately alert each time someone stepped into the room, that he had diligently checked all medication and IV changes that had been conducted during that time—all of which, he recognized, would be a complete waste of time if Natalie woke up and recanted her story about being pushed into the street.

Yet, he somehow knew she would not.

Despite Dr. Weiss's warning, there had been something about Natalie's adamancy, and the look in those heavily lidded gray eyes that made him believe her when she repeated, *He said my name.*

He supposed he might not have given those four words much credence if not for the chilling fax he had received from Manderling Pharmaceuticals and his realization that only a madman could be guilty of the atrocity Dr. Hadden Moore was suspected of having committed. The knowledge that Moore might still be in the city was a major concern. Brady knew that if Moore were guilty, he would realize that having identified Candoxine as the cause of the Winslow barbecue deaths, Natalie had set the police on his trail. The possible repercussions of that scenario, considering Natalie's "accident," were too disturbing to ignore.

Truth is stranger than fiction. Brady was too familiar with that maxim to disregard it.

Brady glanced back at Natalie, recalling the way she had clutched his hand until she fell asleep—so tightly that she had surprised him with her strength. She was so slight that she—

Natalie's eyes fluttered open, interrupting Brady's

thoughts. She stared at him a moment before she said, "Are you still here?"

"Yeah." Brady moved closer to the bed. "Something wrong with that?"

"You were here all night, weren't you?"

Brady nodded.

"Why?"

"Let me see." Brady moved closer still and looked down into her pale face. "You had an accident on the street."

"It wasn't an accident."

"And you said it wasn't an accident, that somebody pushed you."

"Somebody did."

"Maybe I believed you and figured you'd need somebody to stay with you for a while."

Natalie searched his face, frowning.

"And maybe I stayed because I owe you an apology."

"An apology…"

"Because I was tired and irritable that first day I met you and I acted like an ass. Because I was wrong and needed to tell you I was wrong."

"What about the second day?"

Brady smiled. "I was an ass then, too."

Natalie nodded.

"And I also wanted to tell you that—"

A sound at the door turned them toward Dr. Weiss as she stopped still and said, "Excuse me. Am I interrupting something?"

"No." Brady stood up. "Come on in."

Dr. Weiss glanced between them as she approached the bed. She said, "Well, you look a lot better today, Natalie. That's more than I can say for your friend here. How do you feel?"

"Somewhat better."

Brady started toward the door and Dr. Weiss said, "I'll be done here shortly, Detective. Also, there's a uniformed officer waiting for you at the nurses' station. He said you're expecting him."

"Right."

"Brady?"

Brady looked back when Natalie called after him with uncertainty. He responded to her unasked question. "I'll be back."

It occurred to Brady as he stepped into the hallway and the officer at the desk started toward him that he suddenly felt like smiling.

Why?

The answer to that was embarrassingly simple. It was because Natalie hadn't wanted him to leave.

BRADY PULLED THE DOOR of the precinct station house open and strode inside, squinting as his eyes acclimated to the darkness within. He swore under his breath as he tripped over a carton of snack cakes beside the vending machine that was being refilled. He glared at the service attendant, mumbled an apology and moved the carton out of his way, then turned toward the squad room in the rear where Wilthauer was waiting. He was late. It had taken him longer than he had expected to get cleaned up, change his clothes and negotiate the traffic for his morning meeting. The fact that Wilthauer was waiting was already one count against him.

In Wilthauer's office minutes later, with Stansky standing silently nearby, Brady insisted, "You know damned well Natalie Patterson will need protection, at least until she leaves that hospital. She can't protect herself and since she's the possible target of a homicidal maniac and somebody already tried to push her into the path of an oncoming car, I'd say we have no choice."

"Possible target of a homicidal maniac? Don't you think

you're going a little overboard on this, Tomasini? I don't have the statistics, but I'd say similar, unfortunate *accidents* like the one that happened to Patterson, have been known to occur more often than we care to admit in this city."

"It wasn't an accident. Somebody pushed her."

"So she says."

"I believe her."

"Maybe somebody did push her, some careless bastard in a rush who—"

"She said that *careless bastard* called her by name."

"What do you mean?"

"She said he whispered her name before he shoved her into the street. There's nothing accidental about that, and you know damned well I wouldn't be making a case of it if I didn't believe it was true."

"Come on…"

"Natalie's not the type to cry wolf, I tell you."

"You haven't gotten far enough in this investigation to be sure what type this Patterson woman is, or to be sure if this Moore character is still in the country—if he is the perpetrator."

"He's the one. He had motive and the opportunity to obtain the Candoxine. You know that as well as I do. And I'll make you a bet that as soon as we do some checking to determine his location, we'll find out—"

Breaking his silence, Stansky interjected, "I've already checked on Moore's location. There's no record of his return to England…or of his leaving the U.S., for that matter. He's still in this country somewhere as far as the records show." At Brady's inquiring glance, he added, "What did you think I was doing while you were babysitting at the hospital all day?"

Brady looked back at Wilthauer's frown. "What does that tell you?"

"That you're both jumping to conclusions."

"I don't know. Are we?"

Brady stared at Wilthauer boldly. Damn, the man was hardheaded! He'd been able to get a uniform stationed at Natalie's door temporarily, but he knew *temporarily* wouldn't do. He said, "Look, Captain, we can't afford to take the risk. If Natalie gets attacked again and the attack succeeds, there'll be hell to pay. Natalie's the golden girl of the CDC. They won't take it lightly that we didn't protect her."

He knew he had hit the bull's-eye with that thought when Wilthauer hesitated, then responded, "All right. You win. I'll keep a uniform outside the Patterson woman's hospital door until she's released, but remember, we can't provide protection for an extended period. We don't have the manpower to spare, so find this Moore guy and make it quick. Manderling provided us with his picture. Leak it to the newspapers. Notify the networks. Flood the town with his picture, and then get set for the deluge. If he's still around, you'll get him."

"Natalie should be out of the hospital in a few days. She won't be any safer in her hotel room if this guy is really after her."

"I told you, we don't have the manpower."

"Captain…"

"A step at a time, Tomasini." Wilthauer added snidely, "By the way, when did this CDC chick change from *the Patterson broad* to *Natalie*?"

"When she got pushed into the street and was almost killed." Brady's light eyes pinned him. "Is there anything else you want to know?"

Brady was striding out toward the street when the desk sergeant stopped him. Sergeant Mike Santini's full, jowled face reflected his annoyance as he said, "Don't listen to Wilthauer, Tomasini. He was just ragging on you. No matter what he says, we've got enough personnel in this precinct to protect whoever we need to protect. We've got some recruits coming in straight from the academy, and I have in my hand the paperwork for ten more cops who are getting transferred here soon." At Brady's questioning glance, he said, "What? So I heard what Wilthauer said to you. He was yelling so loud that the whole precinct probably heard him."

Right.

Brady turned back toward the door and tripped over the carton of snack cakes still lying beside the vending machine. This time, the service attendant didn't even raise his head.

Cursing, Brady pushed open the door into the sunlight.

"THAT'S QUITE A MAN you've got there."

Natalie stared up at Dr. Weiss. The attractive doctor had arrived a few minutes earlier. Her unexpected remark in the midst of a checkup took Natalie by surprise.

Holding a finger up in front of her, precluding Natalie's response, Dr. Weiss asked, "What do you see? One or two?"

"One."

"Right answer."

"What man are you talking about?"

Dr. Weiss paused to smile knowingly at Natalie. "You don't have to pretend, dear. Your tall, dark and handsome detective let your relationship slip."

"What relationship?"

Dr. Weiss shrugged. "If that's the way you want it. All I know is, I let him know in the most delicate of ways that I was available—which is not my normal procedure with the opposite sex, I might add—but he didn't bat an eye. As a matter of fact, he set me straight about the situation between you two so I wouldn't make a fool of myself—which I appreciated. All I can say is, if I had a man like him, I wouldn't try to deny it."

"I don't know what you're talking about. Detective Tomasini and I are presently working together. We have a *working* relationship."

"That's why he stayed all night by your bedside...because you have a working relationship. That's why he had a policeman stationed at your door, and that's why he looks at you like he's afraid you're going to break."

"He stayed with me because...well, that's a private matter. As for his looking at me like I might break, I think he thinks I might. I probably gave him a few shaky moments with the nightmares I had last night. As for the policeman—"

"He's obviously worried about you, but I did warn him you might hallucinate for a while. Besides, Detective Tomasini doesn't look to me like the type who lets too much scare him."

"I don't know how this misconception got started, but—"

"All right, Natalie." Dr. Weiss cut her short. "I'm sorry I mentioned it."

Natalie raised her hand to her head. She must be more confused than she thought. What was this woman talking about?

At the sound of deep voices in conversation in the corridor, Natalie turned toward the doorway. Brady looked in and said, "Should I come back later?"

"No, Detective, now is fine. I'm done with my examination. Natalie is doing well. There's some residual trauma, but she should be all right in a day or so."

Natalie bristled weakly. "You should probably be directing that progress report at me, Doctor. I'm conscious, coherent and quite capable of comprehending what you're saying—even if my head does hurt."

"Sorry." Dr. Weiss looked annoyed. "In any case, I'll leave you two alone."

It was Natalie's turn to look annoyed.

BRADY HESITATED in the hospital room doorway. It was a little past noon. Only a few hours had passed since he had left Natalie that morning, but the improvement in her condition was easily visible, even without Dr. Weiss's comments. Natalie was propped up in bed, her color had improved and her eyes were clearer.

Yet he was somehow unprepared when Natalie asked abruptly, "What's going on, Brady?"

Brady sat down on the chair at her bedside as he asked cautiously, "What do you mean?"

"First of all, there's a policeman standing guard at my door."

"You said somebody deliberately pushed you into the street."

"Yes, but—"

"But didn't you expect me to believe you?"

Brady saw the way Natalie appeared to assess him, searching his face while hesitating in her response. He wondered what she saw, because he sure as hell wasn't sure. All he knew was that he had told Stansky to follow up on a couple of leads while he checked back on her…because he had needed to assure himself that she was all right. And, hell, she had looked so damned needy and appealing when he'd stuck his head back into the room a few minutes earlier that his heart had done a teenage flip-flop in his chest. Even as annoyed as she appeared to be, he could somehow see past the surface to the confusion and uncertainty that had touched her off. He continued, "The policeman outside is a precaution."

"A precaution…" Natalie's expression twitched. "Does that mean you expect that person who pushed me will…will try to hurt me again?"

"It's just what I said, a precaution."

Momentarily silent, Natalie said, "Tell me the truth."

Her question was flat-out—no minced words—and Brady hesitated.

"I need to know what's going on, Detective."

"Brady."

"Tell me, please."

"All right. Don't get upset." Brady glanced toward the door. "I've got the feeling Dr. Weiss is looking for the opportunity to throw me out of here."

"That's another thing. Dr. Weiss seems to think…I mean she intimated—"

"That we were more than friends?"

Natalie's face colored in response, and Brady could not help but be amused. He responded frankly, "Dr. Weiss was making it clear that she was available and I said that to put her off. I figured her Hippocratic oath would keep her at a distance while I had other things on my mind—like who pushed you into the street."

"I guess you run into that kind of problem quite often."

"What problem?"

"Women coming on to you."

Unsure if she was serious, Brady shrugged. "I wouldn't say it was an everyday occurrence."

Natalie appeared about to respond, then seemed to think better of it.

He frowned as he said, "About the uniform at your door—" Brady did not miss the change in Natalie's expression as he continued, "I think you should know that we received a report from Manderling Pharmaceuticals involving a Dr. Hadden Moore. He's a Ph.D. and one of the researchers who developed Candoxine. It seems he became fixated on Mattie Winslow when he visited the U.S. and went off the deep end when she married somebody else. He spent some time in a mental institution in England before coming back to this country at the time of the poisonings. He had free access to Candoxine prior to his return, and bets are that he's our man. The problem is, we're not certain where he is right now. He may still be in the country—maybe in the city—and in view of what just happened to you, we're not taking any chances."

"You're telling me that a doctor dedicated to science and the saving of lives is possibly responsible for such horrendous crimes?"

"Being a Ph.D. doesn't rule out mania."

"You think he pushed me into the street?"

"I told you, that policeman outside your door is just a precaution."

Natalie paled. "But why would he come after me?"

"I don't think we can look for logic in the reasoning of a deranged individual." Brady moved instinctively closer. He could see fear in the open gaze that searched his face, and he wanted to relieve it. Somehow, he wanted that badly. He whispered, "Look, Natalie, don't worry. Nobody is going to let anything else happen to you, most especially me. Hell, I made enough of a jackass of myself when we first met. I'm working on changing your image of me."

"Why would you care what I think of you?"

"I don't know." Brady smiled. "You tell me."

"Because your professional pride won't let you accept my low opinion of your ability?"

"Maybe."

"That's why I was so angry when you challenged me during the lab tests, you know."

"Is that why?" Brady heard himself say. "Just injured pride?"

The touch of her sober, gray-eyed gaze was almost palpable as Natalie studied his face before responding, "And I couldn't understand why you disliked me so intensely."

"I was prepared to dislike you for reasons that turned out to be…prejudiced against you on the wrong basis, but that's changed. You won me over."

A devastating dimple flashed in Natalie's cheek with her brief smile. Brady's heart did another teenage flip-flop as she said, "I won you over with the warmth of my personality, I suppose."

"That, and a few other things."

"A few other things?"

Brady did not immediately respond. If he were truthful, he'd have to say that his thoughts when he first looked at her were a little more than *She's a babe.* It was more, *Hold on, man. A beer and pizza guy like you who's been around the block a few times would be barking up the wrong tree with a classy act like her.* He'd also have to admit that he'd resented his reaction and tried to deny it. And when he had been forced to look into her professional background and was also forced to admit she was everything she had been represented to be, the truth had only increased his resentment. Yet all resentment had faded when he saw her lying injured and alone in her hospital bed, and his first instinct had been to set things straight.

Brady looked down at Natalie. She was a babe, all right. Although she made no attempt to capitalize on a natural beauty that grew more apparent on close scrutiny, unlike most of the women he had known, she somehow still tied him up in knots without even trying. He wasn't exactly sure what he knew or what he felt when faced with her direct, honest stare that reflected both fear and a determined resolve to comprehend a frightening situation that was inexplicable. All he was certain of was his need to console her. He wanted to explain as honestly as he could that he'd keep her safe. He wanted her to know he meant every word. He wanted—

Brady's thoughts stopped. Natalie was still looking up at him with those gray eyes that somehow turned him inside out with no effort at all.

Yeah, who was he kidding? If Natalie Patterson were any other female, he'd also say he wanted *her.*

Romeo.

The precinct stud.

That was a joke. The only problem was that the joke was on him. Natalie wasn't any other female.

That thought taking precedence in his mind, he said simply, "Don't worry, Natalie. I won't let anything else happen to you. I talked to my captain and he—"

A sound at the door preceded a harshly voiced interjection. "I don't care who you talked to. You're a little late with your reassurances."

Brady's attention snapped toward the door. He stood up at the sight of the uniformed policeman gripping a tall, slender man by the arm as he said apologetically, "I'm sorry, Detective, but this guy has CDC identification. I figured he was all right, but I didn't expect him to barge in here."

Natalie gasped, "Chuck, what are you doing here?"

Chuck…Charles Randolph.

Brady signaled Randolph's release. His lips clamped tight as Randolph advanced into the room and leaned down to kiss Natalie. The familiarity of the gesture tightened a knot in Brady's stomach as Randolph turned back toward him to say, "I heard what you just told Natalie, and what I want to know is how you let this happen to her in the first place."

"Chuck, please." Natalie looked at Brady with a plea for understanding as she said, "I'm sorry. Chuck doesn't understand."

"I understand, all right."

Natalie said hoarsely, "Chuck, this is Detective Tomasini. He's been assigned to the Candoxine case, and he and the NYPD are doing their best in a difficult situation that is only now becoming clear."

"If you mean by 'becoming clear' the fact that there was an attempt on your life, my response is that incompetence isn't to be denied, no matter how good the intentions are."

"Chuck!"

Brady took an aggressive step, his hands spontaneously balling into fists. He halted abruptly when Natalie's complexion turned ashen. He remained silent as Charles Randolph turned to her and said in a softer tone, "I grabbed a flight as soon as I heard what happened. George thought that considering your aunt's age, it was best not to tell her what happened to you until you could call her yourself, and I figured you needed someone here. Besides, I needed to be sure you were all right."

"I'm fine, Chuck, or I will be fine in a few days. I have complete confidence in my doctor."

"This never should have happened." Completely ignoring Brady, Randolph sat beside her bed and took Natalie's hand in his. Brady noted that Natalie made no attempt to withdraw her hand from his grasp as Randolph said, "I'm going to get you out of this city as soon as you're able to travel. It's unsafe for you here."

Brady interrupted, "I don't know if that's a good idea at present. The perpetrator—"

"I don't want to hear any of your reasons for keeping Natalie here, Detective." Randolph turned sharply toward him. "The bottom line is that your foremost interest is in apprehending your *perpetrator*. Mine is Natalie's safety."

Brady glanced at Natalie and frowned. For all his talk about being concerned about Natalie's health, Randolph ignored the steady waning of Natalie's color, as well as the beads of perspiration that had sprung up on her forehead and upper lip. The damned fool was putting stress on her that could only do her harm. He had to defuse the situation, and there was only one way to do it.

Brady said tightly, "I think I should go."

"That sounds like a good idea to me."

"Chuck, please." Natalie looked back at Brady and said, "Maybe that would be best for now."

Brady turned toward the door. He looked back to see Randolph stroke Natalie's cheek, then lean over the bed to press his mouth to hers for a more lingering kiss. Natalie raised her hand to cover his, and the knot in Brady's stomach clenched tighter.

He heard Randolph whisper when their lips parted, "I've missed you, Natalie. I want you to come home with me."

Brady walked resolutely into the hallway.

"Detective." Brady turned to look at the uniformed policeman at the door as the fellow said flatly, "I just want you to know guys like that make me sick. That talk about being incompetent. What does he know, shut up in a lab most of the day with nothing but test tubes and lab rats to keep him company? Besides, who would be the first person he called in case of trouble?"

Brady nodded stiffly without responding. The uniform was right, not that it made any difference with Natalie lying in that bed and Randolph sitting beside her.

Brady walked rapidly down the corridor without looking back.

Chapter Five

Hadden Moore trembled with fury. He stared at the picture of himself in the morning newspaper a moment longer, then threw it down onto the floor atop the week's worth of newspapers he had discarded there.

Bastards! The New York police were determined to find him, so beleaguered were they by the press to put an end to the Winslow barbecue murder case—murders discovered only because of the interference of a laboratory technician trading on his brilliance to make a name for herself.

Hadden paused at the thought. He remembered the words he had whispered into Natalie Patterson's ear before shoving her into the street.

Goodbye, Natalie.

He had been unable to resist speaking her name so she would know that the utter terror she was experiencing was meant especially for her. He had truly believed at that moment that she was receiving full payment for her actions.

But she had survived!

He had thought himself clever in having moved so quickly to discover the hospital room where she was confined, only to find when he went to finish his work that her watchdog was on hand.

Now this—his photo on TV, in every newspaper, plastered on every bulletin board in every public building in the city!

Hadden struggled to control his rage as he glanced around the apartment he had enjoyed for the past several months. High over the city, it looked down on Lincoln Center, the beautiful oasis of culture where he had spent countless enjoyable evenings in the company of the masters. The apartment had appeared luxurious beyond his needs at first, with its ingenious decor and its perfectly situated balcony that allowed him an unmatched view of the city. He had stumbled onto the sublet fortuitously, but now he was being forced out of his haven because of *her*.

Fortunately, he was clever enough never to be stymied by the unexpected. He had prepared for such a situation, although he had never really believed he would have to use his alternate plan. He knew exactly where to go and what to do while he slipped out of sight. Interest would wane as time passed. His picture would no longer be newsworthy. Things would gradually return to normal and when they did, he would slip back into the city where he had no doubt Natalie Patterson would remain.

Why was he certain she would remain in New York? Because she was a heroine in the city. She had made a name for herself here. She was celebrated and feted as an expert for the first time in her career, and his failed attempt on her life had done nothing more than gain her more attention.

Yet he knew well that the limelight did not last long. The Candoxine surprise would quickly become old news when there was little new information to report. And when she least expected it—when *everyone* least expected it—he would strike.

It was a shame. She was such a lovely little thing. Yet a malignancy was a malignancy. He needed to remove it from his life so he could go on.

"I INSIST, NATALIE."

Dr. Gregory looked at her adamantly. It was approaching noon and the summer sun was shining outside the hospital windows as she sat, completely dressed for the first time in a week, ready to go home. The subdued din of the busy hospital progressed in the corridor beyond as he continued, "It isn't an imposition at all. I bought the apartment for my daughter when I married Emily. Justine…" He smiled at her reaction. "Well, my daughter resented Emily when I married her a few years ago, and Emily and I both felt it would be better if Justine had her own place when she started college. Everything worked out quite well in that regard. Justine took in a roommate, and now both girls have decided to spend their junior year in Italy. My wife and I didn't want to rent the apartment out during that time because we didn't want to be bothered with tenants, so it has been empty since Justine and her roommate left a month ago."

Dr. Gregory continued, "My dear, Dr. Minter has confirmed that you'll be staying in the city for an indefinite period while the Winslow investigation continues to develop. You'll obviously need to be totally comfortable as you recuperate fully from your…experience. A hotel room simply will not do. You needn't worry about rent. I'll take care of the details. Our agency won't bother you with expenses."

"You're too generous, Dr. Gregory, but—"

"No buts. Dr. Ruberg has already arranged to have your things moved from your hotel room to the apartment so you can go directly there when you're released from the hospital today."

"I don't expect to remain in New York too much longer, Dr. Gregory. Most of my work on the Winslow case is done."

"I don't think Detective Tomasini will agree. He—"

"I don't think Detective Tomasini's opinion matters, Doctor."

Chuck's interjection from the doorway prompted them to turn in his direction as he entered and said stiffly, "I've already made arrangements to take Natalie home with me as soon as she's released."

Natalie frowned. She had finally been pronounced fit enough to be released from the hospital by Dr. Weiss, and she was glad. She knew a week's stay was almost unprecedented in concussion cases. In weaker moments, she had silently wondered if Dr. Weiss's attraction to Brady had affected her decision to keep her longer than necessary, considering that Dr. Weiss made certain to be present each morning when Brady showed up to update her on the progress of the investigation. In more realistic moments, however, she acknowledged that although she was feeling better with each passing hour, she was still confused and uncertain at times.

Natalie's frown darkened. She had made a mistake in allowing Chuck to believe that there was something between them. A familiar face had been so welcome during her confusion and uncertainty. She had appreciated his concern, but she hadn't felt well enough to argue with him. She realized now that the need to correct her error would be painful for both of them.

Natalie stated with gentle determination, "I'm afraid you misunderstood the situation, Chuck. I agreed to go back to Atlanta with you, but only after I was satisfied that I wasn't needed here any longer."

Chuck appeared briefly stunned. She inwardly winced at the pain that flashed in his eyes as he responded, "Natalie, you're not thinking the situation through clearly. You're not safe in this city. That madman is still on the loose, and the possibility that he has turned his animosity toward you can't be ignored."

"All the more reason for me to remain. The police have provided me with protection here."

"Which they'll terminate as soon as the Candoxine poisonings are no longer news."

"The Candoxine case aside, an attempt was made on my life."

"Do you think that makes any difference? How many people in this city have had attempts made on their lives for one reason or another, and still walk the streets unprotected by the police?" Chuck sat down on the bed beside her and took her hand. "It's the Candoxine case that's fueling all the attention you're getting. Once it's old news, your protection will disappear without notice."

"Brady assured me—"

"Brady." Natalie noted the revealing twitch of Chuck's lips before he continued, "You depend too much on Detective Tomasini's word. He's just telling you what you want to hear, but the truth is that his superior is the one who makes the decision to provide protection. Your *friend* has one thought in mind—finding Hadden Moore—and he's determined to do and say whatever is necessary in order to accomplish that objective and advance his career."

"That's a terrible thing to say, Chuck!"

"It's true. I don't want you to be fooled by him. He's not like us, Natalie. We're professionals, scientists dedicated to serving humanity. He's a policeman through and through, even if he doesn't wear a uniform, and his idea of serving the public is entirely different from ours. He's goal-oriented. He's a detective because he actually thinks like the criminals he pursues. He's as untrustworthy as they are. If you ask me, he even looks like one of them. Oh, he's concerned about the case, all right, but it's not especially the victim that he cares about. It's all about apprehending the criminal. If you listen to him, he'll put you at risk if necessary because he's career-driven and he—"

"If you'll excuse me." Interrupting the heated diatribe, Dr.

Gregory stood up with a tentative smile. "I think it's best if I leave now, Natalie, since you and Mr. Randolph obviously have personal matters to discuss." With an apologetic glance toward Chuck, he placed a card down on the bed beside Natalie and continued, "As I said, Dr. Ruberg has already arranged to have your things moved into my daughter's apartment. I've written down the address and telephone number for you. It'll be much more comfortable for you, no matter how long you decide to use it." He paused. "I hope you'll let me know what you decide to do. The contribution you've made to the West Nile virus project in your spare time while in the city has been greatly appreciated. Dr. Truesdale and I were actually hoping we could count on your continued expertise for a few months in pursuing the avenues you've opened for us. Actually, I've talked to Dr. Minter about it and—"

At Chuck's responsive reaction, Dr. Gregory halted prematurely and added, "But I expect that's a matter to be discussed at a better time."

Natalie waited until Dr. Gregory left before turning to Chuck to say, "I'm sorry. I don't know how many of the things you said are true, but I can't go back to Atlanta with you now, Chuck. I have too many matters to clear up here first. It's a personal decision that I feel is necessary for my peace of mind."

"That's insane!" Chuck moved closer. She felt the agitation that pulsed through him. She saw it in the flush that colored his cheeks and in the tense lines of his face as he paused to search her face. His gaze lingered briefly on her lips before he whispered, "Natalie, you know how I feel about you. I'd be a fool to deny it. I also know you don't return my feelings in the same way, but what I'm saying has nothing to do with that situation. You're in danger in this city."

"If I'm in danger here, I'd be in danger in Atlanta, too."

"No...no, you wouldn't. You'd be out of sight and out of mind. You could go on as if this aspect of your life had never happened."

"But it did happen, and I can't hide from it." Natalie took a strengthening breath as she voiced a reality that haunted her. "I have to face a hard truth. If this Hadden Moore person is responsible for pushing me into the street, he's already traveled across an ocean to exact his revenge on one woman. Certainly he won't hesitate to travel to another city for the same purpose." Her voice briefly trembling, she continued, "Chuck, please understand, I have to stay here until the investigation progresses further...until I can leave the city without fear."

"You can leave this city without fear as long as I'm with you." Chuck's sober brown eyes held hers intently. She read the promise in their depths as he said, "I'd protect you with my life. You know that."

"I don't want it to be that way, Chuck. I don't want you getting involved...putting yourself in possible danger for me."

"I'm involved as long as you're involved."

"Chuck..." Natalie raised her hand to his cheek. Sincerely pained, she said, "I'm so sorry. I have to do it my way. I have a guard outside my door, and Brady informed me that a policeman will escort me to my quarters and stand guard to make sure I'm protected. I can't ask for more."

"Yes, you could, Natalie." Chuck said more softly, "It wouldn't take much convincing to persuade me to stay with you and make sure you're safe."

"Oh, Chuck..." Natalie's regret deepened. "I couldn't ask you to put your own life on hold while I went on with mine. I couldn't ask that of anyone."

Chuck's gaze held hers. "I don't suppose I need to remind you that it wouldn't be a sacrifice." When Natalie remained silent, he drew back with a sad half smile and said, "Well, I guess there's nothing else I can say."

"I have to stay. Please try to understand."

"I have two tickets on the afternoon flight for Atlanta. I told George I'd be back to work tomorrow."

Natalie felt her throat choke tightly. "Don't worry. I'll be safe here. I'll let you know the moment the situation changes and I feel safe enough to go home."

Chuck checked his watch. "I expected to be taking you straight to the airport from here with only the clothes on your back. So much for that daydream." He shrugged and said softly, "I'll have to leave if I'm going to make that flight."

Natalie struggled to maintain control as she said, "Thanks so much for coming here to be with me after the…incident. It meant a lot to me." Chuck did not reply and Natalie continued, "Don't worry, please. I don't know how much longer it'll be before somebody comes up here with my release papers, but I'll be protected every step of the way."

"Let me know when you're settled."

Natalie did not resist when Chuck hesitated briefly, then pressed his mouth to hers for a lingering kiss. His kiss was pleasant. He was a friend…a dear friend.

She said, "Call me when you reach Atlanta. You have my cell phone number."

"I love you, Natalie."

Natalie caught her breath as Chuck walked out into the hallway without waiting for a response.

Alone in the room again, Natalie felt the lump in her throat tighten.

He had said it.

He loved her.

And her only thought was that she wished so desperately that he didn't.

"LOOK, I TOLD YOU that you didn't have to come with me." Brady looked at his partner as Stansky walked beside him down the hospital hallway. "I'll have no trouble getting Natalie safely out of here and installed in her apartment, especially with a uniform taking up the rear. You could've stayed back at the precinct and checked on a few more of those tips from the hotline."

"Thanks, Brady, but no thanks. I'm just as sick as everybody else on the squad is of hearing Santini moan about the transfer paperwork he lost for those new men the precinct is supposed to get and the processing delay it's going to cause. Besides, checking on those tips is all I've been doing for the past three days. You know as well as I do that most of those tips turn out to be either cranks or honest mistakes."

"Yeah, but it only takes one of them to be on the mark and we've got the bastard. Hell, we've got Moore's picture plastered all over the city. Somebody has to have seen him somewhere."

"You'd think."

Brady did not respond. They had arrived at the hospital only a few minutes previously and had parked directly in front of the lobby—one of the perks afforded the city's finest. It hadn't escaped his notice that Charles Randolph was leaving when they arrived—and leaving alone. Brady was only too conscious of the danger that guy presented. He wondered what he would've done if he had seen Natalie leaving with him—if he would have stopped her for her own safety, or if he would've let them go.

Grateful that he now wouldn't have to face that decision, Brady forced back a smile. He didn't like Charles Randolph. He didn't like Randolph's looks, his elitist attitude or his presumptuousness when it came to everything pertaining to Natalie. Thankfully, Natalie took exception to some of those points, too.

How did he know that? The answer was pretty simple. For the past week, he had gone to the hospital to check on Natalie first thing in the morning before he reported to the precinct. He had taken those opportunities to bring her up to date on their progress in the case—which was nil. He had shared every point of information with her, as well as his frustration, and unless he was mistaken, she actually had begun to look forward to his visits.

It amused Brady to think how spontaneous their relationship had become in view of their inauspicious start. He arrived with a cup of coffee from the machine down the hall and sat with her while she ate breakfast. The coffee was terrible, but sharing the time with Natalie wasn't. She was so bright, so quick to seize on every aspect of the case despite her debility. Yet it was the look on her face the few times Randolph called while he was there, that distress she couldn't seem to hide, that had clued him in. The information he had received from his contact in Atlanta was accurate. Randolph had it bad for Natalie, but Natalie didn't return his feelings. He had known instinctively that Randolph would put pressure on her to return to Atlanta with him. The truth was, he might've done the same, but seeing Randolph exit the hospital alone had said it all.

And he wouldn't have missed it for the world.

Brady glanced at Stansky as his partner walked resolutely beside him. Despite the reasons Stansky had professed, he had the feeling Stansky hadn't been completely honest about his determination not to be left behind at the precinct house that morning. He was still wondering when they reached Natalie's door.

Pausing only to speak a few words to the uniformed policeman seated there, Brady walked into the room. Natalie was sitting on the side of the bed. Her dark hair loose on her shoulders, her face devoid of makeup, dressed in sandals and a pale blue shift dress that somehow turned her gray eyes to silver, she looked young and anxious, the antithesis of the image she had tried to present that first day. She said flatly,

"It's twelve o'clock. I've been ready since ten. Am I leaving here today or not?"

She wasn't as fragile as she looked.

Brady inwardly smiled as he replied, "I don't know. Are you?" Pulling the paperwork out of his pocket that he had picked up and signed for at the desk, he said, "Oh, yeah, I guess you are!"

"Brady…"

Her brief smile and that fleeting dimple almost did him in again as she stood up and walked toward him.

"But we have to wait until the wheelchair gets here. A volunteer is bringing one up from downstairs."

"A wheelchair? I can walk."

"Hospital procedure. You have to go out that front door in a wheelchair so the hospital will be relieved of liability." He turned toward his partner belatedly. "You remember Joe Stansky, don't you?"

Natalie extended her hand in greeting. "I'm sorry. I seem to have forgotten my manners, Detective."

Brady slid a casual arm around her shoulders and guided her toward the wheelchair a smiling volunteer pushed into the room. He said, "We're going straight from here to the apartment Dr. Gregory set up for you."

Natalie frowned. "You know all about that, huh? It seems I'm the last to be informed."

"Dr. Gregory called the precinct this morning and made sure we would have a uniform posted there. He wanted to be certain there wouldn't be any foul-ups. So did the captain, so here we are."

"My protectors." She flashed a smile.

The knot in Brady's stomach clenched tight as that dimple winked again.

Natalie's smile disappeared abruptly when she sat down in the chair and Brady propelled her forward.

Brady scanned the area cautiously as they made their way to the elevator. The normal, everyday hospital routine progressed around them—familiar faces doing familiar jobs. He scrutinized the people exiting the elevator intently when it opened, then noticed that Natalie was looking up at him. She said in a strange tone of voice, "You're always the policeman, aren't you, Brady?" She remained silent for long moments, then surprised him by asking bluntly when the doors closed to seal the three of them alone inside the elevator, "Tell me the truth. How do you think this is all going to end?"

The door opened up opportunely, saving Brady from having to reply. He pushed her toward the entrance, silently gratified because Natalie had asked for the truth, and the truth was, he didn't have an answer.

HADDEN MOORE watched covertly as Detective Brady Tomasini pushed Natalie Patterson across the hospital lobby toward the front door. He looked at the fair-haired, slight Detective Stansky walking beside them and at the uniformed policeman following a few feet behind. His stomach churned with agitation. The police were giving Natalie Patterson the VIP treatment, when she was nothing more than a laboratory technician who had used him to take a giant step up.

A giant step at his expense.

Hadden watched as Tomasini pushed the wheelchair through the front doorway. He saw an attendant take the wheelchair as Natalie Patterson stood up and Tomasini took her arm to usher her into the unmarked police car parked illegally near the entrance.

And then she was gone.

All he had needed was a chance, another chance now lost, and now he—

"Get moving, *muchacho*. We ain't got all day to clean up this lobby!"

Hadden's head snapped up toward the man issuing the rude command. He forced himself to smile through the week's worth of beard that he had raised and darkened to match his recently darkened hair, then wiped his hands against his stained coveralls, pulled his cap down farther on his forehead with a subservient stance and began pushing his broom toward the hallway.

"Wait a minute!"

Hadden halted abruptly. He turned toward the maintenance supervisor to see the man glaring at him as he said, "I don't know where you worked before this, but you ain't getting away with half-assed work on this job. Sweep that floor and do it right!"

"Si. Si, señor. Lo siento."

Hadden retraced his steps, his shoulders submissively rounded as he pushed the broom with infinite care while the supervisor watched. He continued on down the hallway after the supervisor had disappeared from sight. He would leave the hospital at his first opportunity, and the derelict foreman who had just tried to humiliate him would wonder what happened to the replacement worker who had shown up briefly for work that morning. But he wouldn't wonder long. Illegals came and went without mention in menial service jobs. He'd just write it off.

Hadden was inwardly amused. Too bad for the ignoramus. There was a sizable reward being offered for information related to the capture of Dr. Hadden Moore, and the fool had missed his chance.

Hadden's satisfaction faded. He had missed an opportunity today, too—which meant he'd have to wait a little longer.

NATALIE WATCHED as Brady and Stansky moved through the apartment with professional thoroughness, silently, their jackets pushed back and their hands on the unbuckled holsters on their belts. Her heart had jumped a beat when she first saw them reach toward their guns. Small and black, the instruments looked so deadly, making her suddenly realize the full extent of the danger possibly facing her.

Her knees weak, Natalie sat abruptly on the living room chair. She did not realize that consciousness was fading until Brady was beside her, asking, "Are you all right, Natalie? Come on, honey, answer me."

Honey.

Natalie responded breathlessly, "I don't like being called *honey.*"

"What about *sweetie* or *darlin'*?"

The world gradually drew back into focus at Brady's deliberately provocative response. She mumbled, "No."

Suddenly swept up into strong arms, Natalie felt the air rushing past her, then felt a soft bed underneath her back and saw Brady looking down at her. He was frowning as her full consciousness returned. He asked, "What happened, Natalie?"

Embarrassed, Natalie replied, "I don't know. Maybe I'm not as recuperated as I thought I was."

Natalie saw Joe Stansky move into the doorway as Brady asked, "Did something scare you—a noise, or something you remembered?"

"No…maybe…oh, I don't know."

Stansky stepped back into the living room as Brady pressed, "Do you want me to call the doctor?"

"No, don't call her." Natalie attempted to sit up.

"Lie down."

She insisted and drew herself to a seated position, "I'm all right. I just got a little light-headed for a minute."

"You almost passed out."

"Not because I'm sick." Natalie hesitated, then said flatly, "Because I'm a wuss."

"A *wuss*?"

Natalie shook her head. "When you and Stansky reached toward your guns as you started checking the rooms—"

Brady went still.

"I feel like a fool."

Brady did not respond.

"I'm sorry. I didn't mean to scare you."

Brady still did not respond.

Natalie shrugged. "I disappointed you, didn't I?"

Unprepared for Brady's reaction, Natalie gasped as he sat on the bed beside her, grasped her shoulders and said in a hoarse whisper, "No, you didn't disappoint me, but you scared me, all right, and I'm not a guy who scares easily." Brady continued flatly, "Look, you don't have to be afraid…of anything. And I don't want you to hold anything back from me because you feel foolish. I need to know you're being honest with me…always."

"I'm sorry."

"Sorry?"

A tear slipped out of Natalie's eye, and she brushed it away angrily. What was wrong with her? She was acting like—

"Natalie…dammit."

Natalie took a breath as Brady slipped his arms around her and held her comfortingly close. The warmth of him…his strength enclosing her… She heard him whisper against her hair, "You had a frightening experience, you were injured and you're still not free of threat. It takes a damned brave person to face the uncertainties you're facing. I want you to understand that."

Brady slowly released her. She felt the intensity in his light eyes as he searched her face in silence, then said, "You're safe here. Nothing's going to happen to you."

Natalie took a breath. "I know. I just got…overwhelmed for a second."

Brady studied her closely.

"It won't happen again."

He remained silent.

"I mean it. It won't happen again."

Brady nodded and stood up. She couldn't quite read his expression as he said, "You'd better rest for a while. Joe and I are going to leave now. I'll be back later." He paused and added, "There'll be a uniform at your front and back door day and night. Don't worry."

Natalie nodded and forced a smile.

She was still smiling stiffly when she heard the sound of the hall door closing behind him.

Silent for a moment, she suddenly burst into tears.

BRADY WAS QUIET as he drove through the heavy afternoon city traffic. He had left Natalie at her new apartment and had not looked back. It was a classy address, all right, just a block from Lincoln Center. She'd probably take advantage of the opera, ballet or whatever arts were presently being offered when she felt a little more secure. It was a part of who she was, while he had lived in the city all his life and couldn't remember the last time he had felt tempted to walk through the Met's doors.

Natalie belonged in this neighborhood because despite her present neediness, she was classy.

Too classy for a beer and pizza guy.

Brady clamped his jaw tightly shut, glad that it was his turn to drive because it gave him something to do with his hands when he felt like punching out a window.

Stansky spoke up abruptly. "Well, I had to see it to believe it."

Brady glanced at his partner. His quiet manner aside, Stansky saw right through him. Yet Brady said evasively, "What are you talking about?"

"Do I have to spell it out?"

"It was time to get back to work. This Candoxine case won't solve itself."

"Yeah…sure."

When Brady didn't respond, Stansky said, "I didn't think I needed to remind you that I'm not as dumb as I look."

Brady cursed under his breath as he blew his horn and drove around a waiting taxi to a chorus of honking horns. When there was no reaction from his partner, he said succinctly, "So, I'm screwed."

"Would you care to elaborate?"

"You have to give me credit for getting out of that apartment before I did something I'd be sorry for."

"Meaning?"

"What the hell do you think I mean?" Brady looked at his partner coldly. "You saw her. She looked scared to death."

"Oh, you mean that hot little cookie who happens to be a research scientist who hasn't fully recuperated from her injury, who is feeling alone and vulnerable, and who was looking at you as if you were the only person in the world she could depend on?"

"Yeah."

"I'm sure you didn't do or say anything to her that might convey that impression."

"I did my job, that's all."

"Sure…real conscientiously."

Brady replied, "Whatever. The fact is, we have to finish up this case in a hurry, or I'm in trouble. Natalie Patterson is out of my league. My head knows it, but the rest of me is fighting like hell to deny it."

Dropping his sarcastic veneer, Stansky said quietly, "Natalie Patterson is feeling particularly defenseless now, Brady. Things will shake themselves into place as soon as she's feeling like herself again."

"By then, it might be too late."

"You're right, you know. She's different from the average woman. She even speaks a different language when she gets together with those on her level, but she's scared and she's looking for somebody to hold on to. Taking advantage of a situation like that might feel good for a while, but it would be a big mistake."

"Tell me something I don't know."

"Just keep in mind that she'll snap out of it."

Yes, but would *he*?

"What about that Randolph character who came from Atlanta to see her?"

"You've got to be kidding!"

"Brady…"

"He's a stuffed shirt, Joe. He'd drive Natalie crazy in any long-term relationship."

"Oh? She needs somebody more like you, huh?"

"Hell, no."

"That's what you'd like to think, though, isn't it?"

"Hell, no!"

"Come on, Brady!"

"I told you, I'm not looking for trouble."

Stansky squinted at him. "What would you call what was going on back there in that bedroom, then?"

"I'd call it self-control." Brady drilled his partner with a look. "Because, if you want to know the truth, I sure as hell didn't want to leave that apartment just then."

Stansky stared at him. "You're serious, aren't you?" He shook his head. "I never thought I'd see the day."

"What day?"

"The day you'd be heading for the short end of the stick."

Brady inwardly grimaced. He kept forgetting. He was the *precinct stud*.

Stansky continued, "Look, Natalie Patterson's had a bad

experience. It has to be hell being stuck in a strange city, just waiting for a murderer to try again."

"I know that."

"So don't forget it."

Brady asked flatly, "How many of those hotline tips did you go through?"

"About a quarter of the pile that was on the desk when I got there this morning."

"We'll finish them up today."

"Today?"

"We need to get this guy soon, or—"

When Brady did not finish his statement, Stansky prompted, "Or?"

Brady responded, "What do you think?"

Silent for a few moments, Stansky shook his head and said, "That's another 'I never thought I'd see the day.'"

"Meaning?"

"That I'd actually be glad I'm not you."

NATALIE SPLASHED WATER against her face, dried it with the luxurious, spotlessly clean towel hanging beside the sink, and looked up at herself in the bathroom mirror. She saw a small, pale face surrounded by wildly curling dark hair, where red-rimmed gray eyes that still held a trace of uncertainty overwhelmed small, pinched, tightly controlled features.

She would not cry again!

Despairing at her reflection, Natalie walked out of the extravagantly tiled bathroom into the bedroom where her few items of clothing hung neatly in one of the two closets in the room, and where her personal items were placed tidily in the top drawer of the dresser. Whoever Dr. Ruberg had sent to move her to this apartment had done a wonderful job. Even the small amount of laundry that she had accumulated had been done for her. A note on the refrigerator indicated that it had been freshly filled with necessities for her use, and that the canned goods in the cabinets were for her convenience. She wondered exactly who was responsible for such considerate treatment. She made a note to find out so she could thank and reimburse them.

It occurred to Natalie as she walked back toward her silent bedroom that the apartment was larger and more beautifully furnished than she could possibly have been able to afford on her salary, and that, in fact, her whole apartment back home would probably fit very well within the perimeter of the living room.

But it was quiet. Much too quiet, and Natalie felt again the rise of tears.

What was wrong with her? She couldn't count how many years it had been since she had last shed a tear. It was humiliating, and if she didn't know it would be even more humiliating, she would've put in a call to Dr. Weiss to see if there was something drastically wrong with her.

Natalie reached for the telephone on the nearby table, then paused with her hand on the receiver. She could call Aunt Charlene, but that would probably be a mistake. She had called her aunt from the hospital to explain about the accident—managing to make only vague reference to Hadden Moore—and had barely been able to stop the frail old woman from getting on a plane and flying to her side. And she knew that wouldn't do. Aunt Charlene's health was failing. A trip like that would probably be more than she'd be able to take.

Of course, she could call Chuck. Chuck would probably be on the ground by now, but she knew that would also be a mistake.

She could call George. Natalie glanced at the grandfather clock in the hallway and grimaced. She had fallen asleep from utter exhaustion after Brady and Stansky left. It was late, and George was probably on his way home by now. She'd have to call him tomorrow.

She could call Marge or Janet, her friends from the CDC, but she didn't know exactly what to say—she'd had an "accident," she was fine, she was going to stay in the city for an indeterminate time…and someone was trying to kill her.

Natalie's stomach did a flip-flop at the thought and she all but ran to the hallway door and jerked it open. The uniformed policeman seated there turned toward her with a frown.

"Is anything wrong, ma'am?"

"No, nothing." Natalie managed a stiff smile. "I…I just wanted to make sure…I mean, I needed to know—"

"There's going to be somebody posted here twenty-four hours a day, ma'am. Those are the orders that have come down through command, so you don't have to worry."

Don't worry. Familiar words.

Brady's light eyes flashed before her, and Natalie took a backward step.

"Thank you, Officer."

She closed the door and walked directly to her bedroom. Her throat suddenly so tight she could barely breathe, she lay down, pulled the covers up over her head and closed her eyes. She wanted to hide, and whatever was the matter with her, she needed to sleep it off.

Hopefully, she'd sleep it off.

DAYLIGHT STILL PREVAILED as Brady made his way silently up the hallway of the luxurious apartment complex. Gun in hand, wearing a Kevlar vest, he turned to look at Stansky, who was walking behind him, similarly attired. He saw the tension in his partner's tight expression, then looked at the black-clad SWAT team behind them.

It had been a long day after leaving Natalie. He had worked his way almost to the bottom of the hotline tips when he froze at the next report. He had somehow sensed that this one was authentic. The description of the subject; the timing of the subject's move to the apartment; the fact that the apartment was sublet and still in the former tenant's name, granting the subject anonymity; the subject's English accent and peculiar behavior during the past week while the manhunt had increased—all noted by a nervous tenant living a floor below in the same building who had shared the elevator with him several times. The tenant positively identified Moore when shown the picture a few minutes earlier, and they had been on their way.

The fact that the bastard's apartment overlooked Lincoln Center only a few blocks from Natalie's present location left Brady cold. He did not want to think how close Moore was to Natalie, or what might have happened if the guy on the floor below hadn't been so observant.

The doorman had not seen the subject leave. He was in there, and Brady was not about to let the opportunity slip past.

Cautioning silence as he and the SWAT team remained concealed, Brady motioned the building manager up to the door. He nodded, and the perspiring manager knocked and said, "Mr. Whittingham, we have a report of a leak in the ceiling of the bathroom below yours. If you'd be so kind as to allow me to check your bathroom."

No response.

The anxious manager looked back at Brady, and Brady silently cursed. If Moore was looking out through the peephole and saw him looking back…

He signaled, and the manager knocked again. "Mr. Whittingham…"

Still no response.

Suddenly unwilling to wait any longer, Brady thrust the manager aside and motioned the team forward.

Entering close behind as the team rammed the door open, Brady hardly heard the echoes of "Clear…clear…clear" as each successive room was declared vacant and safe. Instead, he approached the elaborately detailed desk situated in the corner of the room. He picked up the envelope marked Detective Tomasini.

Jaw tight, he opened it and read:

Dear Detective Tomasini,

I suppose it is superfluous at this point for me to tell you that you are too late. You see, I expected that you would find this apartment sooner or later, but I felt it would be best if I weren't here when you did. I'm sorry to disappoint you. You are so dedicated to putting the Winslow murders to rest, almost as determined as I was to commit the perfect crime.

Does it disturb you to know, Detective, that on several occasions during your investigation, I stood so close to you that you need only have turned around to see me?

It's true.

You're wasting your time attempting to find me, yet I'm sure you'll keep trying. I admire your perspicacity, but you really are out of your depth.

Please tell Natalie I won't forget her—because I won't. As it turned out, when I stood behind her on that street corner and whispered goodbye into her ear a week ago, my goodbye wasn't final. Next time, it will be.

It's too bad. She's a bright girl, but she outsmarted herself, and I must see that she pays.

As you can see, this has all become a game that I am determined to win. I always do, you know.

Sincerely,

Hadden Moore, Ph.D.

"Well, if there was ever any doubt…" Stansky mumbled over Brady's shoulder as he finished reading the note. He added, "But Moore's impressed with himself. He thinks he's smarter than we are and because he does, he'll end up out-smarting himself."

Not bothering to respond, Brady turned toward the officers awaiting his command.

"Seal off the apartment and get a crime scene unit in here. I want this place gone over with a fine-tooth comb. If this bastard left any clue as to where he went or what he intends to do from here, I want to find it."

"Brady—"

Brady turned at his partner's questioning tone. He said emotionlessly, "The bastard said it's all a game to him, and he always wins. Maybe so, but he hasn't taken into account that there's always a first time. Whether he knows it or not, I'm going to make sure this is his."

IT WAS SO WARM AND SAFE, and she didn't want to leave. She heard muffled sounds, but she remained motionless in the strange limbo holding her in its grasp.

Yet the sounds grew louder and a familiar fear made in-roads in her mind. She tried to ignore it, but—

Natalie gasped as the coverlet was ripped away from her face and she heard a male voice curse in the darkness of the bedroom. She shielded her eyes against the sudden glare of the lamp at her bedside. Still disoriented, she stared up to see Brady standing there, his face as hard as marble as he said, "What's going on here, Natalie? I knocked. No, I *pounded* on the door, but you didn't answer."

She took a breath. "I didn't hear you."

"You had the covers pulled up over your head!"

"How did you get in here?"

"How do you think? I have a key."

"A key? Why?"

"I'm the one who should be asking why." Brady turned to

the policeman standing in the doorway of the bedroom. He said harshly, "She's all right, McMullen. Go back to your post."

Brady turned toward her and demanded, "Why didn't you answer the door?"

"I told you, I didn't hear you."

"You had to be deaf not to hear me."

"I said, I didn't hear you."

Natalie watched as Brady took a deep breath, then stared at her in silence. It occurred to her that if anyone had told her a month previously that she'd be lying in bed with a homicide detective looking down at her, she would've said he was insane. But the world had turned upside down in the past month, and it suddenly wasn't as crazy as it seemed.

He was still staring at her, and Natalie said abruptly, "What happened?" When he did not answer, she threw back the coverlet and forced him to step backward as she stood up and repeated, "What happened?"

"Nothing. I'm going home."

Grasping Brady's arm when he turned toward the door, Natalie said, "I know something happened, Brady, or you wouldn't have come here so unexpectedly and you wouldn't be looking at me that way."

He turned back toward her. "What way?"

"I don't know...like you're angry."

"If I'm angry, it's because you scared the hell out of me!" Obviously making an attempt at control, he started again. "I made a helluva racket when I pounded on that door—*which you didn't hear*. Then I came in here and found you covered up like a corpse!"

"Brady!"

"Do you always sleep that way, or did you do it for kicks?"

"That's my business. I wasn't expecting you or anybody

else to come bursting into my room." Natalie paused, then said, "Why did you come bursting in here, Brady?"

"I came back to check on you. You're my responsibility, whether you know it or not."

"No, I'm not. You're not assigned to my protection detail."

"No, I'm the guy who's supposed to find the man who tried to kill you."

Natalie felt her face drain of color. She took a backward step and Brady said, "I'm sorry. I shouldn't have said that."

"No…you're right. I'm the one who's sorry." Natalie raised a hand to her forehead. "I don't seem to know what's right these days. I keep hoping that if I go to sleep, I'll wake up and find out this is all a bad dream."

"If it's a bad dream, it's one I'm sharing." Brady's expression softened. He asked abruptly, "Do you think you can find some coffee in that spectacular kitchen out there?" He hesitated. "You do know how to make coffee, don't you?"

"I'm a scientist. If I can't mix coffee grounds and water and come up with a decent cup of coffee, I should throw in the towel." Natalie frowned. "But you didn't come here for a cup of coffee."

"No, I came to talk to you…to make sure you were all right before I went home." Brady shook his head. A trace of a smile touched his lips as he said, "It's been a damned hard day and I have one more stop to make before it ends, so are you going to make me that coffee or not?"

"What time is it?"

"About nine o'clock. Why?"

"I just wondered."

Natalie did not protest when Brady draped his arm around her shoulders as they walked toward the kitchen. She looked up when he said, "You didn't answer me. Do you always sleep that way, with the blanket over your head? I feel I should be forewarned."

"Why?"

"Just answer the question."

"No, I don't usually sleep that way."

"Does your head hurt? If it does, maybe you should call the doctor."

"My head doesn't hurt."

"So?"

Natalie turned toward Brady when they reached the kitchen. She flicked on the light and replied with a flutter in her voice that she couldn't control, "Wouldn't you give in to some eccentricities if somebody was trying to kill you?"

Brady's strong features were lined with exhaustion—his five o'clock shadow was prominent, his thick black hair was unruly—but there was something about those light eyes and the way he looked at her the moment before he slipped his arms around her and drew her tight against his chest that choked Natalie's throat. Held warmly and protectively in his arms, she heard him say, "Do you believe me when I say I won't let anything happen to you, Natalie?"

Natalie whispered, "I believe it when you're here with me, but when you walk out that door, it's hard to remember."

Brady drew back, a small smile on his lips as he teased, "Natalie Patterson, are you asking me to spend the night?"

Hardly aware of her intention, Natalie responded, "Would you, Brady, just until I get used to this place? It's so…big."

Brady stared at her blankly, and Natalie said in a rush, "You could sleep in the other bedroom. It's all made up, but—" she took a breath "—but it's so far away. What if I take the chaise in the bedroom and you take the bed?"

Natalie saw Brady swallow, and she shrugged. "You'd be comfortable in the bed. I'm smaller than you are and I'll be fine on the chaise."

"McMullen might get ideas if I stay."

"And I might get some sleep."

Silence.

Natalie drew back, her face flushed with color as she said, "Forget it. It was a crazy idea. I don't know what's the matter with me."

"I'll stay."

Her responsive smile abruptly faded as Brady's expression darkened and he said, "But first we have some things to discuss."

THE COFFEEPOT stood empty as Brady concluded determinedly, "By his own admission, Hadden Moore is responsible for those Candoxine killings and for trying to kill you."

Brady and she were seated in the state-of-the-art kitchen, empty coffee cups on the table in front of them. Natalie was uncertain how much time had elapsed since they had come out into the kitchen, or how much small talk they had made before she had finally worked up the nerve to ask him what he meant by *We have some things to discuss.*

She said hoarsely, "He admitted it…all those killings at the Winslow barbecue and the attempt on my life? What possible reason could he have?"

"Mattie Winslow was the woman he wanted, and she *betrayed* him by marrying another man. He got his revenge by executing the perfect crime, only to have you, another woman, find him out. He can't let that go, Natalie. His monumental ego won't stand for it. He has to satisfy himself that everyone will know he's the superior intellect. There's only one way for him to do that."

Natalie felt the color drain from her face.

"You wanted to know the truth."

She nodded. "I can see you've discussed this with a police psychologist."

"I didn't need to. It's common sense once you know the details of Moore's life. He's a sociopath—a handsome, brilliant man at the top of his game, a manipulator who has never suffered a defeat that went unpunished by him." Brady shook his head. "I don't want to think how he handled comparable situations in the past, but this time he went too far. He would've gotten away with it, too, if not for you."

Natalie stared at him.

"Don't worry, we'll get him."

"How?"

"How did we find his apartment today?"

"You were too late."

"We won't be next time."

"How can you be sure?"

"Because I'm as stubborn as that maniac is. He may be a brilliant scientist, but I'm a damned good detective, and all he has to do is make one mistake."

"What if he doesn't make one?"

"He will."

"What if he doesn't make a mistake until...until it's too late for me?"

Brady sat back abruptly, his jaw tight. "I told you. I won't let that happen."

"You can't stay here every night."

"But I'm staying tonight, and we're taking one day at a time."

Natalie stood up abruptly. Her knees wobbled and Brady stood up beside her. "Shaky?"

"I'm fine. I'm just tired."

"Then maybe we should go to bed. And remember, I'm bigger than you are so *I'm* taking the chaise."

"But you'll hang off by at least a foot!"

Standing beside the abbreviated chaise a short time later, Brady cut short her protest by saying, "I'll be fine."

Natalie looked up into Brady's face. It was lined with exhaustion. She said, "All right. If you say so."

Clad in her nightclothes, Natalie exited the dressing room a short time later. She stopped short when she heard Brady talking into his cell phone in the next room.

"I know Sarah's waiting for me, but something's come up. Just tell her I'll see her tomorrow. She's been through this before. She'll accept it."

Struck momentarily motionless, Natalie then reproached herself silently. Brady had said he had one more stop to make before he went home. She should have realized that the absence of a wedding ring didn't mean the absence of a similar commitment—not for a man like Brady. Chuck was partially right. Brady lived in a world far different from the sterile environment she inhabited, and he made decisions accordingly. Yet he had been kind enough to sense her distress and to agree to stay with her. She hoped Sarah understood when she received Brady's message.

Sarah was a lucky woman.

Her throat tight, Natalie attempted a smile when Brady walked into the room and prepared to lie down on the chaise she had hastily prepared. She was right. He would hang off the chaise by almost a foot.

That thought was in her mind when the room was dark and she heard Brady vainly attempting to get comfortable. She said softly, "Thanks for staying with me, Brady. I appreciate it."

A soft grunt was his only response.

Chapter Six

"In my office, Tomasini…now!"

Brady looked up at Captain Wilthauer as the morning sun glinted through the mottled squad room windows behind him. He recognized that tone of voice, and he didn't like it. He noted as he walked through the busy room that Bigelow, seated at the next desk, snickered and glanced at his partner, who seemed to be sharing the joke. A few of the other detectives appeared to be in on it. On another day, he might be just as ready as they were for a good laugh, but presently he wasn't in the mood. Admittedly, he was a few minutes late reporting for work—a situation that had rarely happened before the Winslow case was thrown into his lap—but the previous night had been long and difficult. He was well aware, however, that the cause for his sleeplessness was unrelated to the uncomfortable chaise he had slept on.

He had left Natalie's apartment while she was still sleeping so he could go to his place and get cleaned up, but he had gotten caught in traffic again and had arrived at the office late. He knew that ticked off Wilthauer, but the truth was that he didn't give a damn. First things first, and Natalie was way up there on that scale.

Hardly waiting until his office door closed behind Brady,

Wilthauer said gruffly, "What in hell was that all about last night?"

"Last night?" Brady shrugged. "If you mean routing the SWAT team to Moore's apartment for nothing, you know as well as I do that happens. Stansky and I had a tip, a good one. We just got it a little too late and we—"

"Don't waste your breath! You know damned well I don't mean that." Wilthauer sat down abruptly behind his desk. "What's wrong with you, Tomasini? You know this is a high-profile case and that CDC woman is presently at the center of it. You also know that getting involved with her at this point—especially with your history—isn't smart."

"Getting involved with her?" Brady felt the blood rising to his face. "With my *history*? What is this, that stud thing again? If McMullen had something to say about me—"

"McMullen didn't say nothin'. He didn't have to." Wilthauer stared at him. "I thought you had more sense! Right now, Natalie Patterson is a combination of Albert Schweitzer and Snow White as far as the newspapers are concerned. If word gets out that you two are making it, it'll be splashed all over the tabloids, and the Commissioner will have a fit. He doesn't need any more complications than he's already got in this case."

"You're wrong, Captain."

"Am I?" His bleary eyes holding Brady's intently, Wilthauer asked bluntly, "Where did you spend last night?"

"What business is it of yours?"

On his feet in a moment, Wilthauer leaned forward with the flat of his hands on the desk, glaring, his bulldog persona on full display. He snapped, "Look, Tomasini, whatever you do is my business. A cop is on duty twenty-four hours a day, and what you do reflects on the department—especially when it pertains to a high-profile person in a high-profile case that the Commissioner is especially interested in because the media is hot on his back!"

"Who says?"

"I do, dammit, and I'm telling you now to keep your pants on if you want to stay on this case."

"I'm not going to argue with you. I'm just telling you you're wrong. I stayed in Natalie Patterson's apartment last night, but I didn't sleep with her."

"Oh, is that so?"

"She was scared, and I slept on the chaise in her room."

"You mean she turned you down."

"I mean, she was still feeling the residual effects of the concussion and she was scared to death last night—especially after I told her about Moore's apartment being located so close to hers and about the note Moore left."

"You divulged that information to her?"

"She has a right to know the full extent of the danger she's in. I don't intend to downplay it or keep her in the dark."

"She has a policeman at her door."

"That wasn't enough for her last night."

"You don't expect me to believe—"

"Look, Captain, believe what you want. I'm just telling you what happened. I slept on the chaise. Natalie slept in bed." He shrugged. "And never the twain shall meet."

Wilthauer eyed him coldly. "Is that what dealing with a high-class dame like Natalie Patterson does to you, make you spout poetry?"

Poetry?

Brady inwardly groaned.

Wilthauer continued to stare. "Maybe the twain will never meet—I have to admit, you've got me thinking about that one—but I don't want the media getting wind of this, so my advice would be to talk to the tenant who called the squad room this morning about your sleepover."

"What tenant?"

"His name is Armand Josephs. He lives across the hall."

Brady said, "I've met Mr. Josephs. He's retired. He lives alone. He's a very private person with a heart condition He made it clear that he doesn't want any part of this case and the publicity connected with it because of his heart condition. He never made that call."

"So who did?"

The chill that moved down Brady's spine was reflected in his voice as he responded coldly, "I'm thinking that bastard, Moore, has more nerve than we gave him credit for. I think he was right there in the building, in front of our eyes somewhere, and it's my bet that if there hadn't been a uniform at Natalie's door—"

"He wouldn't be that crazy."

"Who else would be keeping such a close eye on Natalie's apartment? If the tabloids were responsible, you wouldn't have gotten a phone call. You would've read it in the headlines this morning instead."

Wilthauer warned, "If you're making this up to cover for yourself—"

Brady gave a scoffing snort and Wilthauer said flatly, "All right. Talk to that Josephs fella. Then talk to Officers Mc-Mullen and Winters. They're off duty now, but they covered that Patterson woman's door right through the night. Press them. Ask them if they saw anything that was at all suspicious. Officers Jackson and DeMassio are on duty right now. Jackson's fresh from the academy. Make sure he stays alert."

"So you believe me."

"Do what I said! Report back to me personally. I need to know if this Moore bastard is playing with us, because if he is, he'll be sorry."

"I wouldn't say NYPD pride is the highest priority here, Captain."

"Don't preach to me, Tomasini!"

"I'm not." Brady paused, then continued determinedly,

"*That Patterson woman* is scared and she's depending on me to keep her safe, and unless you take me off this case right now, that's what I'm going to do. And I'm going to do it my way—which is any way I can."

"Don't get involved with her, Tomasini."

"Is that all, Captain?"

At Wilthauer's nod, Brady jerked open the door. Stansky looked up as he strode toward his desk and said gruffly, "Let's go. I'll fill you in on the way."

As he followed Brady out the door, Stansky commented, "You took care of Wilthauer's hissy fit, I see."

"Right."

"Where are we going?"

"We're going to Natalie's apartment building. We're going to interview a Mr. Armand Josephs, and every other damned tenant in that place to make sure Moore isn't hiding there right in front of our eyes."

SHE WOULD NOT let the situation get the best of her.

With that thought in mind, Natalie reached into her closet for her denim suit and contrasting shell, the only casual outfit she had brought with her on her supposedly short visit to New York. She put it on determinedly, slipped into her tennis shoes and started for the door. It was past midday, her head ached despite the pills Dr. Weiss had prescribed for her and her muscles were sore. Dr. Weiss had advised that some effects of her injury would fade slowly, but that she was otherwise all right. A short walk would clear her head.

She couldn't let fear dictate her life.

She *wouldn't* let it.

Natalie looked in the mirror as she passed and frowned at the realization that her hand trembled as she pushed a willful strand of hair into place. She had spent the major part of the day on the telephone speaking to Marge and

Janet, her friends at the CDC. They had heard a sketchy report on the case and were anxious for a firsthand account.
They had been shocked and sympathetic and had advised
her to come home. She had reacted by playing down the
danger of her situation and explaining that she needed to
stay until some of the particulars of the case were resolved.
She had hung up from the calls feeling depressed and knowing that the only thing she had accomplished, besides having arranged to have a few clothes shipped to her, was to
make herself feel more uncertain about her involvement in
the case.

She had then called Aunt Charlene and spent a half hour
reassuring the dear old woman that she was all right. She'd
hung up feeling homesick for the first time in years.

She still refused to admit that she'd been waiting for the
phone to ring—bringing with it the reassurance of Brady's
voice. When and how had the man she had formerly despised
suddenly become her friend?

The answer hadn't been hard to ascertain. It was when that
big, intimidating detective had looked at her with a simple sincerity she had never expected to see in those incredibly light
eyes and said, "I won't let anything happen to you, Natalie.
You have my word on that."

Somehow, she knew his word meant something to him; because it did, his word meant the world to her. She felt safe
when he was within sight, although she was not fool enough
to think that the threat lessened in any way.

Tall, dark, and handsome—she supposed some would say
Detective Brady Tomasini amply fit that bill. She wasn't sure
if she agreed, but she knew Dr. Weiss did. She did not doubt
Brady was successful with women, either. He had that down-
to-earth gut appeal. Her old college flame, Billy Martindale,
had had a similar appeal to which she had easily succumbed,
but the disastrous result of that relationship was a lesson she

wouldn't readily forget. Admittedly, it had probably colored her first reaction to Brady. What else could account for their initial, adverse reaction to each other?

Natalie paused on her way to the door. She couldn't continue to depend on Brady for support. She needed to get past her fear. She couldn't expect Brady, or even herself, to respect a woman who was so cowed.

Natalie glanced at her wristwatch. Four o'clock. Her head was pounding. She wasn't quite sure when she'd be in condition to return to the lab and the West Nile virus project she had instituted there, but she was determined to take a first step.

Natalie approached the door. Yet despite her resolve, the thought of a walk around the block left her as frightened as a child.

Natalie pulled the door open and smiled at the policeman seated there. He startled her by frowning back at her as he stood up and said, "Where do you think you're going, ma'am?"

"Where do I think I'm going?" Natalie's smile faded. "I'm going for a walk. I need some exercise."

"No, ma'am. I'm sorry. I can't let you do that." Soberly intent, the policeman blocked her way as he continued, "Detective Tomasini stopped by this morning and said to make sure you stayed inside until he gave the word that you could leave the apartment."

"Detective Tomasini..." Natalie felt a flush rise to her cheeks. "When did he say that? When he left this morning?"

"No, ma'am. He stopped by at midmorning, after he reported to the precinct."

"I didn't hear him knock on the door."

"He didn't knock. He just gave me my orders and left."

"Oh." Struggling against disappointment, Natalie forced herself to say, "Well, he'll approve of my getting a little exercise." She added, "You can come along if that'll make you feel better."

"No, ma'am. Step back inside, please. I have my orders."

"Wait a minute, Officer." Natalie went cold. "Are you telling me I'm a prisoner here?"

"No, ma'am. I'm just telling you Detective Tomasini gave me my orders."

Natalie said stiffly, "What if I decide to go for a walk despite Detective Tomasini's orders?"

"Then I'd have to stop you."

The pounding in her head accelerated, and Natalie was suddenly aware that she was trembling. But this time, it wasn't from fear.

Natalie turned abruptly and pushed the apartment door back open. Attempting civility despite her anger, she said, "Thank you, Officer. I guess Detective Tomasini is the one I'll have to discuss this situation with when he decides to show up."

"Yes, ma'am. I'd appreciate that."

Natalie closed the door behind her. Brady had left before she had awakened that morning. He had been right outside the door later that morning and he hadn't stopped in. She supposed what she could learn from that was that Brady was a professional…a detective intent on solving the case, just as Chuck had said. She couldn't fault him for that. She could only fault herself for misreading his intentions, for believing he had become her friend.

Natalie shook her head, walked back toward the TV and switched it on. She sat down and stared at it blindly. She should've learned from Billy Martindale, but apparently she hadn't.

BRADY STOPPED SHORT as he raised his hand to knock on Natalie's door. He checked his watch. It was the end of another long day that Stansky and he had spent knocking on doors in the apartment building. The first door had been Armand

Josephs's, and his suspicions had been confirmed. Mr. Josephs didn't have any idea what he was talking about when asked about the call Josephs was supposed to have made to the precinct.

Stansky had darted him a look at that moment that had said it all. Brady had stopped only to warn Jackson to make sure Natalie stayed safely inside her apartment before checking his gun and starting for the next door. After endless hours, however, the quest had proved fruitless. Stansky and he had quit for the day, somehow knowing they were wasting their time.

As disappointed as Brady, Stansky had gone home to his wife. Brady had gone directly to pick up Sarah at the veterinary hospital before it closed for the night. His brief call the previous evening to tell the vet he couldn't pick up Sarah had been difficult. The vet had said that the normally placid animal was restless, that she appeared to be waiting for him. He had told himself that Sarah was a cop's dog, and that she was endlessly forgiving of the difficult choices he often had to make that left her in a similar situation. Sarah's delight at seeing him a short time earlier had proved his theory correct and warmed his heart. He had paid the bill and headed home, only to find himself turning his car back toward Natalie's apartment. Twenty minutes later, he had left Sarah in the manager's air-conditioned office in the parking garage, determined to make his stop at Natalie's apartment brief.

The sight of the young officer still seated outside Natalie's door stopped his intended knock as he said, "What happened, Jackson? You should've been relieved of duty here a half hour ago."

"I know." Jackson's freckled face twisted into a grimace. "And my kid's sick, too, but Winters called and said he was caught in a traffic jam and he'd be late, so I guess I'm stuck here for the duration."

"Sorry about that." Brady raised his hand again to knock,

only to hear Jackson caution, "I'd be careful about going in there if I were you, Detective." Brady turned back toward him sharply as Jackson added, "There's one angry lady in there."

"Angry?"

"She came out here about four o'clock and said she was going for a walk."

"A walk?"

"Yeah, like she didn't have a worry in the world."

Brady shook his head, incredulous. "Did she look disoriented or confused?"

"She looked determined. I practically had to threaten her to get her to go back inside."

Brady knocked sharply on the door. He knocked again when there was no response. He had already withdrawn his key from his pocket when the door opened and Natalie backed up to let him in.

She wasn't smiling.

"What's wrong, Natalie?"

Wrong question.

Natalie pushed the door shut behind him, her face flushing with heat as she responded, "Am I a prisoner in this apartment, Brady? If so, I'd like to know because I'm going to call a lawyer and get myself out of here and out of this city as fast as I can!"

"Wait a minute!"

Almost amused, Brady took a step toward her, only to have Natalie back up as she demanded, "Well, am I?"

"Whatever gave you that impression? Of course, you're not a prisoner. That guard outside is there for your protection, and for your protection means not going out for a walk alone until we can be sure you're safe."

"What does that mean, Brady?"

"That means Stansky and I have to make sure the situation is secure."

"Which means?"

"Which means—" Brady sobered and took a breath "—that you can't go out until I say it's all right."

"I can't go for a walk."

"You don't really feel well enough for the exertion, and you know it." Brady looked at the revealing frown lines between her brows. "You have one of those headaches again. Did you take your pill?"

"I'm fine, or I will be if I can get some fresh air."

Brady took another step. This time, Natalie didn't move back, and he said, "Why are you so hot under the collar? What happened?"

"Nothing. That's the trouble. Nothing happened, all day. I just sat here trying to amuse myself between calling a few friends and taking *naps*."

"Don't tell me you're bored."

"I am."

"I guess that's better than feeling sick."

"It isn't. At least if I felt sick, I'd have a reason to lie in bed all day. I'll go crazy in this apartment with nothing to do."

"You're supposed to rest."

"This place is so big that it echoes. It's not conducive to resting."

"You can watch TV."

"I hate TV."

"You could read."

"My head hurts when I read for an extended period."

"So you're telling me you spent the day alone, lonely and bored because you don't have anything to do, because you can't go for a walk and because you don't know anybody in the city who can keep you company."

Natalie nodded. She said unexpectedly, "Pathetic, huh?"

"Yeah." Brady stared at her a moment longer.

Damn.

He said, "I wish I could stay."

She looked disappointed.

Brady's spirits rose despite himself as he said, "Did you want me to stay for a while?"

She shrugged. "I thought you could bring me up to date on the case."

"I got my tail kicked this morning for telling you as much as I did yesterday. The captain didn't think it was necessary."

"That's crazy. I need to know what's happening so I can protect myself."

"You don't have to protect yourself. That's why you have officers guarding your front and back doors."

"I still need to know."

"I agree." He forced himself to continue, "But I'll have to fill you in tomorrow. I can't tonight."

"Oh, you have a date." She took a backward step. "I'm sorry. I didn't think."

"It's not a date. It's a previous commitment."

"Of course."

"Besides," Brady said as he sniffed the air, "I'm hungry and I don't smell anything cooking in that grandiose kitchen."

"I wasn't particularly hungry. I thought I'd order out."

"The story of my life." He shook his head. "But I can't stay. I have to leave."

Tears glinted in Natalie's eyes as she averted her gaze and said, "I'm sorry, Brady. I don't know what's wrong with me. I'm all confused and uncertain. I don't even feel like myself."

He was lost.

Brady heard himself say, "I'll stay for a few hours and we can talk, as long as you don't mind if I bring a friend. She's waiting downstairs in the manager's office."

"A friend?" Natalie looked taken aback. "You're sure she won't mind?"

"She won't mind as long as I'm here with her."

Brady noted Natalie's uncertain expression as she said, "All right…if you're sure. I'll wait to see what she prefers before I order out."

"Order what you like. She's not fussy. I'll be right back."

Concealing a smile and feeling somehow better than he had felt in years, Brady pulled the door closed behind him.

NATALIE LOOKED DOWN at the dog at the end of Brady's leash. Of an indiscriminate breed in shades of black and brown, and sporting a large bandage wrapped around a shaved portion of her belly, the dog looked up at Brady worshipfully as he said, "Natalie, I'd like you to meet Sarah."

"Sarah? *She's* your friend?"

"The best friend I've ever had."

Natalie stared at Brady blankly.

"What's the matter? Don't you like dogs?"

"I like dogs." Natalie took a breath and managed a smile. "I like them very much. I just didn't think…I mean, I thought you meant…"

Rescuing her opportunely, Brady explained, "I was supposed to pick up Sarah at the vet's last night, but I figured another day in the veterinary hospital wouldn't hurt, considering the circumstances."

"Considering that I panicked at the thought of staying here alone."

Brady made no response.

"What happened to her?"

"She needed an operation."

"What was wrong with her?"

Brady's face colored surprisingly as he replied, "Female problems, but she's all right now."

Natalie smiled, warmed by the cold nose that nuzzled her hand. "She's friendly."

"Not always, but she seems to like you." Brady said abruptly,

"And she's as hungry as I am. The vet said he didn't feed her because he didn't want her to get carsick."

"I ordered Italian."

"That's good. Sarah likes Italian." Brady smiled as he unfastened Sarah's leash. "Considering my name, I guess you figured I'd like Italian, too, and you're right."

Sarah's and Brady's plates were empty an hour later, but Natalie's food lay almost untouched as she asked, "You're saying you believe Hadden Moore was right here in the building or was close enough to know that you spent the night?"

"You wanted to know the truth."

"Yes, but—"

The fear in Natalie's eyes tightened the knot deep inside Brady. Intensely aware of the multitude of emotions she raised inside him, he took her hand in his. It was small and fine-boned, delicate, just like she was—although he knew those same hands had ably conducted scientific research that had left other competent researchers in the dark.

Brilliant, yet vulnerable.

A world apart from him, yet tantalizingly, briefly within his reach.

Never more aware of those contradictions and the dangers they represented for them both, Brady said earnestly, "Natalie, that should be reassuring to you. If Moore was that close and didn't act, it was because he realized you were well protected. What he probably doesn't realize is that he got Captain Wilthauer's back up by pulling that stunt, which worked out well because Wilthauer's now prepared to make sure the NYPD continues to protect you as long as it remains necessary."

"With an officer at both doors of this apartment, you mean?"

"And with Wilthauer's best detectives on the case so you'll be completely safe."

"Wilthauer's best detectives…"

"Stansky and me."

"And you're modest, too."

Natalie almost smiled, but Brady did not. Instead, he glanced at his watch and forced himself to say, "It's getting late. Sarah needs to be settled in for the night, and so do I. I have to go."

"Oh."

Brady swallowed at the sound of that *oh*. He looked at Natalie, and his heart did that teenage flip-flop thing again in his chest. Those damned gray eyes were looking up into his with an appeal that she did not speak, but that he heard clearly—too clearly for him to be feeling what he was feeling. The situation was obvious. He was the detective who was protecting Natalie while her innocent life was being threatened by a madman; he was the only individual in a strange city who had taken the time to treat her like a human being instead of a scientific commodity; he was the only person who had walked through her apartment door who acted as if he cared more about *her* than the situation she was in.

He stared at her, wondering what it was about Natalie Patterson that knocked him off his feet. She was a babe, all right—even if she seemed to do her best to nullify her appeal with unattractive clothes and a lack of makeup that somehow had the reverse effect, leaving him salivating. The hard truth was, if she were any other woman, she'd be in his arms right now. He'd be tasting those lips she was presently biting to still their trembling, and he'd be crushing her so close that those shudders occasionally shaking her narrow shoulders would cease. He'd be running his hands through her dark, silky hair as he whispered words such as, *I want you, Natalie, honey— it's an ache that won't quit. I can't seem to think of anything else when I'm with you and it's driving me crazy.*

He'd probably be doing his best to override any objections

she might be thinking of making, too—which he knew only too well would be a mistake for both of them, and which he somehow knew left him as vulnerable as she was. He heard himself say, "Why, did you want Sarah and me to stay here tonight?"

Natalie looked down as Sarah nuzzled her free hand. She said, "Do you think she would mind?"

Aware that he was only digging himself in deeper, Brady responded, "Not unless you object to her snoring."

Natalie's small smile tore at Brady's heart as she replied, "Aunt Charlene had a pug while I was growing up. No dog snores louder than a pug."

All right.

Brady stood up abruptly. "I have to take Sarah out for a walk. I'll be back."

"Brady," Natalie stood up beside him and said soberly, "I appreciate it…really. I feel like you're the only person who understands. I mean, everybody's been very generous since I got here, but—"

She took a breath, her eyes filling. His resolve almost undone, Brady kept his hands at his sides as he repeated, "I'll be back."

Brady picked up Sarah's leash and the canine pushed herself to her feet. As he turned toward the door, Natalie said, "Thank you, Brady."

Brady figured it was wiser to keep walking.

Out in the hallway, he looked at the officer sitting there and said, "When did you get here, Winters?"

"About an hour ago."

He instructed tightly, "Make sure you stay alert. Moore won't give up easily and we have too much to lose here."

"Will you be coming back to the apartment tonight, Detective?"

Brady frowned. "Yeah. Why?"

"Just wondered."

Doing his best to ignore the officer's knowing glance, Brady walked toward the elevator and rang the bell.

FROWNING, HADDEN WATCHED as Tomasini walked his canine toward him on the busy street. Dressed in old clothes and worn tennis shoes he had picked up at a used clothing store, bearded and with his hair darkened as he shuffled around garbage barrels standing on the curb for morning pickup, he knew he was all but invisible in a city where the homeless were a fact of life. It amused him to know that even were he questioned, he was more than capable of convincing even the most astute police officer that his masquerade was authentic. Among his many accomplishments, he was not only a linguist, but he was also an accomplished actor who had been wise enough to douse his clothing with alcohol to affect his present facade. He doubted that the renowned NYPD was aware of his lesser-known list of accomplishments—which gave him the edge he sought.

Hadden's unshaven jaw tightened as he pulled open another plastic bag and retrieved an aluminum soda can to add to those in the filthy sack he carried. Despite his brilliance, however, his calculated call to Tomasini's captain that morning had been a waste of time. Tomasini had not been removed from the case as he had hoped, and if he did not miss his guess, the determined detective was preparing to spend the night in Natalie Patterson's apartment again. Actually, he admired the detective's dedication to his work. Were he in Tomasini's position, he would probably have taken advantage of the opportunity with Natalie Patterson that had been dropped into his lap. He hoped the detective was enjoying his little peccadillo, because he intended to see to it that it would be short-lived.

Unable to resist the temptation, Hadden turned toward

Tomasini as he came abreast of him. He grasped his arm as he mumbled, "A quarter for a—"

The sudden growling lunge of the canine at Tomasini's side thrust Hadden backward with a gasp of genuine fear. He stumbled, overturning the barrel and falling. He was speechless under the brief heat of Tomasini's gaze as the detective pulled his dog back and ordered sharply, "Find another street to work, buddy. This isn't a good place to be right now."

Hadden stood up, grabbed his sack and staggered away without pausing until he was out of sight. He straightened up and looked back in the direction from which he had come when he turned the corner. His decision made, he walked toward the spot where he had parked his "borrowed" car.

Hadden unlocked the car door and started it up the moment he got inside, frustrated by the realization that he could no longer afford to play the game while the odds were presently stacked so high against him. It had become necessary for him to leave the area for a while so the situation could cool down. He consoled himself that time was on his side and that when interest in the case had sufficiently faded, he would again have the advantage.

Hadden carefully guided his vehicle out into the waning traffic. He would put his alternate plan into effect and regain the advantage.

Hadden frowned at the thought. He was a patient man, but he disliked delay. Yet he was also a realist who faced hard truths, and delay had become a necessity.

Despite it all, he was certain he would win the game in the end, no matter how long it took.

He always won.

It was just a matter of time.

Chapter Seven

"You know you're making a big mistake, don't you?"

Brady had figured something like this was coming. Stansky had been too quiet since picking him up at Natalie's apartment house that morning—a first since he had started staying there almost three weeks earlier. Those same three weeks had been a test of his self-control that Brady had never expected he would be capable of handling.

So far, so good. Those teenage flip-flops in his chest continued every time Natalie's dimple winked in his direction—yet he'd been able to resist the temptation to gather her into his arms whenever an unexpected sound startled the smile from her face; to resist comforting her with the brush of his lips and the warmth of his body; to put the brakes on believing that she wanted him as much as he wanted her.

Yet those dark wisps of hair that clung to her cheek when she awakened still tempted his touch, the sight of her parted lips still whipped up a hunger inside him unlike any he had ever known and the simple sight of her still left him aching.

Frowning, Brady took a steadying breath. In the last three weeks he had graduated from sleeping on Natalie's chaise, to the parlor couch and then to the extra bedroom. Natalie had panicked when he had attempted to shut the bedroom door behind him. Not that he could blame her. The investigation into Hadden Moore's whereabouts had almost come to a standstill. Even the hotline tips had all but ceased. To the NYPD's knowledge, Moore had neither left the city nor the country, yet he was untraceable within those confines. For all intents and purposes, Hadden Moore had disappeared into thin air.

Brady consoled himself that despite the lack of progress on the case, Natalie appeared to be adjusting. He knew nightmares haunted her, but her headaches seemed finally to have been brought under control, enabling her to return to work on the West Nile virus project she had begun at the NYC Public Health lab. Yet nagging at the back of his mind was the realization that Wilthauer wouldn't be able to continue the protection he had provided her much longer—which could easily reverse every positive step she had taken.

Another truth was that he was becoming increasingly protective of her and she was becoming increasingly dependent on him. Something had to give, and it now appeared Stansky knew that as well as he did.

"Did you hear me, Brady?"

"I heard you."

"Yeah, sure…but did you really hear me? And don't try telling me this thing between you and Natalie Patterson is none of my business, because I'm involved in this Hadden Moore case and everything connected with it, whether I like it or not. And whether you like it or not, your personal reaction to Natalie Patterson's situation is affecting it."

Brady glanced at Stansky coldly. "I suppose I could've avoided this conversation if I hadn't asked you to pick me up at Natalie's apartment this morning."

"So why did you?"

"Because my car's in the shop getting the alternator fixed. Look, I told you before, there's nothing going on between Natalie and me."

"The sad thing is that I believe you—but I also know you, and I know this 'platonic thing' will get thrown out the window sooner or later if you don't make some changes soon. I suppose my next question is whether ethically speaking—" Stansky paused, then continued. "Cancel 'ethically speaking.' I don't want to get into that, but I suppose what I wanted to ask was whether you really want to take advantage of the situation."

"Natalie feels safe with me. That's all there is to it."

"You're kidding yourself. Whatever you've got going on in your head, you're her hero. You're protecting her, watching out for her in a way that's above and beyond the call of duty, while she's scared to death that maniac is going to come after her again. That puts a lot of stress on 'platonic.' Add to that the fact that you're hot for her, that you're normally the last person who'd let something like that get past him and that some misguided women actually find you somehow appealing. If you need a reality check just about now, try remembering the way that Patterson chick looked at you that first day in the lab, as if you were from a different planet."

"Maybe, but we're on the same planet now."

"Temporarily."

"Maybe 'temporarily' would be all right with me."

"I don't think so."

"So you're a mind reader now."

"No, I'm not, but if 'temporarily' was all right with you, you'd already have made your move. The fact that you haven't says it all." Stansky continued more softly than before, "I'd have to be blind not to see the way you look at her, man!"

"So?"

"So, you know if you got anything started, it would only come tumbling down between you two as soon as this Hadden Moore thing is cleared up."

"What if we don't find the guy?"

"That's a hell of a thing to base your future on."

"My future?"

"Come on, face it. You're not thinking of a one-night stand."

Brady shrugged.

Stansky stared at him. "Let me ask you something. What do you talk about when you're with her in that apartment?"

"What do you think we talk about? The case!"

"That's all?"

"And her work."

"Her work?"

"On the West Nile virus."

"Great. I suppose you understand every word she says."

"Just because I don't understand all the technicalities, doesn't mean I can't appreciate the contribution she's making."

"Yeah…and I guess that makes for stimulating conversation." He didn't wait for Brady to respond. "She's an intellectual. At the risk of repeating myself, she's out of your league."

"Screw it, Joe! Maybe it's none of your business what we talk about in private!"

Stansky persisted. "Do yourself a favor, Brady. Don't put yourself in a position where you can't win. Do your job and forget the rest. That's the only way to be fair to yourself and to her."

Silence.

"You know I'm right."

Silence.

"Brady…"

Brady said abruptly, "Turn right at the next light."

"Why?"

"Just do it!"

Waiting until Stansky made the turn, Brady directed,

"Slow down. That's right. Pull up in front of the doughnut shop."

Stansky looked at him.

"I'm hungry. I didn't have any breakfast."

Stansky glared. "Bastard."

Brady shrugged. Well, maybe he was.

SHE WAS FEELING BETTER. She had returned to the lab and her work on the West Nile virus. She was almost her former self.

Not.

Natalie glanced up at the lab doorway. She sighed silently with relief at the shadow of the uniformed policeman there. The West Nile virus project was important and she was making significant progress in a direction that pleased Dr. Gregory immensely. But the project had become more than a contribution to her—it had become a lifesaver, a way to keep her mind occupied so she wouldn't see danger in every shadow.

Brady's image cut into thoughts of her research, and Natalie smiled. It had taken her a while and considerable contemplation, but she had decided that he was handsome after all. More importantly, she knew she couldn't have made it back to this place of semisafety in her mind if not for him. She recalled waking up in the middle of the night gasping, hardly able to breathe because the sound of Hadden Moore's voice saying, *Goodbye, Natalie,* resounded in her dreams. It was Brady whose arms held her safe. Somehow, the same light eyes that had mocked her so openly the first time she met him now stirred a warmth inside her that nudged out the cold knot of fear.

Brady's image as he had appeared when emerging from the spare bedroom that morning returned unexpectedly to mind, raising a flush to Natalie's cheeks. Dark hair still tousled from sleep, barefooted, wearing only pajama bottoms, he had still carried himself with instinctive caution as he approached the kitchen. He paused briefly when he saw her in the kitchen doorway, and he smiled. She remembered the jolt that had shuddered through her at that smile, and the restraint she had employed to keep from walking straight into his arms.

Strangely, nothing had seemed more right at that moment.

Even more strangely, nothing seemed more right to her even now.

Natalie sighed. But Brady had merely walked past her into the kitchen for a cup of coffee.

The sharp ring of the telephone cut into Natalie's thoughts. She frowned as she reached for the receiver, then sucked in her breath at the sound of the familiar voice inquiring, "Natalie, is that you?"

"Yes, it's me, Chuck." Natalie continued with true sincerity, "I'm so sorry! I forgot to call you back yesterday, but the director of the National Institute of Allergy and Infectious Diseases called me, and I was distracted. I hope you forgive me."

"Of course."

There was resentment in his voice, but Natalie continued, "The director surprised me with his call. He seems to think there might be a correlation between their research and the research I'm doing here on the West Nile virus." Excitement tinged her voice. "One of their paths is support of West Nile virus vaccine approaches, including chimeric vaccines, naked DNA vaccines and vaccines containing cocktails of individual West Nile proteins. In a nutshell, our conversation led me to believe I can actually contribute to the progress they've already made at NIAID. It's exciting, Chuck. Exhilarating, really."

Growing interest tinged Chuck's voice as he said, "You're referring to the Acambis vaccine, of course."

"Right. It seems my name came up in relation to the expansion. To tell you the truth, I'm flattered they even heard of me."

"I don't think you should be surprised, Natalie. Your Candoxine discovery has gotten a lot of play in the media. The follow-ups written about you included your interest in West Nile virus research." He added softly, "You deserve the recognition. I'm proud of you."

Natalie was touched at Chuck's sincerity. Then he asked, "How is the Candoxine case coming along, by the way? I haven't heard much about it in the media lately."

Natalie's enthusiasm went cold. "The case is coming along slowly."

"No progress?"

Suddenly defensive, Natalie snapped, "There haven't been any other attempts on my life. I'd call that progress."

"I'm sorry. I didn't mean to make you angry." Chuck's remorse was obviously genuine as he continued, "I was just wondering…I mean…well, I miss you. And to be truthful, I'm intrigued by this West Nile virus research you're doing. I thought I'd come up to the city to see you this weekend if it fit in with your plans."

"I don't have any plans, Chuck. I haven't had any since the Hadden Moore thing happened."

"So…would it be all right if I came?"

"Of course it'll be all right." Natalie swallowed, uncertain of the reason for her sudden discomfort as she added, "Just as long as you don't mind having the NYPD a part of your life for the weekend."

"I won't mind."

"Come then, Chuck. I'll be interested in your opinion on the chimeric virus vaccine once you've had an opportunity to learn more about it."

Their conversation dwindled to a halt, and Natalie hung up. She looked up abruptly and saw Brady standing in the lab doorway.

NIAID…CHIMERIC VACCINE…ACAMBIS VACCINE…
Hell, it was all Greek to him!

Brady hesitated in the lab doorway, never feeling more like an outsider. A call from Stansky's wife telling Joe that their five-year-old son had fallen and had needed to be taken to the emergency room for observation had sent his partner directly to the hospital after he had dropped Brady off to pick up his car. Their conversation that morning was behind them, but Stansky's straight talk had lingered in Brady's thoughts despite his pretended dismissal of it. The fact that he was alone for lunch had seemed a made-to-order opportunity for him to clear up some things on his mind.

He asked, "Am I interrupting anything?"

"No." Brady silently cursed the dimple that winked in Natalie's cheek as she smiled, glanced at her watch and said, "It's time for lunch and I'm hungry. We can go down to the cafeteria to eat if you like." She glanced at the uniformed policeman standing silently at the door. "It'll give Officer Clark a chance to eat on time, too."

"Yeah…" Brady looked at the officer and said, "You heard her, Clark. Take a break."

Brady was halfway through his roast beef sandwich and an extended, meaningless conversation when he asked abruptly, "Who were you talking to on the telephone when I came in?"

"Chuck Randolph. Why?" When Brady did not immediately respond, Natalie said, "He was curious how everything was going on the case."

"I don't suppose he was too happy to learn there's no progress to report."

"I don't know about that." Natalie avoided his gaze as she said, "I'm still alive, which I doubt I would be if not for you and the NYPD."

"It's been three weeks, Natalie. For all we know, Moore isn't even in the area anymore."

"I suppose that's why there's still a policeman stationed outside my door."

"That's a precaution."

"It's a necessity."

"A temporary necessity."

"Brady, please!" Natalie whispered fervently, "I know you're trying to make less of the danger for my benefit, but I know the truth."

"Stop it. We're going to get him. It just might take a while."

"I know." Natalie breathed deeply. "I'm sorry. I guess all this talk about progress has stirred things up for me."

Brady's expression hardened. "Did Randolph say something?"

"He doesn't understand, Brady. Everything follows a natural progression in our work. We follow certain steps and we arrive at our results, whether they're negative or positive. He doesn't factor in the human element involved in a case like this."

"Did he try to undermine you—try to tell you that you were in danger even with us protecting you, because if he did—"

"No, of course not! We talked about the West Nile virus project. Chuck is interested in the progress I'm making. He's coming up this weekend to learn more about it."

"He's coming here to the city to learn more about vaccines." He nodded. "Sure."

"It's no reflection on your work, Brady. I know you're doing all you can."

"It's not enough, and you know it."

"It's enough for me."

Natalie's whispered statement froze Brady's reply on his lips. Natalie was suddenly clutching his hand, and she was looking at him with wide gray eyes that had turned to liquid silver. It was all there, exposed for him to see. Stansky was right. He was her hero right now, the man saving her from a killer. She hadn't even liked him the first time she'd met him, but now he was her lifeline, the only person who made her feel safe while her life hung in the balance. The problem was, it wasn't like that for him. She had knocked him off-kilter from the first moment he'd seen her.

Stansky was right. Sooner or later, that sterling coat of armor she saw him wearing would tarnish and *he* would be all that was left. He didn't want to be around for Natalie's rude awakening. He somehow knew he wouldn't be able to bear it.

"Brady?"

She was waiting for his response.

Brady was about to reply when a voice beside their table inquired, "Do you mind if I join you?"

Brady looked up, relieved to see Dr. Gregory standing beside the table with tray in hand. He noted the hesitation on Natalie's face and he responded, "Not at all, Doc. Natalie and I were just discussing her West Nile project."

Dr. Gregory settled his tray and pulled up a chair as he continued, "Your work here has been brilliant, Natalie. I'm very pleased that it's being recognized. I'd like to discuss some of the points covered in my conversation with the NIAID director when you get a chance."

"Yes, of course."

Brady drew himself abruptly to his feet. "I have to go back to work."

Responding to Natalie's soft sound of distress, Dr. Gregory said, "I hope I'm not driving you off, Detective."

Brady forced a smile. "No, of course not. I have to meet my partner at the station house in an hour. It'll take me just about that long to make it through the traffic. He'll be pissed if I keep him waiting." He turned to Natalie. "Officer Clark will walk you back to the lab. I'll see you later."

Brady strode resolutely toward the cafeteria doorway.

It was the hardest thing he had ever done.

Forty-five minutes later, Brady walked across the station house floor toward Wilthauer's office. His expression was set when Wilthauer looked up at him questioningly and he closed the door behind him.

NATALIE WAITED ANXIOUSLY for the elevator door to open. She glanced at Officer Clark where he stood beside her and smiled. The afternoon had stretched tediously onward after Brady left the cafeteria. Actually, she wasn't quite sure what had happened. It could have been Chuck's comments about the lack of progress on the case that had started everything rolling. Or maybe it was the change she had sensed in Brady since they had parted that morning. Whatever, she'd had the feeling Brady was assessing her in some way and that she had come up short.

The elevator opened and Natalie stepped out of the car and started toward the door where Officer Flynn was waiting. She heard the relief in Officer Clark's voice when he officially turned his watch over to the younger policeman and allowed her to enter the apartment.

Natalie was never quite certain who would be guarding her door, considering that NYPD personnel seemed to change on a day-to-day basis. Brady and his partner were the only constants. She wondered how she could have made it without him.

Natalie turned the key in the lock, pushed the apartment door open and walked inside. A sound from within the apartment halted her thoughts abruptly, and fear shot up her spine. She called out sharply as she took a backward step, "Who is it? Who's there?"

"It's me. I'm in the bedroom."

Brady.

Her heartbeat gradually returning to normal, Natalie started toward the sound of his voice. Her smile froze on her face when she reached the bedroom doorway. Brady was in his shirtsleeves, his tie hanging loosely askew as he packed the small suitcase he had brought with him a few weeks earlier.

In answer to her unasked question, Brady said emotionlessly, "I've been taken off the case, Natalie. Wilthauer assigned the case to a new team. He figures a fresh outlook might start things moving again."

"What do you mean? That's crazy!"

Brady looked up at her and shrugged. "I don't know. Maybe he's right. Maybe it's time to get some new blood in on the case."

Natalie shuddered.

"Sorry. Poor choice of words."

A slow breathlessness began to overwhelm her. Natalie said, "But that doesn't mean you have to leave."

"Yes, it does. O'Reilly and Potter have their own way of handling things. They wouldn't appreciate my interference in the case."

"You wouldn't be interfering. You'd just be staying here…as a friend."

"Chuck Randolph is coming to visit this weekend. He can keep you company."

"Is that it, Brady? Chuck is just a friend, but you're more than that. It's different between you and me. I feel safe with you. I know no one will ever hurt me while you're here."

"No one will hurt you with O'Reilly and Potter on the case, either, Natalie. They're good cops and excellent detectives. They won't let anything happen to you."

Natalie attempted a smile. "But you and Stansky are the best. You said so yourself."

"Yeah, well, maybe I exaggerated."

Natalie stared at Brady in silence, her chest heaving. Brady looked the same—tall, handsome, light eyes—but no, those light eyes were now cold.

She questioned, "What happened, Brady?"

Brady slapped his suitcase closed. "I was taken off the case—that's what happened."

"No, there's something else."

Brady replied softly, "Look, Natalie. You're going to be all right. You've come to depend on me. That's my fault. I shouldn't have let that happen. That was my first mistake."

"Mistake…"

"That's right, a mistake. It's the NYPD that's protecting you, Natalie, not me. You don't owe me anything."

"And what you're trying to say is that *you* don't owe *me* anything, either. Is that right?"

Brady ran an anxious hand through his hair. "I suppose."

"I don't want to stay here alone, Brady."

"You won't be alone."

"You mean the uniforms at my door? They won't be there when I start seeing movement in the shadows of my room during the night."

"You'll get used to it."

"I don't want to get used to it! I want you to stay." Natalie caught her breath. "Stay just for a little while…at least until I get to know O'Reilly and the other detective better."

"I can't be your security blanket, Natalie. That's what I am to you, you know. But that's my fault. I made a mistake."

"No."

Brady picked up his suitcase and said softly, "I have to go."

"Don't leave, Brady. Stay a little longer. Just a few days until I can get used to the idea."

"It's not goodbye forever, you know. I'll keep in touch. I'll call you for dinner sometime."

"Sometime…" Natalie shuddered.

"Dammit, Natalie, you're not making this very easy."

"I don't want you to go."

Brady stared at her. "I have to, you know."

"No."

Brady started toward the door.

"No! Don't go, Brady." Natalie threw herself against him. She clutched him tight, unable to think past the sensation of Brady's strong, hard body pressed tightly against hers as she cried, "Please don't go!"

SHE WAS SO CLOSE. Brady could smell the warm, female scent of her, could feel her softness as she struggled to hold her fear at bay. She looked up at him, a tear spilling out from the corner of her eye as she waited for his response.

His response was simple. He wanted to kiss her. He wanted to wrap his arms around her and make her a part of him. He wanted never to let her go. He wanted her to know that, and he wanted her to know she was his first thought on awaking and his last thought before falling asleep.

But he also wanted to tell her that for the first time in his life, that wasn't enough. He wanted to explain that with her, it was different. He needed more. He needed her to see him as a man, not as the person who presently kept a psychopath from her door.

The problem was, things had somehow slipped past that point with Natalie. He wanted *her,* but she wanted the man she *thought* he was.

It was a lopsided relationship. What he felt for Natalie demanded more.

Brady lowered his mouth to Natalie's parted lips. He kissed her, his mouth pressing suddenly hard and deep, his arms snapping around her as he indulged every emotion rocketing through him.

Then he snapped back. He held her at arm's length as he stared down into her startled expression.

Temporarily.

No. That wasn't good enough with Natalie.

Releasing her abruptly, Brady said, "I'll keep in touch, Natalie. O'Reilly and Potter will do a good job for you, but I won't be far away if you need me."

Natalie did not respond. Brady knew he would never forget the way she looked at him—silent and frozen to the spot as he picked up his suitcase and walked out the doorway.

HADDEN MOORE SIGHED and slipped down farther between the clean, cool sheets on his bed and looked at the television screen that flickered in the darkness of his room. Another day was coming to an end, and it amazed even him how well things were progressing according to his plan.

Hadden glanced at the newspapers piled beside his bed and smiled. The media reported less and less every day about the progress on the Winslow poisonings case. He knew the reason was simple—there was no progress to report. He had seen to that.

Hadden chuckled. He had no doubt the police were continuing with their investigation, but he also knew the weather would soon change. Fall would come in, then winter. The Winslow barbecue deaths would seem out of season, and they'd then be replaced with another story.

He was patient. He could wait for that to happen before continuing with his plan. It was brilliant, of course, like every other plan he had ever conceived.

Hadden went still, his attention caught by a familiar image on the television screen across from him. It was Natalie Patterson, walking rapidly toward the NYC Department of Health lab building. She looked thinner. She was unwilling to speak to the reporters who stretched their microphones out toward her as she turned briefly toward the camera. Her small, petite features drawn into a frown and her narrow eyebrows drawn tight over large, gray eyes, she looked much like a delicate fawn caught in impending disaster.

Hadden raised the remote and increased the volume to hear:

…but Natalie Patterson, the CDC employee well-known for her brilliant work in the Candoxine poisonings, has not been idle during the present lapse of progress in the case. She has been working in conjunction with the New York City Department of Health to research the West Nile virus that has threatened the New York City area and many other areas of the country. She has joined pioneers in the study of the virus and her work has been recognized as exceptional.

Kudos, Ms. Patterson! You make us proud.

Brilliant? Exceptional?

Hadden remained motionless as he stared at the television screen.

Chapter Eight

November

"Don't do this, Captain. It's a mistake. Moore is waiting for this to happen."

"You don't belong in here, Tomasini." Captain Wilthauer looked up from behind his office desk. "You gave up the Candoxine case, remember? As a matter of fact, you asked me to assign it to another detective because you said you were getting too personally involved. I did you a favor and granted your request. O'Reilly and Potter are good detectives with a combination of twenty-two years on the job. They've covered all the bases and you know it. So get out."

Brady's jaw twitched. "I told you I was getting too personally involved. I didn't say I wouldn't be following the case."

"I have no problem with your following it, just as long as you remember you don't have the first word anymore. O'Reilly is the principal on the case now and he's all right with the department's decision to remove Natalie Patterson's protection."

"I know." Brady glanced back at the squad room floor through the glass that enclosed Wilthauer's office. O'Reilly's balding head shone with perspiration, a signal that the middle-aged detective was getting irritated as he watched the

progress of the meeting between Brady and Wilthauer. He
knew O'Reilly sensed what Brady and Wilthauer were discussing, since the news that the Patterson protection detail
was being scrapped had swept across the squad room floor
like wildfire. He also knew that O'Reilly didn't like him
questioning that decision, but Brady didn't give a damn.
Wilthauer was right. O'Reilly and Potter had done as good a
job as could be expected since they had taken over the Candoxine case almost four months previously, considering that
as far as the NYPD knew, Hadden Moore had dropped off the
face of the earth. Brady also suspected that O'Reilly believed
he had dumped the case when he saw it was going nowhere—
which was far from the truth—but Brady hadn't been of a
mind to make explanations. He still wasn't.

"Hadden Moore is a psychopath, Captain. Look at his past
history. He was brilliant at Manderling Pharmaceuticals, but
obviously unstable. When Manderling finally saw the need
to have him committed, Moore obviously played the game,
content to wait out six months in the institution that would
make his 'cure' appear plausible. He returned to Manderling
and waited even longer while he accumulated enough Candoxine in small amounts for its disappearance not to be noted,
then waited just long enough so his return to the U.S. would
not appear suspicious. When he finally arrived in the States,
he killed Mattie Winslow, six more members of her family,
and maimed several others without blinking an eye, just to
serve Mattie Winslow the punishment he felt she deserved for
marrying somebody else."

"So? Is that supposed to mean something?"

"It means Moore is patient, determined and ruthless. He
admitted that he tried to kill Natalie Patterson and failed. He
won't accept failure. He's just waiting until it's safe to try
again."

Silent for a moment, Wilthauer shook his head. "No, I

don't think so, and neither does O'Reilly. Ask him. He's been following through on all the evidence on the case for the past four months. He thinks Moore has given up his revenge on Patterson and has left the country somehow."

"Moore wouldn't do that. He's out there waiting for his chance to strike again and you're serving it to him on a silver platter."

"That's enough, Tomasini!" Wilthauer stood up, his jowled face reddening. "I looked at the situation, considered the facts, and I agree with O'Reilly and the Commissioner that Natalie Patterson doesn't need protection any longer. That's it! Over. Done. *Fine, capisce?*"

Brady's heart was pounding. He had thought he was doing the right thing when he backed away from the Candoxine case months earlier. He had truly believed he was too caught up in his mixed-up feelings to act responsibly either in a professional or a personal capacity. Hell, he had wanted her so badly….

But months had passed, he had purposely put physical distance between Natalie and him so he might get a clearer perspective, and nothing had changed. He still wanted her. The only difference was that Natalie had put more than a physical distance between them. He had noted the difference in her tone in his weekly phone calls to check on her during the past few months. On the few occasions when he arranged to have dinner with her, she wasn't the same. He wasn't sure which had hurt more—that guarded look in her eyes or his own certainty that, in spite of it, he had done the right thing.

The right thing…because Chuck Randolph had come increasingly into the picture with weekend visits that Natalie appeared to appreciate. He didn't like Randolph but, admittedly, the bastard spoke her language. Every time he'd seen them together, they never seemed at a loss for conversation, and Randolph had actually made Natalie smile.

Brady had consoled himself, however, that unless he read the signs wrong, the relationship between Natalie and Randolph was strictly friendly—at least on Natalie's part. And he was glad. As far as he was concerned, Randolph was a hardass who thought he knew it all, even if Natalie seemed to like him.

Brady asked, "Have you told Natalie the department made the decision to remove her protection?"

"Not yet." Wilthauer drew back, frowning. "She's coming in here this morning. The Commissioner felt that in view of the cooperation she's afforded the department in the past, she should be informed face-to-face, so we can explain our position."

"Right." Brady's jaw tightened. "When is she coming in?"

"She should be here within the hour." Wilthauer added, "And I'll handle it, understand? The only other persons I want in this office when she's here are O'Reilly and Potter. You and Stansky have other important cases on your plate, so get moving."

"All right." Brady added, "But for the record, you're making a mistake."

"Tomasini…"

Brady walked out of the office without replying.

NATALIE GLANCED OUT the window of the taxi at the gray clouds darkening the late morning sky overhead as her cab darted through the heavy traffic. It was going to rain, which she had learned was not an unlikely expectation for New York City in November. Gray days had become the norm since the month had rolled in a week earlier, but she hadn't really given the weather, anything or anyone a thought, so engrossed had she become in the West Nile virus project that now was her major focus.

Or so she told herself.

The cabdriver pulled up in front of the precinct station house. Natalie dropped the fare into his hand. She stepped out onto the sidewalk and walked slowly toward the doorway, ignoring her NYPD shadow as he slid his police car to a stop nearby. She had a bad feeling about this summons to the precinct. She'd had less and less communication with the department as the months had rolled on, and media coverage of the case had come to a virtual standstill. Wilbur O'Reilly and John Potter, the two detectives who had replaced Brady and Stansky on the case, were nice men, but she hadn't become too friendly with them. They had done their best to keep her up to date, even if she had the feeling that her situation had changed of late.

Natalie shrugged. The only problem was that the idea of "new blood" stimulating results in the case had fallen flat. Hadden Moore's whereabouts remained as much a mystery as the man himself.

The cool wind blew her dark hair into disarray, and Natalie pulled her coat tight around her neck. She had become accustomed to the wind that gusted through the caverns of the city, carrying with it minute particles that stung her eyes and occasionally bit sharply into her cheeks. But her mind was far from the weather as she pulled the heavy, precinct door open and stepped inside. Taking a moment to smooth fly-away strands of her hair, Natalie approached the desk, only to be waved inside without a word by the desk sergeant. She had the feeling he had been waiting for her arrival. That thought somehow raised a wave of apprehension as she walked into the squad room and headed for Captain Wilthauer's office.

Despite herself, Natalie scanned the room for the sight of a familiar face—Brady's face, to be exact—but he wasn't there. She smiled at Stansky and stopped to say a few words as she passed his desk, but she didn't like the way the other detectives avoided her glance. She liked it even less when Wilthauer stood up behind his desk, frowning when he glimpsed her approaching through the glass office walls, and when O'Reilly and Potter fell into step behind her as she entered the office.

Moments later, Natalie stood stock-still, shock radiating through her as Wilthauer said apologetically, "I'm sorry, Miss Patterson. The department's official position is that Hadden Moore has left the city—possibly the country—and unless we obtain evidence to the contrary, your protection is being suspended."

At Natalie's silence, Wilthauer continued, "The department sincerely regrets having to take this step, but the manpower problem in this precinct is critical, and since there appears to be no present threat—"

Hardly aware that the color had drained from her face, Natalie responded, "No present threat? Hadden Moore tried to kill me. Then he came to my apartment building the same day I moved in. He could've had only one purpose in mind when he did that, and if it wasn't for the protection the department provided for me—"

"That was almost four months ago, Miss Patterson."

"Moore waited almost a year to get revenge on Mattie Winslow."

"The circumstances in that case were different. He had a vested interest in his supposed vengeance on her."

"He has a vested interest in his supposed vengeance on me, too."

"But the situation has changed. The police department is aware of Moore's crimes and is on the lookout for him now. He won't risk getting caught. And the fact is, if he was going to try to harm you again, he would've tried already."

"You're speaking as a rational man, Captain. Hadden Moore isn't rational. He's insane. He doesn't see things the way a normal person does, or he wouldn't have tried to kill me in the first place."

"Miss Patterson…"

"Wait a minute. Let me get this straight." Natalie attempted a stabilizing breath. "You're telling me that no matter how I protest this decision, you're just going to…abandon me to this killer?"

"We're not abandoning you. The conclusion has been reached that any further threat from Hadden Moore is unlikely, that's all."

Natalie looked at the two detectives who had remained silent throughout the discussion and said, "Detective O'Reilly…Detective Potter, you know the background here. Don't you have anything to say?"

His expression unreadable, O'Reilly replied, "We'll continue to work the case, of course, ma'am, but the decision to cancel your twenty-four-hour protection came down through command, and unless we come up with something definite to change things, the department's decision stands."

Incredulous, Natalie shook her head. "I don't believe this. So what am I supposed to do now?"

O'Reilly replied, "My best advice to you is to return to Atlanta. You know, out of sight, out of mind."

"Do you really believe I'll be safe in Atlanta?" Natalie was starting to shake. "Or are you figuring that once I'm there, you won't have to worry anymore about what happens to me because I'll be the problem of the Atlanta Police Department?"

"Those are . harsh words, Miss Patterson," Captain Wilthauer said, frowning. "I can only suggest that if you have family in the Atlanta area, you might stay with them temporarily. You'll probably feel safer."

Natalie returned hotly, "You know what Hadden Moore did to Mattie Winslow's family. Do you really believe I'd entertain that thought for a moment?"

"Miss Patterson…"

"No! We're talking about a psychopath here, a psychopath who has already proved his murderous intent. Don't you care?" Natalie took a few steps in retreat. "He's going to try to get me one way or another if you let him."

"I'm sorry. There's nothing I can do."

Her knees suddenly weak, Natalie turned blindly toward the door. She staggered and would have fallen if not for a sudden, strong grip that stabilized her.

She looked up.

Brady.

A tremulous smile curved her lips as Brady slid a supportive arm around her. Her voice choking as she stared up into his tight expression, she heard herself say, "Dammit, Brady, what took you so long to get here?"

"THEY CAN'T DO THAT, can they, Brady?"

Brady sat opposite Natalie in her apartment kitchen, the place where they had spent numerous evenings in easy conversation. Her face was ashen, and her expression was stressed. Their conversation was filled with tension as Natalie pressed, "They can't just remove my protection, can they? It's not safe. Hadden Moore is still out there."

Brady stared at Natalie, a sense of déjà vu sharp in his mind. The discomfort between them had disappeared the moment he had touched her in Wilthauer's office. The only problem was that other feelings had returned, as well.

With Wilthauer's direct order in mind, he had remained concealed in the squad room when Natalie arrived there earlier, but he had watched the progress of her conversation with Wilthauer through the glass partition. He had seen Natalie suddenly go still when Wilthauer dropped the bomb that her protection was being cancelled. He wasn't sure exactly what happened after that, except that he had started toward her the moment she started shaking and within minutes, she was in his arms.

Wilthauer hadn't said a word when Brady escorted Natalie out of the squad room—Brady supposed because he had actually done Wilthauer the favor of handling the situation. Or possibly Wilthauer had remained silent because he had known nothing he could have said would have made any difference. Whatever. Brady had ushered Natalie into his car and headed back to her apartment, where he knew she felt safest. It had not escaped his notice that there was no longer any guard at her door when they arrived, and his stomach had clenched tight. He had rushed her inside without taking into consideration the way he would feel when they were finally alone in that apartment, sitting face-to-face, with his same hunger for Natalie again racing through his veins.

"Answer me, Brady, please."

Natalie's soft urging brought him back to the present. Struggling to find the right words, he ventured, "What do you want me to say, Natalie? You already know the answer to your question. As far as the NYPD is concerned, Hadden Moore isn't an immediate threat any longer."

"You know as well as I do that doesn't mean anything."

"The department doesn't agree. The media pressure is off and the powers-that-be figure Moore's too smart to try again with the whole city on the lookout for him."

"That's it, then? What about the police department psychiatrist? Doesn't he have anything to say about it? He can't possibly agree with their conclusions."

"Dr. Rightgart gave his opinion on the subject and the result is obvious."

Natalie shook her head. "I don't know what to do, Brady. Should I go back to Atlanta like O'Reilly suggested and hope Moore won't follow me?"

"I think that would be a mistake."

Natalie began trembling again as she replied. "Are you

also saying I should just stay here and wait for Moore to strike again?"

Aware that mere words would not suffice, Brady drew Natalie to her feet and slid his arms comfortingly around her.

Brady's arms closed around her, and Natalie leaned into his strength. Brady hadn't responded—or maybe he had. In his arms, she was home…safe now, where she was supposed to be.

She burrowed closer, uncaring that Brady had not answered her question because she wasn't afraid anymore. Brady was with her. It was only when he left that the fear returned.

Natalie closed her eyes as Brady's strength encompassed her. She wanted to tell him how much she had missed him and how she had longed to ask him to come back each time he had called to check up on her during the months they were apart. She wanted to tell him that she had looked forward to those few times when they had dinner during their separation, but that she had been afraid of looking weak and dependent, and had ended up acting stiff and cold. She wanted to tell him how many times she had relived his kiss, how many times that memory had gotten her through the long, dark nights that she spent alone. She wanted to tell him that. But she knew what he'd think.

I can't be your security blanket, Natalie.

Natalie drew back abruptly and said, "You're not my security blanket, Brady. You know that, don't you? You know you mean more to me than that."

"Do I?" Brady's gaze burned into hers and his voice grew hoarse. She sensed a meaning far beyond his words when he said, "What do I mean to you? Tell me, Natalie. I need to know."

Natalie looked up at him intently. Brady was dear to her in so many ways that were suddenly clearer to her than they had ever been. She had missed him desperately—the way he looked at her, as if he really cared what happened to her; the warmth of those sudden smiles that touched her heart; the way he listened to her when she talked, and the candid comments or direct challenges that followed. His wry, surprising humor. His upfront, unvarnished view of the world, and his pride in the sometimes disheartening but necessary work he felt compelled to do. But most of all, she had missed the surprising, unexpected gentleness and understanding that was so much a part of his personality but that in no way negated the instinctive toughness necessary in his sometimes thankless job. She needed to tell him all those things and to say she didn't want to lose him again, because the first time had been too hard.

Responding truthfully as best she could, Natalie whispered, "I don't really know that answer. All I do know is that I missed you terribly while you were gone, Brady. Somehow I didn't feel complete without you. And I know no one can hurt me as long as you're with me—not because I know you'll always do your best to protect me, but because everything slips back into place when you're here. I feel whole again."

Brady responded, "Be careful what you say if you don't want me to take things the wrong way."

Natalie's reply came from the heart. "There is no wrong way, Brady."

Hoping desperately that Brady would understand what she was trying to say, Natalie lifted her mouth to his.

NATALIE OFFERED HIM her lips and Brady accepted them, his heart pounding. His arms snapped around her to crush her close as he intensified their kiss, hardly believing that he was holding her as he had dreamed of holding her, hardly believing that he was kissing her as he had wanted to kiss her since the first moment they had met.

He loved her. That truth rang through Brady's mind as he

indulged the warmth of her slenderness pressed tight against him. He bathed her face with kisses, slid his lips down her throat past the pulse throbbing wildly there. Her skin was soft under his lips. The taste of her was sweet.

Her knees buckled, and Brady lifted Natalie up into his arms and carried her to the bedroom. She was so light, a feather in his embrace as he lay her on the bed and stretched out beside her.

His heart leaped as he pressed himself fully against her. She was beautiful…so beautiful that his heart ached with the joy of her.

Sweet desire. Loving moments. A growing heat that would not be denied.

Sliding himself atop Natalie at last, no longer able to restrain the heat building inside him, Brady groaned as their naked flesh met. He probed her intimately. His heart thundered as he slid himself inside her.

Warm…moist…she enclosed him, and he briefly closed his eyes as she met his thrusts.

Brady felt the moment approaching, but he forced himself to pause. Natalie's expression was anxious…expectant, and the joy of the moment was almost more than he could bear.

Natalie's slender body convulsed rapturously, with a suddenness that carried Brady with her to mutual, exhilarating climax.

Raising his head in the breathless quiet that followed, Brady looked down at Natalie. Her eyes were closed, her lips parted. He pressed his mouth lightly to hers. She did not respond and a knot of anxiety tightened slowly inside him. He whispered with a trace of uncertainty, "Talk to me, Natalie. Tell me you wanted me to make love to you. I need to hear you say the words."

Brady held his breath in the momentary silence before Natalie's heavy eyelids lifted and she whispered, "I wanted it, Brady, because…because I know now that I wanted you."

His throat too tight for response, Brady drew Natalie close again with a loving reply that went unspoken.

THE GRAY AFTERNOON was at its height when Natalie stirred, then glanced at the empty bed beside her. Momentarily disoriented, she searched the room with her gaze. She was covered with a light sheet and her clothes were neatly folded on the chair beside the bed, but Brady's clothes were gone and he was nowhere to be seen.

Uncertainty made slow inroads into her mind. The apartment was dark and silent. Where was he? Where had he gone? Surely he wouldn't have left without a word…not unless—

Natalie snapped to a seated position in bed and stared into the afternoon shadows of the darkened room. Her unsteady breathing was the only sound in the silence.

No, she heard a stealthy step.

Natalie's heart pounded. Somehow frozen to the spot, she listened as the footsteps drew closer.

She gasped aloud when a shadowed figure appeared in the doorway.

"I didn't want to wake you up while I dressed. Are you hungry? I made sandwiches."

Natalie remained rigidly still, her response caught in her throat as she struggled to catch her breath.

"What's wrong, Natalie?" Brady was at her side in a moment. His hand on the gun strapped to his belt, he scrutinized the shadows, then turned back to her and demanded, "What happened?"

"Nothing. Nothing's wrong. I'm sorry. I must've fallen asleep, and then when I woke up—"

Brady's light eyes went cold. He stood up slowly, his hand dropping away from his holster as he continued, "And when you woke up—you remembered what happened and you didn't understand what came over you, or how you ended up in bed with me—is that it?"

When Natalie did not immediately respond, Brady turned away.

Aware that she was naked under the sheet and somehow unwilling to stand up, Natalie called after him, "I don't regret anything that happened between us, Brady. For a moment, I was just—" she took a breath "—I don't know…scared."

Brady turned to search her expression. He walked slowly back toward her and crouched beside the bed. Still clutching the cover tightly against her, Natalie stared at him anxiously. A wry smile touched his lips as he said, "There'll be no surprises for me if that sheet slips." Natalie did not respond, and his smile faded. He said more softly, "Don't worry. I told you…no strings attached, if that's what's bothering you."

Not allowing her time for a reply, Brady stood up abruptly and said, "Come on, get up. We have a lot to do. I have a very placid but deserving female waiting for me in my apartment who won't be able to wait too much longer before she needs to go out for a walk." He added, "I figured we'd take her for a walk together before I packed up my suitcase and my dog and moved back in here for the duration."

Natalie took a breath. "For the duration?"

"For as long as necessary."

Brady slipped his palm against Natalie's warm cheek as he whispered, "No strings, Natalie…for as long as you want me to stay, and not a minute longer."

Standing up before she could reply, Brady turned back toward the doorway and said, "Hurry up. Those sandwiches are waiting."

WHAT WERE THEY DOING up there in that apartment?

He didn't like waiting.

Hadden Moore looked up at Natalie's apartment window, his patience short as he stood on the windy street below. Four months was a long time to wait, and he was still waiting. However, the wait had proved advantageous in a way, since it had allowed him time to do some engaging thinking.

Hadden smiled. He had known the media would get tired of the Candoxine mystery. He had also known that when the media lightened its scrutiny, the order would come down through command for Natalie's police protection to be cancelled.

Poor Natalie. He sympathized with her. It was difficult to be helpless.

Hadden's smile faded. He had made good use of his idle time during the past few months by learning more about Natalie Patterson. He knew he had plenty of time before making a very important decision. Natalie wasn't going anywhere for a while. She was smart enough to know that even if she left the city, he'd follow her.

Two familiar figures suddenly walked out onto the sidewalk from the fashionable building, and Hadden took a spontaneous step backward. Judging from Tomasini's possessive grip on Natalie's arm, he suspected he knew the reason they had been delayed.

That complicated things. Yet complications had always challenged him, and Natalie was such a lovely little thing.

Hadden watched as Tomasini drew Natalie toward his car. Succumbing to impulse, Hadden strode toward Tomasini as the detective settled Natalie into the passenger side. He bumped into Tomasini roughly, then said, "Oh...sorry," without waiting for Tomasini's reply as he strode away.

Hadden paused at the corner and looked back to see Tomasini's car pulling out into traffic with its precious cargo. The fool! Tomasini had not recognized him and had missed out on another opportunity to easily apprehend him.

Hadden had no doubt that he would win in the end. Strangely enough, however, for the first time, he wasn't sure what he wanted the ending to be.

NATALIE STOOD BACK a few feet as Brady pulled a key from his pocket and unlocked his apartment door. The whining on the other side stopped the moment he pushed the door open, and Sarah greeted them with enthusiastically wet, sloppy kisses.

"I know what she wants." Amused, Brady grabbed the leash hanging nearby and snapped it onto Sarah's collar. "Don't bother taking off your coat, Natalie." When Natalie did not immediately respond, he said hesitantly, "Or you can wait in the apartment if you'd rather. It's safe here for the time being, as long as you keep the door locked."

A chill ran down Natalie's spine and she responded, "No, I could use some exercise."

"Sarah makes sure I get that, day and night."

Natalie responded with an attempt at lightness, "It's obvious that her big, brown eyes can talk you into anything."

"Yeah. I suppose you could say the same thing about big, gray eyes."

Sarah whined a little louder, and Brady said, "We'd better hurry."

Walking with Brady and Sarah was an unanticipated, simple pleasure. The chill in the air was invigorating, Sarah's enjoyment contagious. And the moment when Brady slipped her hand through the crook of his arm and she leaned spontaneously against him…well, she wasn't quite sure what she felt, except it was good.

When they returned, Brady closed the apartment door behind them and headed for the bedroom. Sarah trotted behind him, leaving Natalie alone in a living room that was comparable to her quarters back in Atlanta—meaning small and spare.

Natalie scanned the room. No TV, and furniture that, though neatly arranged, showed definite signs of wear. She knew the look—donated, or secondhand store treasures. She walked toward the kitchen and smiled. It was pristine, evidence that Brady most likely ordered out more often than not. She followed the sounds of Brady's packing to his bedroom. The room contained a big, comfortable-looking bed with a comforter thrown casually across it, a large, flat-screen TV and on the floor an oversize pillow covered with dog hair where Sarah obviously lay each night, watching him adoringly. Manila file folders lay randomly placed on a nightstand, with a stained coffee cup beside them. Various books were strewn on the floor beside the bed. She scanned their covers— mostly instructional—but the volume on criminal psychotic behavior caught her eye.

Natalie's sense of well-being went cold.

"What's the matter? Don't you approve of my housekeeping?" She felt the intensity of Brady's scrutiny, then saw him glance at the books on the floor.

"I'm just tired, I guess."

Brady snapped his suitcase closed, signaled Sarah to her feet, and took Natalie's arm, saying as he moved her toward the door, "Let's go. This place depresses me, too."

Natalie had stopped shaking by the time Brady opened her apartment door. Once inside, the look in his eyes did not quite match his tone as he glanced at his watch and said casually, "Why don't you order something for us to eat while I unpack?"

"Chinese?"

Brady grimaced.

"Italian?"

"A girl after my own heart."

Natalie walked toward the kitchen telephone as Brady turned toward the bedrooms with his suitcase. She found takeout menus and ordered what she knew were Brady's favorites. Then she followed the sound of his movements to the doorway of the spare bedroom. She watched as Brady unpacked the last of his things and picked up his empty suitcase.

When he looked up, Natalie said, "Are you trying to tell me something, Brady?"

His shirtsleeves were rolled up, his collar was loosened, his dark hair was tousled as if he had raked it absentmindedly, and his jaw was beginning to show the edge of five o'clock shadow, but Brady's light-eyed gaze assessed her closely as he responded, "Maybe I am. I said no strings, and I meant what I said."

"No strings. Is that for my benefit or yours?"

"I don't know." Brady watched her walk toward him. "You tell me."

"It's for your benefit, if you sleep in this room." Natalie halted a few steps away from him and continued softly, "I mean, it's all right with me, too, if you want to keep things casual between us, or if you figure things will work out better that way, but as far as I'm concerned, that isn't what I want. Not because you're a security blanket for me, Brady. Because for me, that's the way it seems right."

Natalie saw the almost indiscernible twitch of Brady's lips and the slow heaving of his chest before he replied, "You're sure about that? I told you, this isn't a conditional arrangement. I'll stay just as long as you want me here, whether it's in the spare bedroom or—"

Hardly able to speak past the emotion suddenly choking her throat, Natalie said softly, "*Or* is better for me, Brady."

Brady dropped his suitcase and took her into his arms. He whispered against her mouth, "That's all I wanted to know."

Chapter Nine

The November morning sun shone brightly through the window blinds, reflecting a slatted pattern against the Oriental hallway runner as Natalie started toward her apartment door. She patted Sarah's head in passing. Sarah was a dear. The canine hadn't taken long to settle into her routine at the apartment. Brady took her out for her walk when he woke up, a dog walker took her out at noon and Sarah was then content to wait until Brady returned to go out again. It didn't seem to make any difference to Sarah if Brady was home on time or if he returned hours late from his job. The canine seemed to know that Brady would not desert her.

Natalie acknowledged with a wry smile that it was much the same with her. All was right with the world now that Brady was back in her life. The threat against her remained, but panic no longer ruled her life. Brady was there for her, always there, in every way.

Natalie recalled the previous evening when they had retired. She had climbed into bed and into Brady's arms. The simple joy of it, the solace, the sense of being complete… She hadn't ever expected to feel the way she felt when he was near, or when he made love to her. It was as if—

Natalie glimpsed the hallway clock as she passed it and

gasped. She was late! She had woken up on time. She couldn't imagine how she had fallen behind schedule.

Natalie grabbed her coat, her lips twitching at the silent acknowledgement that she might have lost time when Brady had pulled her into his arms in the kitchen earlier and proved to her that his desire for her wasn't limited to the evening hours. Or maybe their prolonged shower afterwards accounted for it.

The memory of Brady's calloused hands moving sensuously against her skin set a flush of heat to her cheeks. But late or not, she didn't regret a moment of it, which surprised her. Her work in the lab had always been her first concern. She had never expected that lying in a man's arms could feel so right, or that she could share herself so completely with a man without losing her individuality and sense of direction as she had done once before. She supposed she should have realized that Brady wasn't like Billy Martindale. Billy's life had revolved around himself, and he had expected the woman in his life to share that fascination. Brady wasn't like that, and his wry sense of humor didn't fool her for a moment. She sensed his pride in her when she talked about her work, even if she might sometimes lose him along the way. Actually, she supposed it was the same kind of pride she felt when he talked about *his* work, whether she understood the intricate workings of a detective's mind or not.

In truth, Brady never ceased to amaze her. The constant state of alert under which he functioned had surprised her at first. He sometimes seemed so relaxed, but was on his feet, gun never far from his reach, at the first unexpected movement or sound. His systematic efficiency was equally surprising. He had spent the evening hours of the first night he moved in with her on the telephone. In the morning, a bodyguard was waiting outside her door, ready to accompany her to work, and a future schedule was in place. Bodyguards now accompanied her everywhere—two retired policemen whom Brady knew personally and could trust. They left when Brady walked through her doorway each evening. Brady became her bodyguard then, and she couldn't have been happier.

Natalie pulled open the apartment door and smiled at the familiar figure waiting there. Larry Segram was in his late fifties, balding and slightly overweight, but he was sharp, alert and always on time. He had three daughters, a good pension from the police department and was a partner in a detective agency with another retired policeman. He loved his work and was good at it. It showed in his smiling disposition when he fell into step beside her and said, "Good morning. I'm driving my wife's car this morning, Natalie. You'll like riding in a new BMW much more than you did that junk we've been traveling in all week."

Natalie laughed as the elevator doors closed. "I'd ride with you anytime."

"Thank you, ma'am." Larry chuckled. "I wish my wife could hear you say that. Maybe she'd appreciate me more. Anyway, with Harvey taking over at one o'clock, and with him driving you home in a Cadillac, I figured I had to do better than a five-year-old Honda."

Natalie did not reply. Harvey Pasternak—tall, fit, in his late fifties, with a full head of gray hair and a less communicative personality—was her alternate bodyguard. She liked him, but Larry was a darling. Her father's personality was a bit shadowy in her mind, but she would like to believe he had been like Larry.

Natalie's thoughts halted as the elevator doors opened in the lobby and Larry stayed her with a light touch on her arm. He scouted the space briefly, then urged her toward the exit and the car waiting at the curb. He laughed at the No Parking sign he had ignored and said, "Ain't it great! I'm not a cop anymore, but nobody can touch me when I'm parked in front of this building, illegally or not."

Yes, Brady never ceased to amaze her.

Smiling, Natalie walked toward Larry's car.

IF HE DIDN'T KNOW BETTER, he'd think by the smile on Natalie Patterson's face that she didn't have a care in the world.

Hadden stood boldly on the street outside Natalie's apartment. He watched Larry Segram's car pull away as they headed for the Health Department lab. Yes, he knew all about Larry Segram and Harvey Pasternak, her new bodyguards. It was unfortunate for them that they didn't know all about him.

The BMW disappeared from sight, and Hadden walked toward the spot where he had parked his car out of sight. Natalie Patterson was sleeping with Brady Tomasini during the night and was protected by his "buddies" during the day. But she wasn't as safe as she thought she was.

The game was about to resume.

LARRY SLID HIS CAR into a designated parking spot at the Health Department lab and Natalie warned, "You know you can't park here, Larry. These spots are reserved. I don't mind walking from the parking garage. It's not far."

Larry was smiling that way again, and Natalie shook her head.

"All right, don't tell me."

"Brady said that long walk from the parking garage could be dangerous. Dr. Gregory agreed."

"This is Dr. Gregory's parking spot?"

"Don't worry about it. He's parking in the handicapped parking spot around the corner."

"That's illegal!"

"Not for him."

Natalie groaned and got out of the car. She clipped her ID badge on her coat as she entered the building and started toward the lab with Larry walking beside her. She'd have to talk to Dr. Gregory about this and make sure he took his parking spot back. The last thing she wanted Dr. Gregory to think was that she was some kind of prima donna who thought she should have special privileges. She halted briefly at the sight of Chuck standing in the lab doorway.

Intensely aware of Larry walking close behind her as she approached the lab, she said, "I didn't know you were coming to the city, Chuck. What are you doing here?"

"That's what I've been asking myself." Chuck did not smile as he glanced at Larry beside her. "Well, are you going to invite me inside, or are we going to stand out here in the hallway and talk while your bodyguard listens to every word?"

"Chuck!" Larry's expression was as cold as ice as Natalie turned to him and said, "This is Chuck Randolph, a friend from the CDC, Larry, and I apologize for his rudeness."

"Don't apologize for me, Natalie. I didn't say anything that wasn't true. This man was hired as your bodyguard, wasn't he? You don't owe him anything."

"He may be my bodyguard, but he's also a friend." Turning back to Larry, Natalie said, "Please excuse us, Larry."

Chuck followed her into the lab where Natalie turned toward him hotly and said, "I don't know what's gotten into you, Chuck, but I won't stand for that kind of behavior. Larry is a friend."

"And your bodyguard, I know. It's too bad I had to find out what was happening secondhand from Dr. Minter."

"I'm sorry. I suppose I should've called you, but so much has happened in the last week that I lost track of time."

"I guess that's true."

Annoyed at the hint of sarcasm in his tone, Natalie said, "It's a little early to come for the weekend, and you would've called if you intended coming for a visit. So what are you doing here, Chuck?"

Chuck leaned down unexpectedly and kissed her mouth. Frowning, he replied, "I guess that's what I'm doing here."

At a loss for words, Natalie did not reply as Chuck went on, "Dr. Minter told me everything, about the police removing your protection, about Detective Tomasini moving in with you to provide you protection, and about the bodyguards Tomasini set up. To be perfectly honest, that old man outside looks like he wouldn't know which way to turn if Hadden Moore showed up."

"I don't like your attitude."

"And I don't like what's happening, Natalie."

"It's not really your concern, is it?"

"I thought I was a friend. A friend cares."

Unwilling to pursue that line of thought, Natalie replied, "You don't have to worry about Larry. He's a retired policeman. He knows his business."

"He's over the hill."

"He isn't. And even if he was, that gun in his holster has the effect of shedding the years quickly."

Chuck sneered. "Who told you that? Your boyfriend?"

"If you're referring to Brady—"

"Of course, I'm referring to Tomasini. He's taking advantage of you!" His anger intensifying, Chuck continued, "I could see he had a thing for you the first time I saw him. He knows the two of you couldn't make it any other way, so he took the first opportunity to appear indispensable. But he isn't indispensable, Natalie."

"If you came here to run Brady down, Chuck, you're wasting your time."

"I came here to take you home with me."

"What?"

"I spoke to Captain Wilthauer before I came here. He and Detective O'Reilly agree that the best thing for you to do right now would be to return to Atlanta. No one believes Hadden

Moore is still in the area, but even if he is, you'd be better off away from New York."

"I don't agree, and neither does Brady."

"Brady." Chuck made a scoffing sound. "He has another agenda."

"You don't know Brady. He cares what happens to me."

"So do I."

"And he knows the kind of man Hadden Moore is. He knows Moore is still a danger to me, and that he'll be a danger to me no matter where I go."

"Tomasini brainwashed you."

"No, he didn't. He didn't have to. Moore did that when he pushed me in front of that car."

"You have to try to put that behind you, Natalie, for your own sake."

"So Moore will be free to try again, you mean?"

"So you can go forward. You'll be safe if you come back to Atlanta with me."

"I won't be safe anywhere until Moore is caught."

"That isn't true."

"It is true. I wish I could make you believe me."

"Wishing doesn't work, Natalie. If it did, you'd be wearing my ring right now, and you'd be safely back in Atlanta with me."

Natalie's anger fell flat. She said, "I'm sorry, Chuck."

"So am I, but that doesn't change things, does it?" Chuck paused before continuing more softly, "Natalie, please listen to me. You have to leave New York. Even if my ring plays no part in your future, your place is back at the CDC in Atlanta. That's home. That's where your true future lies."

Chuck was obviously sincere, and Natalie replied, "I know you mean well, but I also know I'm doing the right thing by staying in New York until everything is settled here."

"You're making a mistake, Natalie."

"I'm not."

Chuck frowned as he said, "My flight back doesn't leave until tomorrow. I have a ticket for you, too, Natalie. Give me a chance to convince you to use it."

"You're wasting your time."

"Have dinner with me tonight. We can talk about it."

"I can't. Brady—"

"Tomasini again? Tell him I'll watch out for you this evening. He can take the night off."

"Chuck, try to understand. Hadden Moore is a killer, and Brady is a professional. Brady knows how to handle situations like the one I'm in."

"That aside, he wouldn't like you having dinner alone with me, is that right?"

Natalie replied gently, "I suppose that's right, because it would bother me, too, if Brady had dinner alone with another woman."

"Are you trying to break something to me gently, Natalie?"

"Very gently."

Chuck stared at her for an extended moment, then said, "But that doesn't change anything about your present situation. You should come back to Atlanta with me, and you know it."

"Chuck…"

"All right, dinner is out. How about lunch? You get an hour to eat. We can talk then." When she hesitated, he added, "I've come a long way. An hour isn't too much to ask, is it?"

"No, I guess not."

"Well, that's something, anyway." When Natalie protested his reply, he said, "I guess I should quit while I'm ahead. I'll see you at twelve."

Natalie watched sadly as Chuck disappeared through the doorway.

"You never learn, do you, Brady?"

Brady glanced at Joe Stansky as the smaller man walked beside him past a row of brownstones where carefully tended flowers bloomed in fenced off squares of soil near the curb during the summer. The intent was to brighten an area of cracked sidewalks and endless traffic, and to foster a neighborhood feeling in an area that appeared uncertain in which direction it was heading. But summer was gone, the flowers were dead and the neighborhood looked dismal.

They had parked their unmarked car at the end of the street and were presently approaching the residence of a fugitive's brother. They didn't expect to learn much from his protective sibling, but they both knew it was a part of the game of watch and wait that they needed to play out.

Silently checking house numbers as they walked, Brady responded as casually as he could manage, "What do you mean, I never learn?"

"You know what I'm talking about."

"Maybe I do. Maybe I wondered when you'd finally get around to commenting about it again, and maybe I hoped you wouldn't because it's still none of your business."

"This Natalie Patterson situation…"

"Oh, here it comes…your sage advice."

"Brady, dammit, how many times do I have to say the same thing? You may be riding the crest of the wave with her right now because you're her hero, and because you're taking care of her when the NYPD turned her out, but sooner or later it's going to end. She can't stay grateful forever."

Brady glanced at the brownstone at the end of the street. It was indistinguishable from the others except for the large numbers that almost screamed twenty-four. He said, "There's the one we're looking for. Menendez should be home. His boss said he was laid off until they could get financing for the concrete on the complex he's constructing straightened out. If I don't miss my guess, he's inside watching TV with his old lady. If he won't tell us where his loser baby brother is, we can just go back to the car and wait for him to show up. He will, sooner or later. He always does."

"That's if 'baby brother' didn't already get the money he needs for his fix by robbing another bodega and putting a bullet in the counterman just for kicks, like he did the last time." Stansky frowned. "And don't change the subject. I asked Janie's opinion about all this last night, and she agrees with me."

"You're kidding. You discussed my private life with Janie?"

"You know how my wife feels about you, Brady. She thinks you walk on water, that you've got what it takes to get any woman you want, and even she thinks you're making a mistake setting your sights on a babe who'll drop you as soon as the heat is off the case."

"Natalie's not like that."

"No, I don't think she is, but I don't think she's thinking clearly right now, either. Who would, with a homicidal maniac on her trail?"

"So you agree that Moore will come after her again."

Stansky paused, then nodded. "Yeah, I do. But I also think that doesn't give you a free pass into her life. If you want to help her, help her, but don't get yourself personally involved."

"Too late…way too late."

Joe stopped in his tracks. "What do you mean?"

"I mean I'm as personally involved as I can be, and for the first time, it feels right."

"What does that mean?"

"Do I have to spell it out for you?"

"If you mean what I think you mean, you're crazy, man!"

"Maybe." Brady stopped in front of the brownstone steps.

His expression changing, he said, "Are you ready in case 'baby brother' is in there right now?"

At Stansky's nod, they walked up the steps, rang the bell and waited.

THE CLATTER OF DISHES and silverware banging against metal trays and the buzz of enthusiastic conversation as the lunch hour progressed did not distract Natalie as she sat opposite Chuck in the lab cafeteria. Chuck had arrived at the door of the lab as the clock struck twelve, and Natalie had almost smiled. She had forgotten his fetish for punctuality, which she supposed was a by-product of the exacting work they did. She had suffered bouts of the same disease at times…but Brady seemed to have worked miracles on that debility for her.

Natalie forced her mind back to Chuck's ardent appeals. She glanced at Larry where he sat a few tables away, casually crushing saltines into the soup of the day. He had forgotten the crackers on the counter when he paid for his meal and had gone back to pick them up, bringing to mind a time in her youth when she would not have thought of eating soup without them. But those times had changed. Survival was presently her first concern.

With that thought in mind, Natalie picked up her half-eaten sandwich and said as Chuck finished speaking, "Please…I told you. You're wasting your time. There's nothing you can say that will change my mind. I'm staying here until…until my situation is settled. So can't we just enjoy this hour together with some pleasant conversation?"

"Pleasant conversation?" Chuck glanced at the table where Larry was busily consuming his soup. "With your bodyguard sitting a few feet away, watching everything we do? Doesn't he make you feel uncomfortable?"

"No. I like him, and I like knowing he's there. I also like the retired policeman who's going to take his place after lunch hour is over."

"Harvey Pasternak. I know."

"Captain Wilthauer really filled you in, didn't he?"

"No, Dr. Minter did."

"Dr. Minter?"

"Dr. Minter called your boyfriend—"

"He called Brady? When?"

"After you informed him that you'd be staying in New York with the West Nile project for an indefinite period. Dr. Minter was worried about you. He wanted to know if you were safe."

"Brady didn't tell me he talked to George."

"He wouldn't."

Natalie stared at him for a silent moment, at a loss for words, then said softly, "Chuck, you're young, intelligent, good-looking…you have a good sense of humor. You're a real catch for any young woman."

"Except you."

"I appreciate you in other ways."

"Other ways that don't really make a difference to a man who loves you…a man who wants to know you're out of harm's way even if you don't feel the same about him."

"Please, set your mind at rest. I'm as safe as I can be here. No one will be able to—"

Startled, Natalie looked up at Larry as he loomed unexpectedly beside them. He stumbled against the table, pushing it with a harsh, scraping sound that elicited Chuck's protest. Natalie was unable to speak. Larry's breathing was rapid, his eyes bulging and his hand was shaking as he pushed a note toward her on the table and gasped, "Call Brady…now!"

Natalie glanced down at the four words on the note, then jumped to her feet as Larry fell, overturning the table with a loud crash.

Larry began convulsing at her feet.

Shrill screams echoed in the suddenly silent cafeteria. Long moments passed before Natalie realized that the shrill screams were her own.

BRADY DROVE with siren blasting.

Taking a curve wildly on the busy city street, he heard Stansky mumble words of caution, but he was immune to his partner's plea. The message that Larry Segram had been taken down by a mysterious attack in the lab cafeteria had come over the police radio while Stansky and he had been patiently waiting for "baby brother" to show up at the Menendez brownstone. He had taken over the wheel and headed for the hospital where Larry had been transported. The ensuing report on the police radio had warned to be on the lookout for Hadden Moore, who was believed to have been involved, and Brady had pressed the gas pedal to the floor.

He laid his hand heavily on the horn as he rounded a corner, unmindful of pedestrians who angrily jumped out of the way. He hadn't expected Moore to make that move, but from the information Stansky had been able to obtain from headquarters while they traveled toward the hospital, there was no doubt that Moore was responsible for whatever chemical had been slipped into Larry's food because the note Larry had belatedly found on his tray was clearly from him.

It read simply, *My regards to Natalie. HM.*

Panic unlike any he had ever experienced pulsed through Brady's mind. The bastard was crazier than he had thought! Yet he should've realized that any man who would kill six people and cripple several others for life just to get revenge on a woman who had jilted him was insane. And Moore's sights were now set on Natalie—*his* Natalie of the wide, gray eyes that turned him inside out with a glance, *his* Natalie who was sweeter in his arms than he had dreamed was possible, *his* Natalie—the woman he loved.

Brady slid his vehicle to a stop at the emergency room entrance. He jumped out of the car and said, "Park it. I'm going in." He flashed his badge at the uniformed policeman who met him in the corridor with a pad in hand, but waved him off when he saw Harvey Pasternak and Chuck Randolph in the waiting room. Natalie stepped into sight from behind Randolph's lanky figure, her face a ghastly white and her cheeks tearstained. Beside her in a moment, he pulled her into his arms and whispered, "Are you all right?"

"I'm fine. It's Larry. Moore did this to Larry, Brady. Larry is in a coma. He may die—because of me!"

"No, not because of you. Because of Moore."

Curving his arm around her, Brady turned as Pasternak reported, "I got to the cafeteria right after it happened. It looks like Moore slipped something into Larry's soup and Larry didn't see the note until it was too late. He obviously tried to warn Natalie as soon as he realized what was happening. That bastard Moore must have been right there in the cafeteria all the while, probably watching as the whole thing went down and nobody noticed him!" Harvey's jaw twitched with suppressed emotion. "Larry's wife is with him now."

"What's his prognosis?"

Natalie responded, "Larry started vomiting in the ambulance. The doctors pumped his stomach as soon as he got here, but they don't know if Moore used Candoxine again. If he did—"

Natalie's voice failed, and Brady took a stabilizing breath. He looked up at Chuck Randolph, who stood silently a few yards away. He was pale, yet he returned Brady's stare hotly as Brady questioned, "What are you doing here?"

"I came to convince Natalie to come back to Atlanta with me. Now I'm more sure than ever that's where she belongs."

"Are you?" Brady snarled. "That shows how wrong you can be. Natalie's not going anywhere."

Chuck countered, "You're trying to tell me she'd be better off here in this city with a maniac on her trail?"

Natalie looked up as Brady replied with ominous softness, "I'm not *trying* to tell you anything. I'm saying it right out. Back off, Randolph! You're out of your element here. Go back to Atlanta where you belong and stay there!"

Natalie's soft protest was interrupted as a doctor stepped into sight in the corridor. He glanced at Brady's badge as he approached and said, "Are you in charge here?" At Brady's nod, he said, "The patient is conscious but he's still in pain. That's all I can say until we can do some further testing."

"Can I talk to him?"

"It won't do any good. He's confused. He's not fully cognizant of what happened right now."

Brady heard heavy footsteps behind him and turned to see O'Reilly and Potter arrive, with the uniformed policeman and Stansky behind them. Stansky remained silent as Brady said, "It's all yours, O'Reilly. Tell Larry's wife I'll be back later. I have to get Natalie out of here now."

"Wait a minute, Tomasini! We need to question her."

"Randolph can tell you what you want to know. He was there, and Larry will supply the rest. We're leaving."

"Where are you taking her?"

"What do you care?" Brady's response was vicious. "Your professional evaluation was that Moore wasn't an imminent threat and Natalie didn't need protection."

"We don't know for sure that Moore's responsible for what happened here."

"Don't we?"

Flushing, O'Reilly snapped, "So maybe the situation has changed."

"Not as far as I'm concerned." Brady curled his arm more tightly around Natalie and said, "Come on. We've got things to do and I'm not letting you out of my sight."

Natalie hesitated. "What about Chuck?"

"What about him? O'Reilly can talk to him and he can get his own transportation back to his hotel."

"Chuck and I need to finish our conversation."

The plea in Natalie's eyes halted Brady's reply. Silent for a moment, he said, "He can come to the apartment tonight if it's that important. We'll both be there."

Unwilling to wait any longer, Brady moved Natalie rapidly down the hospital corridor as she turned back to say, "Tonight, Chuck. Okay?"

Brady did not bother to look back for Randolph's reply.

HADDEN WATCHED as Tomasini ushered Natalie out of the hospital emergency room and into his car with a tight grip on her arm. Stansky followed close behind, taking up the rear with a look in his eyes that bode poorly for anyone who got in their way. They were both such efficient detectives. He had no doubt they would both be effective bodyguards, too.

But despite it all, they had walked right past him!

Hadden subdued the urge to laugh out loud as he watched Tomasini seat Natalie in the passenger side of the front seat, then go around the car to take the wheel. With Stansky riding shotgun in the back seat, Tomasini obviously felt in full control of the situation. Unfortunately for him, he was wrong. It was he, Hadden Moore, Ph.D., who was in complete control of the situation. And it was *he* who would soon be in the position to decide exactly what Natalie's fate would be.

Hadden's thoughts sobered as Tomasini's car disappeared into the swiftly moving traffic. Actually, Natalie was more than lovely. Unlike most other women—unlike Mattie—she was more handsome upon closer scrutiny. He liked that. And unlike Mattie, Natalie approached his level intellectually. He liked that, too…very much. Yet, there was more to learn before he could make a decision.

He needed to be sure.

"I WANT TO BE put back on the case."

Captain Wilthauer looked up from his desk with a frown. He glanced at the squad room beyond his closed office door to where Stansky was talking to a very nervous and white-faced Natalie and said abruptly, "What in hell is she doing in the squad room?"

Brady responded tightly, "I figured it was the safest place for her right now. If Moore got to her the way he got to Larry this afternoon, you wouldn't have a chance to reinstate her police protection and the media would crucify you."

Wilthauer countered, "You're worried about me, are you? And who says I'm going to reinstate her police protection?"

"You'd be crazy not to."

"That's your opinion. We haven't even determined positively if that note was actually from Moore."

"It was."

"The Commissioner is going to want proof."

"And in the meantime, Moore is free to make as many attempts on Natalie's life as he wants, is that it?"

"I'm the boss here, Tomasini."

Brady took a backward step and smiled. "That's right, you are. You did me a favor by removing me from the case when I asked, and I appreciated it. Unfortunately, requesting to be removed from the case was a mistake on my part."

"You said you were getting too personally involved to stay on the case."

"Yeah, well, now I'm too personally involved to stay out of it."

Wilthauer scowled. "That figures."

"As for Natalie's police protection, you can wait for more substantial proof that Moore's back on the scene if that makes you happy. I'm not going to say you'll be sorry for your hesitation, because I'll make sure Natalie's safe, one way or another."

"Meaning?"

"Meaning if you don't put me back on the case and don't restore Natalie's police protection, I'll take a leave of absence so I can provide it for her."

"And if I don't grant it?"

"That's your choice. It won't change my plans."

Wilthauer dragged a hand across his face. "Look, Tomasini, I don't want to get into a pissing match with you. That wouldn't do either one of us any good. You know my situation here. This case was high-profile and if Moore's back on the scene, it'll be high-profile again, but I've already made O'Reilly the primary on the case."

"So, change it. The situation has taken another turn and having O'Reilly as the principal on the case doesn't fit anymore. O'Reilly and Potter will probably end up working on the case, anyway, once it's official that Moore is back."

"That doesn't mean O'Reilly will like taking your orders."

"I don't care what he likes."

"I know, but I have the responsibility here. And as far as police protection is concerned, the okay needs to come from higher up."

"Your recommendation is all that's needed."

"Why do I have the feeling you have more faith in that statement than I do?"

"Don't worry about it. Once the media gets wind of what happened today, you won't have any trouble reinstating Natalie's protection."

"Yeah, sure, and in the meantime we have a manpower shortage."

Brady frowned. "That's crap and you know it. That influx of personnel Sergeant Santini was expecting finally came through a few weeks ago. What about those men?"

"They're not in my domain."

"That's a poor excuse."

Wilthauer hesitated, then said, "All right, you've got it—everything you want. I'll take care of it. Just make sure you don't blow this chance I'm giving you."

"Thanks."

"Don't thank me. Just get that Moore bastard!"

Brady pulled the office door closed behind him and walked out into the squad room. Natalie searched his face as he approached and that teenage flip-flop thing happened again in his chest.

Hell, he was pathetic.

At her side, Brady slid his arm around her and said as Stansky awaited his report, "We're back on the case. Natalie's protection will be reinstated, too."

The firming of Stansky's jaw said it all.

Natalie leaned against him and briefly closed her eyes. His throat suddenly tight as he looked down at her, Brady said softly, "Let's go home."

CHUCK GLANCED AROUND Natalie's apartment as he entered. Evening had come, and Chuck was right on time. A twitch in his cheek betrayed that he was angry despite his smile. He confirmed Natalie's assessment by saying, "I see you have a uniformed policeman at your door again. Your boyfriend was true to his word, but I don't think I'd feel so good about depending on his word if I knew my life depended on it."

"Chuck, please…" Natalie glanced toward the kitchen where Brady was making coffee. Brady and she had come back to the apartment immediately after leaving the precinct station house. Stansky had stayed to discuss the case while she trembled and fought back tears during their careful questioning. She had made a complete fool of herself despite her struggle to present a calm demeanor, yet Brady had seemed to understand. His arm around her and his voice gentle, he had been the calm after the storm. She knew if Stansky had not been present, she would have buried herself in his arms, wanting never to emerge. After Stansky had left, she had done just that.

It seemed ironic that only a few hours later, she was hoping Brady would leave the apartment so that Chuck and she could talk freely.

But that obviously wasn't going to happen.

Chuck followed her glance toward the kitchen and frowned at the clatter of dishes. "Tomasini's in the kitchen, isn't he? What's the matter? Doesn't he trust you to talk to me alone? Or maybe he doesn't trust *me*."

"That's right, I don't trust you, Randolph."

Brady strolled back into the room with a cup in hand and Sarah walking close behind. He was wearing those jeans that hugged his narrow waist and hips and emphasized the long length of his muscular legs, and a casual knit shirt that looked comfortably worn while still managing to convey the fact that Brady was all man from head to toe. His attitude was casual, but the look in his eye told Chuck he had kicked back and was settled in with Natalie for the night.

The message was clearly conveyed, and Natalie felt a flush rise at Chuck's poorly concealed discomfort. Irritated by Brady's obvious strategy, she hinted broadly, "Chuck and I were in the middle of a conversation when Larry…" She stopped and started again. "Chuck and I were in the middle of an important conversation this afternoon that we didn't get to finish."

She waited for Brady to make a move. He didn't. Instead, he sat down and put his coffee cup on the table.

Deciding on a more direct approach, she said, "I don't think you'll find this conversation too interesting, Brady. I mean, maybe it would be better if you—"

"What Natalie is trying to say is perhaps you should butt out and let us talk privately, Tomasini, if that doesn't go against your grain."

"Chuck!"

"But it does 'go against my grain,' Randolph." Ignoring Natalie's reaction to Randolph's rudeness, Brady smiled. But Natalie recognized that smile…and she shivered.

BRADY BARELY MAINTAINED his smile. If he'd had his way, he would've given that damned uppity, stuffed shirt Natalie called her "friend" the bum's rush the minute he tried to walk through the apartment doorway. That didn't happen, but Brady was resolved to make sure Randolph didn't have *his* way, either.

Brady took a sip of coffee. It was only partially brewed. He had poured it before it had finished—simply because he had been determined not to give Randolph more than a few seconds alone with Natalie. Like Randolph said, it wasn't that he didn't trust Natalie. He didn't trust Randolph.

The coffee was weak as water, but Brady swallowed resolutely and said, "Go ahead, talk. I won't interrupt."

Natalie said, "Brady…please, this obviously isn't going to work. There are some things Chuck and I have to settle before he leaves town, so either you can go into another room, or we will."

"Why?"

Natalie's wide gray eyes appealed for understanding, but Brady refused to relent. One look at Randolph was all he had needed. Randolph was desperate for Natalie, and the thought that a common player like Brady was sitting where he wanted to be was killing him. Brady knew if he were a bigger person, he might even feel sorry for the poor sap, but the relationship between Natalie and him was too new and too precious for him to risk it.

But Natalie was still looking at him that way, and his resolve faltered. For her sake, it was time to stop playing games.

Brady said earnestly, "Okay, Randolph. Truce. Unless I'm

mistaken, we both want the same thing here—Natalie's safety—so let me explain some things to you. Truthfully, if I believed Natalie would be safer in Atlanta, I'd tell her to go, but both Natalie and I know she won't be. Hadden Moore is a psychopath. He's become fixated on Natalie. It doesn't matter what city she's in or where she goes. He'll follow."

Frowning when Natalie began trembling, Brady stood up and slipped his arm around her as he continued, "Look, Natalie has twenty-four-hour police protection again for an indefinite period. I've been reinstated as the principal on the case, and while she's being protected by New York City's finest, I intend to find Moore and put him behind bars so she'll never have to worry about him again."

"That all sounds very fine, but how do you expect to catch Moore? You don't have a clue where he is or how he manages to slip in and out of places right under your eyes!"

"Neither do you."

"I'm not the detective on this case."

"That's right, you're not, but you're the man who claims he'll take care of Natalie and protect her if she leaves the city with you. How do you expect to do that?"

Suddenly flustered, Randolph shook his head. "Moore won't follow her. That's just a ploy you're using to keep Natalie here."

"Can you guarantee he won't?" Brady persisted, "Can you guarantee that Natalie will be able to walk the streets of Atlanta and never be bothered by Moore again? Because if you honestly can, I'll let her go with you gladly."

Brady waited for Randolph's reply. He knew full well what he had just said to Randolph was a bald-faced lie. There was no way he'd turn Natalie over to Randolph, no matter what Randolph said.

When Randolph did not respond, Brady eyed him more closely. A knot suddenly squeezed tight inside him when

Randolph looked at Natalie with true pain in his gaze. The realization hit Brady that the guy didn't just want Natalie…he *loved* her.

A victim of that same, incurable malady, Brady empathized with him. Tightening his arm around Natalie, he said more softly, "I know, you can't make that guarantee, Randolph, but I'll give *you* a guarantee if that will make you feel any better. I guarantee that I'll take care of Natalie and make sure Moore doesn't get to her. I'll make sure Natalie gets the most professional protection available—not just because it's my sworn duty as a city detective, but because she means as much to me as she does to you."

Randolph started to speak, but Brady interjected, "Look, save your breath. Natalie's not going with you. You can keep in touch, visit anytime you want, but if you really care about her, don't ask her to leave the city. You'd be signing her death warrant."

Brady felt the jolt that shook Natalie at his statement. He looked down at her, regretting the need for his blunt statement as he slowly released her. He looked back at Randolph, and said, "I'll leave you both alone for a while so you can talk, but do me a favor. Don't try convincing Natalie to do something that you know will hurt her in the end. You couldn't live with that, and neither could I."

Randolph's color had paled, and Brady knew he had won. Yet that thought gave him little satisfaction as he walked into the bedroom and closed the door behind him.

Sitting on the side of the bed a short time later, Brady could not believe what he had done. The living room had been too quiet for his liking after he left. The thought that he had to have been crazy to turn Natalie over to that stuffed shirt's machinations reverberated in his mind. He had felt sorry for the guy because the poor sap loved Natalie, while forgetting he was just another poor sap who loved her, too. If Randolph wasn't as honest as Brady thought, he was even now convincing Natalie to leave with him. Brady would never forgive himself if that happened.

The bedroom door opened at that moment. Brady stood up as Natalie entered. In answer to his unspoken question, she said simply, "He's gone."

Holding back tears, she walked silently into his arms.

Chapter Ten

Natalie's mind was far from the brilliant glow of the morning sun beaming through her apartment window as she stood motionless by the kitchen sink. Another morning and another day of uncertainty.

A week had passed since Hadden Moore's attempt on Larry's life. She had consoled herself each time that Brady and she had visited him since then that Moore hadn't used Candoxine to poison Larry. Due to that fortuitous circumstance and the quick work of the paramedics and hospital staff, Larry was expected to recover completely. Yet that detail did not alter the horror of Moore's cold-blooded attempt to communicate with her through the senseless murder of a friend.

Thankfully, Chuck had returned to Atlanta. His departure had lifted a weight from her shoulders that she knew she would not be able to bear if Moore—for no other reason except that Chuck was an old friend—chose to turn his homicidal attentions on Chuck next.

To her mind, the attack on Larry had proved that everyone she touched—her fellow workers, friends, even casual acquaintances—were possible targets for Moore's merciless attack. Most frightening of all was her realization that the bed they shared made Brady a likely candidate for that madman's illogical desire for vengeance. She rationalized that fear by telling herself that Brady was a part of the police team investigating the Candoxine deaths and was involved in the case anyway.

There was the possibility, of course, that Moore would tire of toying with her and make another attempt on her life. She almost wished he would so she would know exactly where she stood.

Natalie brushed away a tear. Providing her with bittersweet solace was her realization that the horrendous circumstances now enveloping her had brought Brady fully into her life. Far from the boor she had first believed him to be, Brady was all she had ever dreamed of in a man. Behind that sometimes brusque male persona, he was always loving, understanding—almost painfully so—engaging, so quick-minded and sharp that he sometimes left her in the dust of his rapid thought processes, and tender. She remembered the previous night when he held her in his arms—his softly whispered consolation when she briefly surrendered to anxiety, the calm reasoning he had used to soothe her anguish, the gentle perceptiveness of his lovemaking and the calm that then displaced her fear.

But that was last night. With the first, gray light of dawn, fears, uncertainties and a deep-seated sense of horror returned.

Where was Hadden Moore? Why had the police been unable to discover how he had gotten into the cafeteria unnoticed that afternoon, and how he had escaped without anyone even having been aware that he had been there? He was a shadow, a will-o'-the-wisp with evil intentions, a demon.

At a touch on her shoulder, Natalie turned with a gasp to see Brady standing behind her. Frowning down at her, his light eyes concerned, he said, "Talk to me, Natalie."

"What is Moore waiting for, Brady?" Not bothering to

hide the return of her anxiety, Natalie asked, "What is he trying to accomplish with this sick game he's playing?"

"He's an egomaniac, Natalie. He believes he's intellectually superior to all of us and no one can stop him until he's ready to stop. The fact that he *believes* that's true will be his downfall. With each success, however minor, he's getting cockier. I've seen it a hundred times. That cockiness will drive him to push things to the limit, and during that process, he'll make a mistake. All we need is *one* mistake, Natalie. We're waiting for it, and we'll get him when it happens."

"But when, Brady? At what price? Larry almost paid for Moore's cockiness with his life."

"It won't happen again." Brady's gaze tightened. "Everybody connected with this case—the uniformed policemen at your doors, your police escorts, right on up the line through the task force Wilthauer authorized, and even the Commissioner—is on special alert. We know what Moore's capable of now. We know what lengths he'll go to in order to accomplish his purpose. The best thing you can do right now is remember that the work you're doing in the Health Department lab is important. If you do your job and we do ours, Moore doesn't stand a chance."

"But you have no clues…no leads…nothing. All you can do is wait for him to make his next move, and by then it may be too late for someone."

"Look at me, Natalie." Brady's gaze was intent and his strong features tightly composed as he said, "Detective work is sometimes slow, methodical and often tedious, but we *will* get him."

Natalie stared up at Brady as countless doubts assailed her.

"Don't look at me that way, Natalie."

"I want to believe you, Brady." Natalie searched his light eyes for a sign of doubt. She saw none, and her throat choked tight. She attempted a smile. "I'm sorry. I just get…overwhelmed sometimes."

"When you do, try remembering that the detectives on this case are good at their job. As for myself, I've got a strong, personal interest in getting Moore."

A smile hovered briefly on Natalie's lips. "For me it's more than a personal interest. It's like…if I didn't have you to talk to…to convince me that you'll get Moore, and if I didn't have you to make me feel that this whole craziness will come to an end and life will go back to normal again, I don't know what I'd do."

"Oh, yeah," Brady said unexpectedly, "life will definitely go back to normal again, but the big question remaining then will be, will you still love me the morning after?"

Shocked at Brady's comment, Natalie said, "If you're referring to that security blanket thing again—"

Ignoring Natalie's response, Brady looked up at the kitchen clock and said, "Oops, don't look now, but you're going to be late for work again if you don't hurry up and get dressed."

Natalie unconsciously touched the worn robe that covered her pajamas and shook her head. She had gotten out of bed with the intention of making coffee, and she hadn't even combed her hair; yet the coffeepot was still empty and she was still a mess. Brady, on the contrary, had showered, shaved and was dressed for the day in a simple dark suit and a blue shirt and tie that matched his eyes. He was a formidable hunk if she ever saw one. She wondered how she had expected to convince herself that he wasn't.

She said in her own defense, "The problem is that you wake up ready and raring to go, and I wake up like a sleepwalker. How did we ever get together?"

"I don't know." Brady shrugged, a half smile on his lips. "Maybe it has something to do with the way we make use of the previous night."

Natalie's eyes widened.

"No?"

"Brady, you have no couth!"

"I know, so the question remains, will you still love me the morning after?"

When Natalie could not help but smile, Brady slipped his arms around her and hugged her tight. Finally separating himself from her, he said softly, "Come on, get dressed. Officer Vance is waiting."

"Officer Vance? What happened to Officer DeMassio?"

"Every uniform in the precinct is vying for duty as your police escort. Captain Wilthauer figures this duty might last a while, and he wants all the men to get their feet wet. Besides, he doesn't want to make any of them think he's playing favorites."

"Oh, sure!"

Brady leaned closer, his lips only inches from hers as he said, "You're a babe, whether you know it or not."

"A babe? I don't think so!"

"I *know* so, but I've got the jump on all those guys. So, hell, let them suffer."

With a kiss that was hard and quick, Brady whispered a few carnal words that made Natalie catch her breath. He grabbed his coat near the door and left with a short laugh trailing behind him.

BRADY'S LAUGHTER FADED the moment he closed the apartment door behind him. His expression suddenly solemn, he glanced at Officer Clark where he stood beside the doorway and asked, "Where's Natalie's escort?"

"Here I am, sir. I was early, so I went for a cup of coffee."

Brady looked up as Officer Vance walked up behind him. Vance had been recently assigned to the precinct and to the case. Most of the detectives on the squad knew Larry Segram and liked him, and for that reason were glad when the task force to catch Moore was formed. But Brady knew most of the new men had no personal interest in the case—except perhaps one. As he had said, Natalie was a babe, and the thought of staying close to her for whatever reason wasn't hard for any red-blooded male to take.

The green-eyed monster reared its head and Brady frowned. It didn't escape his notice that Vance and most of the uniforms who would be guarding Natalie were years younger than the detectives on the squad. He scrutinized Officer Vance briefly. The saying "there's something about a man in a uniform" lingered in his mind as he eyed the officer more closely. Actually, Vance was just a little too good-looking and perhaps too pleased with his assignment to suit him. As a matter of fact, so were DeMassio and Clark—and every other damned uniformed cop who would be protecting Natalie during the day instead of him.

Yeah, he was jealous, and he didn't like it.

Brady retorted, "Just make sure you're here when Natalie walks out that door, Vance. I don't want any foul-ups."

"Don't worry, sir. I'm on it."

Right.

Brady rang the bell for the elevator and took a last, scrutinizing look down the hallway before stepping inside. Thoughts of the reassuring words he had spoken to Natalie that morning moved through his mind. He wished he were as confident as he had sounded. The truth was, he wasn't sure what to expect, except that if Moore had anything to say about it, it wouldn't be good. It was up to Joe, him and the other detectives on the squad to stop Moore before anything could happen.

The elevator doors opened and Brady walked out with a cautious glance in each direction before starting toward the car in front of the building where Joe waited. He knew he wouldn't easily forget the way he had felt when he walked into the kitchen just minutes previously and saw Natalie standing stock-still by the kitchen sink with an empty coffee-pot in her hand and a look on her face that said the horror of her situation had returned. Her dark hair still ruffled from sleep, her delicate features pinched, barefooted, with that ratty, blue robe she loved so much tied tightly around her waist, she had looked like a little lost orphan. Yet when he had turned her toward him and she had looked up at him with those questioning gray eyes, it had been all he could do not to sweep her up into his arms with more than sympathy in mind. But she was scared to death, and he couldn't blame her. All that psychobabble that he had quoted to Natalie aside, Moore still remained a deadly enigma. There was no way of telling what he would do next or when he would try it. And there was nothing he could do about it aside from tediously slow detective work that ended up with watching, waiting, and wondering.

He was sure of only two things. The first was that something *would* happen soon.

The second was that he was seriously crazy about a babe who might end up *not* loving him the morning after.

NATALIE WALKED BRISKLY into the Health Department building, her expression sober as she clipped her badge onto her coat lapel. She glanced at Officer Vance as he walked beside her. He was young, probably not more than a few years older than her own twenty-four years. He had thick blond hair, se-rious blue eyes, and a look about him that said he probably only shaved twice a week. Yet he was so intense, so deter-mined to do his job well that he made her nervous. He had driven slowly through traffic and had parked cautiously in Dr. Gregory's parking spot. He had ushered her out of the car and into the building at a pace just short of a run. He was pres-ently propelling her down the hallway with a look on his face that said he expected Hadden Moore might pop out of one of the doorways at any moment.

Natalie breathed a sigh of relief when she reached the lab and looked inside. Several technicians were already busily at work, a welcome bit of normalcy that soothed her agitation. When Officer Vance attempted to accompany her inside, she halted him, saying, "That won't be necessary, Officer. There's no one inside the lab that I'm not familiar with. It probably would be better if you waited here."

"You're sure, ma'am?" He glanced inside again. "Every face is familiar to you?"

"Yes, I'm sure."

Natalie entered the room, exchanged her overcoat for her lab coat, and smiled when she saw Dr. Ruberg approaching. The older woman said, "Good morning, dear. As you know, I just returned from vacation and I wanted to say hello." Her expression sobered. "And I wanted to tell you how bad I feel about what happened in the cafeteria a week ago. Everything was progressing so calmly when I left. Your work was going well, and Dr. Gregory was immensely pleased with the progress you're making in your research. He thinks so highly of you and the work you've accomplished, and I must say I agree."

"Thank you so much, Dr. Ruberg. I don't really think I've been doing my best work most recently, but I appreciate your confidence in me."

"My dear, considering the circumstances of the past week, I'd say you are working exceptionally well. You haven't lost a step in your research, and your direction has only seemed to clarify."

"Thank you again."

Dr. Ruberg paused, as if to consider her next remarks. She began, "As you also probably know, I'm due to retire next year."

"No, I didn't." Surprised, Natalie continued, "I'm sure everyone will be sorry to see you go, even if you probably have great plans for your leisure time. You'll leave a real void in the department."

"I appreciate your kind words because I know you're sincere, Natalie. Perhaps it's vanity on my part, but I like to think my position in this lab wouldn't be filled too easily. I do think, however, that with a little training, you could fill the opening exceptionally well."

"Dr. Ruberg…I don't know what to say!"

"Don't say anything, dear. I won't retire until the middle of next year and you have plenty of time to think over what I've said. I just wanted to let you know how much Dr. Gregory, Dr. Truesdale and I appreciate your work here. I also want to add that I'm so sorry about all the difficulties you've encountered. It seems totally inappropriate somehow that a person who has uncovered a heinous murder plot perpetrated by a deranged member of the research community should suffer for her acuity."

Natalie did not respond.

"My only consolation is that the police are taking your situation very seriously. I know you'll be safe, and I know the police will bring this matter to as swift a conclusion as possible. Aside from that fact…"

Natalie steeled herself as a familiar twinkle appeared in the older woman's eyes and she continued, "I'm very pleased to hear that you've changed your opinion of Detective Tomasini."

"Yes, I have," Natalie began cautiously. "Brady has been a great help to me. I've grown to rely on him, and I admit to being wrong in my first judgment of him. He's far from the Neanderthal I originally thought he was."

"Of course he is. Years spent on the Homicide Squad in a city as diverse as New York are bound to have a cynical effect on a man. Being exposed to the worst of humanity day after day can't be pleasant. I think he's to be commended for doing a difficult job, and doing it well according to all the reports I've seen."

"Reports?"

"My dear, you must have realized that Dr. Gregory and Dr. Truesdale were as skeptical as you were about Detective Tomasini when they first met him. Dr. Gregory is a very thorough fellow. He made it a point to find out more about him, and what he learned put his mind at ease. Evidently, Detective Tomasini and his partner, Detective Stansky, are considered complete professionals who are an asset to their squad."

"I know."

Dr. Ruberg leaned toward her to continue more softly, "And the truth is, I hated the thought of having that much man slip past you."

At Natalie's startled expression, Dr. Ruberg laughed aloud. "Surprised you, didn't I? I suppose in more ways than one, but the fact is, I had a very successful marriage of thirty-seven years before my husband died. I know the value of a personal life in the kind of work we do, and you were such a serious young woman with so much to offer that it concerned me. Of course, no one but a fool could miss the interest I saw in Detective Tomasini's eyes when he looked at you. I was a bit worried about your negative reaction to him at first, but I can see that the dear man was successful in dismissing it. In any case, I'm pleased. I'm glad you didn't let him get away."

Appearing amused at Natalie's embarrassed silence, Dr. Ruberg concluded, "As far as your work is concerned, I'd appreciate it if you'd consider my thoughts on a future here. I think it would work out advantageously for all."

Natalie watched Dr. Ruberg walk back through the lab doorway, somehow stunned at the woman's bluntness. Her thoughts came to an abrupt halt as she neared her station. She noted the amused glances of the technicians nearby when she paused in front of the vase of long-stemmed roses beside her microscope. Beautiful, red and fragrant, enclosed in an elegant crystal vase decorated with a simple red bow, they were absolutely breathtaking, and Natalie's throat was suddenly tight. Brady knew she had been tense since the incident in the cafeteria, but she hadn't expected this.

Natalie unpinned a small envelope from the ribbon, suddenly frowning as another thought struck her. She had had a tense conversation with Chuck the previous day. They had both been upset at the end of the exchange, and it would be just like him to send flowers before calling her again. Chuck's disapproval of Brady had become a point of contention between them, but she supposed she couldn't expect him to understand how she felt about Brady. Actually, Brady didn't like Chuck, either, and a dozen long-stemmed roses from Chuck wouldn't make him like Chuck any better.

With those thoughts still trailing through her mind, Natalie pulled the card from the envelope. Color drained from her face as she read:

Dear Natalie,
    So near and yet so far, but I haven't forgotten you.
We'll meet again.
HM

Suddenly shuddering, Natalie looked up at the bloodred roses.

That image was the last she saw before everything went dark.

"It wasn't Officer Vance's fault, Brady. The flowers were waiting for me when I arrived at the lab. He was as surprised to see them there as I was."

Brady did not respond as they sat opposite each other in the silence of the apartment they shared. The word *surprised* irked him. He knew he would have more to say to Officer Vance when the task force met again the following day, but one glance at Natalie made it obvious that other matters took precedence for the moment.

Natalie asked tensely, "How did Moore do it, Brady? Why did he do it? What possible reason could Moore have for sending me roses?"

Brady hesitated. The radio call reporting that Natalie had received a communication from Hadden Moore had turned Stansky and him immediately in the direction of the lab, but he hadn't expected to arrive to find Natalie sitting on the couch in Dr. Gregory's office, so white and shaken that she could hardly speak.

The rest of the afternoon passed in a blur as he sealed off the building and ordered a thorough search, telling himself that he would not allow another opportunity for Moore to claim that he had walked right past the bastard without seeing him. Brady had then personally interviewed all the employees present when the roses were delivered. He had concluded with a few more sharp words to Officer Vance before Stansky and he had then escorted Natalie back to her apartment, with Vance following silently behind them in his car.

The sedative that the doctor had given Natalie did its work at last. Natalie fell asleep shortly after arriving back at the apartment, leaving him time to do some heavy thinking. She had awakened as the sun was setting, with her agitation returning.

Responding to Natalie's question, Brady said, "Isn't it obvious why Moore sent those roses? His attempt to kill you failed. He knows he can't get near you now because of your police protection, so he's satisfied to terrorize you instead."

"Terrorize me…"

"He's accomplishing his purpose, isn't he?"

Natalie's white face grayed, and Brady took her arm. "Maybe you should take a few of those pills Dr. Greenspan left for you."

"Tranquilizers aren't what I need, Brady."

Seating her cautiously, Brady said, "Tell me what you do need, then, Natalie."

"I need…I need…"

Natalie covered her eyes, at a loss for a response, and Brady's heart wrenched as he crouched beside her and whispered, "We traced the flowers back to a homeless man, Natalie."

"A homeless man?"

"The florist said the homeless man gave him your name and the lab's address, paid in cash, and gave him a sealed card to enclose with the roses. The homeless guy bragged that a man came up to him on the street and asked him if he wanted to make some money, and when he said yes, the man paid him for sending the flowers. The only problem is, nobody from the area recognized this homeless character. It seems he popped up out of thin air to send the roses, then disappeared the same way afterward. Police cars are continuing to canvass a ten-block radius, but I have a feeling we're not going to find him."

"Why?" Natalie started to shake. "Do you think he's… dead?"

"No. I think the reason we won't find him is because he doesn't exist."

"What do you mean?"

"I think the homeless man was Hadden Moore." Natalie gasped as Brady continued, "That's the only thing that makes sense, Natalie. Do you know how much money a dozen long-stemmed roses costs?" And when Natalie shook her head,

Brady said, "Trust me. The price is outrageous. Moore would never have trusted a homeless man with that much cash. Then think about how much bragging Moore has already done about being able to walk right past me and the police without being noticed."

"Maybe he was lying."

"I don't think so. I've thought it over and I think he disguised himself somehow. I think he did the same thing when he sent the roses so the clerk wouldn't be able to identify him."

"Surely he couldn't have disguised himself that completely."

"Joe has the clerk back at the station right now. He's with a sketch artist but I don't expect anything to come of it. If that homeless person did exist, he doesn't anymore. And if he didn't, Moore will never use that disguise again."

Natalie said through trembling lips, "You're telling me that Hadden Moore could be anybody, then. He could be the man walking beside me on the street, the person sleeping on a park bench, a messenger sent to deliver a specimen, a clerk in the corner store…"

"It's not as bad as you think, Natalie. Police protection is keeping Moore at a distance from you. That's why he's trying to terrorize you in this way…because he can't get to you."

"The police can't protect me forever, Brady."

"They won't have to. Moore won't wait forever. He's going to try something else…some other way to communicate with you." Brady cupped Natalie's face in his hands as he said, "I know this is hard. I know you think Moore is winning the game. Maybe he does, too, but he isn't. He's doing exactly what we want him to do, Natalie. He's getting bolder. He's trying harder. He can't get to you, so he's going to make a mistake."

"So I should just feel good about this whole thing, is that

it, Brady?" A hysterical note rose in Natalie's voice as she said, "I mean, should I be glad that a maniac's failure to kill me is going to make him keep after me until he makes a mistake?"

"Natalie…"

"No, please tell me. Is that it?"

Silence, then Brady's succinct response. "That's it."

Natalie raised a hand to her forehead, and Brady drew her closer as he said, "I won't let him get to you, Natalie. I promise you that."

Natalie's bewildered expression tore at Brady's heart as he gathered her against his chest. He felt her shuddering as he whispered against her hair, "Do you believe me?"

No response.

Desperate to console her, Brady drew back to hold her at arm's length from him. Seeing Natalie's lifeless color and trembling lips was almost more than he could bear. He whispered, "I'll get him. He'll never touch you. You have my word, Natalie."

Natalie maintained her silence, and Brady suddenly realized that this time, promises were not enough.

BRADY WALKED across the squad room floor toward Wilthauer's office. Despite the newly formed task force and uniformed personnel assigned to the case, they were no closer to finding Hadden Moore. Brady was angry, mainly at himself, for the lack of progress on the case, but right now he had something else on his mind.

Wilthauer waved Brady in as he approached the door. Wilthauer said flatly, "You look like hell, Tomasini. What did you do, sleep in that suit?"

"As a matter of fact, I did." Brady knew his hair was ruffled, a day's growth of beard shadowed his chin, his suit was wrinkled and his tie hung loose from his open shirt collar.

Making no attempt at further explanation, Brady continued, "I did some heavy thinking last night and I came to a decision. I think it's time to change our tactics, Captain. I think it's time to put Natalie in a safe house where Moore can't get to her."

"What?"

"She's a target. Moore didn't send those roses without something in mind. He wants her *and us* to know that he's going to come after her again. It's his way of flaunting himself, of rubbing our noses in the fact that he's outsmarting us."

"He can't outsmart us forever."

Brady nodded. "No, he can't. I expect we'll get him sooner or later, but it's the *later* that I'm worried about."

Wilthauer almost growled, "Are you trying to tell me that you think Moore will get to Natalie Patterson right under our noses?"

"I think he could."

"Dammit, Tomasini! If you think he can, what are you doing about it?"

"I'm requesting that Natalie be placed in a safe house—somewhere where Moore can't find her until we find him."

Wilthauer shook his head. "I don't believe you're saying that. Do you realize how long that woman might have to spend in seclusion? Do you realize what it would cost the city to keep her incognito? Do you really understand what you're asking, Tomasini?"

"I think I do, but I also think we don't have any choice. Moore is getting bolder and he's going to try something again soon. We might not be lucky enough to save her next time."

"What are you trying to do, frustrate the bastard? If he really is as crazy and determined to get Natalie Patterson as it seems, you may drive him into doing something even crazier than his attack on Larry Segram."

"And that'll be his mistake."

"At what cost?" That question resounded with dark familiarity in Brady's mind as Wilthauer continued hotly, "I'm not about to sanction anything that might result in some kind of bloodbath."

"That's not Moore's style."

"No, killing seven members of one family and maiming several others in order to get revenge on *one woman* is his style. The man's a nutcase, and I'm not about to do anything that might drive him over the edge!"

Brady said flatly, "Then you're willing to accept the risk that the CDC's golden girl will suffer the same fate as Mattie Winslow. You know damned well if that happens, the FBI will step in immediately. The only reason they've had only minimal participation in the case so far is because they're more deeply involved in matters on a national level right now."

Uncertainty crossed Wilthauer's face. Brady knew his hot buttons, not the least of which was FBI interference that would bring the police commissioner down on him hard. He hesitated briefly, staring at Brady, then said, "I hope you have some kind of a follow-up plan if I agree to this safe house idea."

"With Natalie out of the picture, Moore will be frustrated, all right. He's in the city. We know that for sure, and he's so damned egotistical that he's bound to try something to force our hand because he figures he's home free whatever he does. But we've got a full task force in place, and when he tries it, we'll get him."

"You make it sound so easy."

"It won't be easy, but it'll work."

Wilthauer paused, then said, "Okay, you got it—safe house, the whole deal. But this had better work, Tomasini. Your job's on the line here, you know."

Brady gave him a look so dark that Wilthauer said, "Get out of here. I have some phone calls to make."

BRADY WALKED BACK into Natalie's apartment building with Wilthauer's warning resounding in his mind.

Your job's on the line here, you know.

Hell, more than his job was on the line.

Brady punched the elevator button and waited impatiently for the doors to open. Wilthauer was right. He had slept in his clothes...on the couch, where he had held Natalie until she had fallen asleep, still shaking with fear. Reluctant to wake her, he had simply gotten up when morning had dawned, covered her with a nearby throw, and left, determined to talk to Wilthauer. It had come to him sometime during his sleepless night as Natalie slept fitfully in his arms that, without his having realized it, Natalie was being used as bait for a homicidal maniac. She was a walking target, and neither he nor Natalie could take much more of it.

With a few mental calculations, Brady realized as the doors of the elevator opened to Natalie's floor that he could have her installed in the safe house by the end of the week. She'd be safe, then.

Brady resolutely approached the apartment door.

"A SAFE HOUSE?"

Exhausted after a restless night, Natalie stood up. She had fallen asleep on the couch and slept there through the night. One look at Brady confirmed that his holding her in his arms to dispel her fears hadn't been a dream at all. His clothes were wrinkled, he needed a shave and he looked as if he hadn't had more than an hour or two of sleep—which he probably hadn't, considering the size of the couch they had shared.

Embarrassed guilt touched Natalie's mind. She was suddenly unrecognizable to herself. When had the wuss returned, the spineless coward who thought of nobody but herself? When had she become a person who laid the weight of her anxieties on the man who worried more about her than he worried about himself?

Brady said, "Captain Wilthauer is making the arrangement as we speak. A protective detail will move you out of this apartment sometime during the night. It will take you to a place where you'll be safe from Hadden Moore's intimidation, held incognito and fully protected until we can locate him."

"What kind of a place? Here in the city?"

"Right."

"How will I get to work each day without Moore being able to discover where I'm staying."

"You won't go to work. You'll stay in the safe house."

"I'll stay in the safe house with whom?"

"A female detective will most likely be assigned to be your direct contact, while other officers will be assigned to your protection outside the house."

"How will you be able to come home undetected at night? Moore will find a way to follow you."

"I won't come home. We won't be able to have any direct contact until the situation stabilizes."

"What?"

"I said—"

"No."

"What do you mean, no?"

"I won't do it."

"You don't have any choice."

"Don't I?"

Brady's jaw hardened. "Captain Wilthauer is putting himself on the line to protect you."

"Call him. Tell him to call the whole thing off."

Brady looked at her incredulously. "This is for your own good! You'll be safe, safer than I could ever guarantee you'd be under the present circumstances."

"But my life would be put on hold indefinitely. That's what you're saying. My job suspended…all contact with the outside broken. I'd be a nobody with nothing to do."

"Is that worse than living in fear, Natalie?" Brady covered the distance between them in a few steps and gripped her arms. He said earnestly, "We'll get him, Natalie, but in the meantime you'll be safe. I should've done this at the beginning. If I had, a lot of Moore's terrorizing could have been avoided."

"Hindsight is always twenty-twenty, Brady. Besides, if you had made these arrangements at the beginning, we wouldn't have discovered each other."

Brady frowned.

Brady's hands were still warm against the sleeves of her robe when Natalie said softly, "Answer me truthfully, Brady. Are you tired of me? Is that what this is all about?"

"*Tired* of you?"

"Have you stopped respecting me because of the way I've been acting? Because I wouldn't blame you if you did. I'm not sure if I've stopped respecting myself."

Brady stared at her, his light eyes direct as he whispered, "Is that what you think?"

"What other reason could there be?"

"The reason I gave you, that's what! You'll be safer in a safe house than you are here. Moore won't know where you are. You'll be using a false name and identity, and—"

"And I wouldn't be a real person anymore. Most of all, I wouldn't be able to see you."

"You'd be safe, Natalie."

"You said I'm safe here with police protection."

"You'd be *safer* in a safe house."

"But I'd cease to exist as a person."

"It would only be temporary."

"How long is temporary? A day? A week? A month? Longer?"

"I don't know."

"And I wouldn't see you at all."

"Maybe…occasionally."

Natalie scrutinized Brady's unreadable expression. Funny…she had been completely at ease in being herself with Brady. There was no artifice, no worrying about how professional she looked or how she came across in whatever she said. She was herself 24/7 with him; despite it all, she had felt instinctively that he cared deeply about her—maybe almost as much as she cared about him. But perhaps that had been a mistake. Maybe she had been asking too much by expecting him to accept the change Hadden Moore's actions had wrought—her transformation into a selfish, self-centered, frightened coward.

"Natalie…"

"I'm sorry, Brady. My mind is made up. I'm not going to any safe house. I'm not going to let a psychopath turn me into somebody that I'm not."

"He wants to kill you, Natalie."

"He wants to kill Natalie Patterson, the person I am. I'm proud of the things I've accomplished, Brady. I don't want to change myself into somebody else just to escape him. I wouldn't be proud of the person I'd be if I ran away."

"You're not thinking clearly, Natalie."

"Yes, I am. Please tell Captain Wilthauer that I'm satisfied with the arrangements I have here and I want to keep them." She hesitated before adding, "That doesn't mean…I mean, if you'd prefer to make other personal arrangements, I'll understand." She took an unsteady breath as she continued, "I mean, if you've become uncomfortable with the situation…if you feel you'll be able to do your work more easily from a different base and you'd—"

Natalie gasped as Brady pulled her close and covered her mouth angrily with his. She groaned softly as he separated her lips and drove his kiss deeper. They were both breathless when he pulled back from her and whispered, "Don't say another word, dammit!"

"But—"

"I said, not another word!" Breathing heavily, Brady said, "I don't regret a moment we've spent together, do you hear? The only thing I regret is that Moore still thinks he can get to you, and my own uncertainty about what he's going to try next. But not the time we've spent together, do you understand? Not a second…not a moment… Hell, the thought of you being in that safe house where I couldn't touch you…where I couldn't tell myself you needed me—"

"I do need you."

Uncertain what she had said to cause Brady's spontaneous frown, she said, "You're the only good thing that's come out of this crazy situation."

"Your security blanket."

"No! I told you, you're more than that to me."

Suddenly at a loss to explain her feelings, Natalie hesitated and Brady said sincerely, "Maybe I'm your security blanket and maybe I'm not, but that's all right with me. You can wrap yourself up in me for as long as you want."

Drawing back to look down at the furry animal that had walked into the room to stand beside them, he said, "Besides, Sarah has gotten accustomed to this apartment. She likes it."

Briefly unable to speak, Natalie patted Sarah's head. She looked up at Brady and asked, "Will Captain Wilthauer be angry with you because I refused to go to the safe house?"

"I don't know, but I guess I'll find out." Brady reached for the phone and Natalie slid closer. She rubbed herself gently against the warmth of his body as he talked, enjoying the intimacy that temporarily drove all negative thought from her mind. Shivers traversed her spine when the proof of his response hardened against her while his conversation with Wilthauer continued. Brady's breathing was irregular when he hung up at last and said, "Wilthauer wasn't happy, but he was smart enough to put off talking to the Commissioner until I confirmed the idea with you."

"I'm glad." Breathless, Natalie pressed herself closer, her lips moving against his throat as she said, "I wouldn't want to cause any trouble."

"We're wasting time." Brady curled his arm around her, cupping her breast as he urged her forward and said, "Let's mess up that bed we didn't sleep in last night."

Brady's hand moved sensuously against her hardened nipple as she walked with him toward the bedroom. Yet Natalie couldn't resist saying, "Don't you have to go back to work?"

"Forget it." Brady closed the bedroom door behind them and pushed her ratty blue robe from her shoulders. "I have other plans."

ON THE STREET OUTSIDE, Hadden looked up at Natalie's apartment windows. The roses he had sent the dear girl the previous day had been lovely, but they'd gone unappreciated. That saddened him, but he was amused at how perfectly his plan was progressing.

He wished he could compliment Brady Tomasini for his sense of deduction. It would have been a waste of valuable time if Tomasini had really believed he would be able to locate the homeless man who sent the roses. As it was, only a perfunctory search had been made for the character he had invented and used so well. Of course, that disguise would no longer be useful to him, but he didn't care. It had served its purpose.

Hadden looked up at Natalie's windows a few moments longer. He wondered what Tomasini and she were doing now. He suspected he knew. They were a lovely couple. Unfortunately for them, that pairing would not last long.

Chapter Eleven

Natalie smiled at Officer DeMassio as he slid his car expertly into Dr. Gregory's parking space in front of the Health Department building. Natalie was aware that her smile was stiff and her brave facade was a trifle forced as DeMassio exited the car, scanned the area cautiously and walked around to open her door. She was pleased that specific officers had been assigned to her protection detail. She liked the idea of exiting the apartment each morning and finding a familiar officer waiting, rather than seeing an unfamiliar face.

She supposed Brady had noticed her concern. Either that, or it was his own thoroughness that made him check the background of each man assigned to her protection detail. He had provided her with an alphabetical list of their names, had made sure she knew each man on sight, and had instructed her firmly that she was not to budge from that apartment at any time if any officers other than them were guarding her door or standing ready to escort her.

Natalie recited their names in her mind: Officer Bill Clark—formerly assigned to her detail, thirty-six, balding brown hair and eyes, married, two children; Officer Carmen DeMassio—another familiar face, thirty-two years old, dark-haired and ruddy complexioned as his name would indicate, married, two children; Officer Jeremy Dillon—a transfer, thirty-one years old, dark hair and eyes, lightly scarred from a recent car accident, divorced, no children; Officer Timothy Flynn—thirty-two, red hair and brown eyes, unmarried and she suspected from his lighthearted attitude that he never would be; Officer Martin Jackson—a recruit, twenty-five years old, dark hair and eyes, married, one child; Officer John McMullen—reassigned to her detail, twenty-nine, brown hair and eyes, divorced, one child; Officer Robert Vance—also familiar, twenty-seven years old, blond, blue-eyed, unmarried and still intense; Officer Eric VanDunk, new to the assignment, thirty-seven, dark hair and eyes, married with two children.

Natalie was aware that Brady did not fully approve of the fact that a few of the officers assigned to her were unmarried, and it amused her that so unimportant a detail should annoy him. The detail functioned efficiently. She never went unprotected, and although she found the close scrutiny of the unit embarrassing at times, she was grateful those men were there.

Natalie was also determined not to allow herself to become a victim of Hadden Moore's intimidation again.

True to that determination, Natalie walked down the Health Department hallway with smiling nods at familiar personnel as she passed. Officer DeMassio accompanied her into the lab—pursuant to Brady's strict orders—and checked the area before she was allowed to proceed to her workstation to start the day's work.

She had been working for more than an hour when she realized she had forgotten to check her e-mail for a response from the CDC lab on a slide she had sent to them for confirmation. Her fingers clicked automatically on the keys as she perused her e-mail. They froze in place when an e-mail with the signature HM popped up onto the screen. Her heart pounding, Natalie read:

Dear Natalie,

Your refusal to accept the confinement of a safe house pleased me. As you must have realized, your residence there might have made things more difficult for me; yet overcoming difficulty has always been my forte. I admit to being impressed by you, Natalie, and I am so seldom impressed by a woman. I know what you must think of me, but you are wrong—just as I was wrong when I reacted in anger against you without considering the further implications of your Candoxine discovery in the Winslow liver samples.

I now concede that your discovery was brilliant work, not a stroke of luck as I originally believed. Your ongoing research on the West Nile virus and the attention you've gained from NIAID because of it is proof of your acumen. I admire the progress you are making. I admire intelligence. I know if we could meet face-to-face, I could make you understand that I was justified in the supposed "crimes" I committed. I would like to explain that seeming contradiction to you.

We must meet. I'll arrange it.

HM

Natalie's heart was still pounding when the e-mail disappeared from the screen. When her anxious attempts to restore it failed, she glanced around her at the other technicians working at their stations. She glanced at the doorway to see De-Massio on guard there. Standing up as calmly as she was able, Natalie walked to the empty office nearby, and picked up the telephone.

At the sound of the gruff male greeting on the other end, Natalie managed, "Brady?"

"What else did the e-mail say?"

"I told you." Natalie struggled to retain a steady tone as

she replied to Brady's rigorous questioning, "Moore said he was glad I refused a safe house, that he's impressed by my work and he wants to meet with me."

"Not a chance."

Stansky echoed Brady's spontaneous response as Brady's intense scrutiny continued. Strangely enough, the time that had elapsed between her call to Brady and his arrival at the lab was a blur in her mind. All she remembered was that she had followed Brady's instructions by informing DeMassio of Moore's communication and had allowed DeMassio to take over from there. She was secluded with DeMassio in the empty office when Brady and Stansky arrived, with Doctors Gregory, Truesdale and Ruberg, as well as the rest of the lab techs, kept at a distance. As shaken as she was, she had still realized the reason for her seclusion—the necessity for Brady to talk to her before anything she said could be tainted by the comments of others. Yet she was puzzled by Brady's peculiar intensity.

It was not until Brady said abruptly, "You'd better sit down before you fall down," that she realized she was trembling.

Somehow annoyed by his tone, Natalie snapped, "I'm fine. I'm not going to fall down, so don't baby me." Natalie saw the flicker of Brady's dark brows before he said, "Okay, have it your way, superwoman." He glanced at Stansky before continuing, "I want you to be more explicit about the e-mail. I want you to tell me exactly what Moore said."

Stansky moved up cautiously behind her, and Natalie controlled her annoyance. She was *not* going to pass out again. She would not allow fear to regain control.

Brady pressed "I need to know what he said as exactly as you can remember. It's important, Natalie. Every word is important."

"I can't tell you *exactly* what he said." Her frustration rising, she continued, "I told you, the e-mail disappeared from the screen so abruptly that I didn't have a second chance to read through it."

"We have a computer expert working on that now. If we can get it back, we will, but in the meantime I need—"

"I know what you need, Brady, and I'm doing the best I can." Natalie sat down abruptly on the chair behind her. Mindful of her stress, Brady pulled a chair up beside her and said softly, "Take all the time you need, Natalie."

Brady was leaning toward her. His expression was resolute, yet there was a look in his eyes that said it was as difficult for him to retain his professionalism as it was for her to keep from abandoning herself to the sanctuary of his arms.

But she was done with hiding in Brady's arms. She was a grown woman…a professional. She needed to act like one.

Natalie responded as levelly as she could. "Moore said he was impressed by my discovery of Candoxine in the Winslow liver tissue samples, and with my work on the West Nile virus." She paused as a thought struck her and she said, "He knew NIAID had contacted me about my work on the virus. How could he possibly have known that?"

"Maybe he read it in the papers somewhere."

"Dr. Gregory made a point of withholding that information from the media. He didn't want to put any pressure on me."

Brady did not reply and Natalie leaned toward him earnestly. "Moore said he admires my acumen…my intelligence…the progress I've made in my work. How could he possibly have any idea how my work is progressing?"

"He may be trying to con you."

"No, the tone was different, almost deferential."

"He's a psychopath, Natalie. He'll do whatever he can to gain your confidence…or your sympathy."

"Sympathy?" Natalie's back went rigid. "He killed seven people and then he tried to kill me! How could I ever sympathize with that?"

Stansky interjected softly, "We don't know what he's thinking. That's the problem right now, Natalie."

All attention turned at that moment toward the computer technician who appeared in the doorway, looked at Brady, and said, "I can't do anything with that computer here, Detective. I'm going to have to take it back to the lab with me so I can work on it." He added, "But don't get your hopes up. It looks like tracing that e-mail might be a lost cause."

Brady glanced at Stansky when the fellow left, then turned back to Natalie and said, "Well, that's that. Unless we get lucky, that e-mail is lost somewhere in cyberspace where we can't trace it."

"I don't know what difference that makes." Natalie felt agitation rising. "I told you what it said."

"I know." Brady abruptly drew Natalie to her feet. "What do you want to do now?"

"What do you mean?"

Brady smiled gently. "Darlin', you just had a communication from a man who admitted murdering seven people and who tried to kill you."

"Don't call me *darlin'*."

Ignoring her comment, Brady continued, "You don't have to work so hard to appear unaffected, Natalie. That would shake anybody up." He searched her face. It occurred to Natalie that what he saw concerned him when he asked, "Do you want DeMassio to take you back to the apartment so you can pull yourself together?"

"No, Dr. Gregory and Dr. Ruberg have been very patient and they're waiting to talk to me. I don't want to keep them waiting any longer," she said adamantly. She continued, "They have a right to know what's going on so they can make any decisions they need to make. If they want me to continue with my work here—"

"I don't think there's any doubt about that," Brady interrupted gruffly.

"If they do, they have a right to expect a certain amount of work from me, and I intend to do it. I won't let Hadden Moore intimidate me."

Momentarily silent, Brady checked his watch and said, "Okay. Stansky and I need to follow up on some things, too. I'll come back to pick you up before you leave."

"That isn't necessary. DeMassio can take me home."

"Clark will be on duty by then, but I'll take you home."

"Brady—"

"I said, I'll take you home."

Surprising her, Brady curved his arm around her and walked her toward the door as he continued, "If you decide you want to leave here any earlier, call me and let me know."

"I won't. I told you, I'm going to work the rest of the day."

"All right." Brady's arm tightened around her as they reached the doorway. He leaned toward her unexpectedly and kissed her. His mouth lingered briefly on hers, the reluctance in his gaze as he drew back striking a similar chord inside her as he said, "I'll see you tonight. If you remember anything else in the meantime, call me."

Turning toward Dr. Ruberg as the concerned woman approached, Natalie did not see the intense instructions Brady gave DeMassio before he and Stansky strode toward the street.

"I NEED A LIST of all the Internet cafés in Manhattan, starting with those in the general vicinity of Natalie's residence, O'Reilly." Holding his cell phone to his ear as Stansky guided their car deftly through the heavy afternoon traffic, Brady ordered, "When you get it, fax it to me here in the car and we'll split it up between the rest of the task force so we can cover the locations as quickly as possible. We might get lucky."

Brady hung up and turned toward Stansky. "It doesn't

make sense that Moore would send that e-mail to Natalie from his own computer with the thought that we might be able to trace it back to him somehow. Unless I miss my guess, he used an Internet café."

"I don't like the sound of this, Brady." Stansky's fair complexion flushed as he offered, "I know you won't want to hear what I'm going to say since you've got a personal interest in this case—"

Brady glared when Stansky hesitated, but Stansky persisted, "Natalie said Moore's tone was almost deferential. That change in tone sounds ominous to me. Moore despised her enough to want to kill her just a few months ago. Now he's saying he admires her intellect and the progress she's making in her research. And he wants to meet with her…"

Brady nodded, his jaw tight. "The problem is, I don't know which is a greater menace—his open threat on Natalie's life, or his claim to admire her."

"Of course, it could be a ploy to gain Natalie's confidence."

"That's crazy, and you know it. Moore's an intelligent man. He can't possibly hope to gain the confidence of a woman he tried to kill."

"Yeah, but we both know Moore's isn't functioning on all circuits."

Brady gave a harsh laugh. "And he can still run circles around us intellectually."

"But not rationally. That's where we can get him…with reason. Speaking of reason," Stansky said, "do you remember that list of British import specialty stores we were covering in the hope that the management might be able to recognize Moore as one of their customers?" At Brady's nod, Stansky continued. "I happen to know there's an Internet café just a few stores down from one of the most popular British stores in Manhattan—Ronald's Beef and Bitters."

Brady glanced at Stansky. "Let's go."

NATALIE FOLLOWED Brady wearily through the apartment doorway. More exhausted than she was prepared to admit, she had barely managed a courteous few words to Officer Dillon, who stood outside the door. But it appeared from the responsive smile he flashed that the quiet officer more than understood. She stood in the apartment foyer and patted an exuberant Sarah as she waited for Brady to do a cursory sweep of the rooms, a precaution he refused to surrender despite the fact that the apartment did not go unsurveilled during the day.

Waiting only until Brady returned to motion her forward, Natalie hung up her coat and closed the closet door. She watched as Brady made a phone call that would bring a dog walker to take Sarah out, then waited again. Brady had been unusually silent as they had driven home from the lab. She knew that wasn't a good sign, and she wasn't sure if she was up for any more bad news that day.

The day had turned out to be excruciatingly long after Brady left. Her conversation with Dr. Ruberg and Dr. Gregory had been positive and supportive in every way, but it had left her feeling strangely depressed. Their enthusiasm for her work appeared undaunted, but the feeling that she was presently more of a problem for them than they deserved remained. She had spent the rest of the day attempting to prove her worth but had been unable to concentrate, and the day had turned out to be a total waste. It occurred to her as she misplaced another essential series of notes that Brady had probably been right. She should have gone back to the apartment to pull herself together—but that would have meant surrendering to Moore's terrorizing tactics, which was no longer an option.

Brady turned toward her and, not ready to hear what he had to say, she offered as lightly as she could manage, "I'll order out. There's a great Portuguese place one of the technicians at work told me about that does takeout. It'll be something different." She paused when Brady made no response. She swallowed tightly when he looked at her without a trace of a smile and said, "I think you should rethink that safe house offer, Natalie."

"No."

"Don't be stubborn!" Angrily closing the distance between them, Brady grasped her arms and warned, "You said it yourself. Moore's tone toward you has changed. He's getting increasingly unpredictable. You're protected here, but it's impossible to estimate what he's going to try next."

"No."

"He said he admires you, Natalie. He said your work is brilliant and the attention you're getting for your research into the West Nile virus is stimulating to him."

"He didn't use that word."

"That's a technicality, and you know it! By the way, our computer lab was able to retrieve your e-mail and to locate its source."

Natalie's heart leaped. "Well?"

"It came from an Internet café not far from the lab." At Natalie's gasp, he said flatly, "And nobody remembers anybody that resembled Hadden Moore ever being there."

Natalie's legs went out from under her, and she sat abruptly. Brady sat beside her and said, "So, now you know how close he can get to you without our knowledge. He's probably been closer than that, considering he seems to have a pipeline into your life that we haven't discovered yet."

"But he can't touch me…you said that yourself. If he could, he wouldn't be sending me e-mails."

"The way things are going, it's just a matter of time."

Natalie stared into Brady's sober gaze. She responded without emotion, "So you're telling me you're giving up."

"No, I'm not! I'm telling you you'll be safer if you're at a location where Moore can't find you. We'll get him, Natalie, but your safety is the major concern here."

"I'm as safe as I'll ever be when I'm here with you."

"Natalie…" Brady's full lips twitched with suppressed emotion.

"I know you'll do your best for me."

"That's not the point."

"It *is* the point." Breathing heavily, unaware of the hoarseness that had crept into her voice, Natalie whispered, "I want to be with you, Brady."

"I can't be with you all the time. The investigation is going forward, tediously slowly, and I need to be a part of it."

"That's good enough for me."

"It shouldn't be!" Brady smoothed back a dark strand of hair from her face as he whispered, "I want to know you're safe. I want to be certain that Moore can't get to you. That sick bastard's feelings for you are turning from hatred to admiration, Natalie."

"That doesn't make any difference to me."

"It should. You know what happened to the last woman who turned him down."

Natalie's breathing seemed to stop.

"Natalie?"

Natalie took a shuddering breath. "No safe house. I want to stay here with you."

"Natalie…dammit!"

Brady crushed her breathlessly close. He kissed her—hard, pent-up feelings and frustrations driving his kiss deeper as Natalie's response surged with unexpected heat. This was what she wanted…Brady's arms around her, Brady's touch against her skin, Brady's deep voice whispering soft intimacies that settled in her heart. This was what she needed…to know he wanted her as much as she wanted him.

Brady separated himself from her abruptly to whisper, "Making love won't make it all go away, Natalie."

"Making love with you is right, Brady, no matter where or when." She curled her hand around his neck as she whispered, "Tell me it's right for you, too, so at least that much will be right with my world."

"Hell, Natalie, I don't want to—"

Brady's head snapped upright when he heard a knock on the hallway door. On his feet in a moment, his hand on the gun at his waist, he asked, "What is it?"

"The dog walker is here, Detective."

Natalie heard Brady's soft curse as he jerked the leash off the hall chair and snapped it onto Sarah's collar. She glimpsed the smiling teenager who accepted the leash and noted that Officer Dillon made a point of looking in the opposite direction as Brady pushed the door closed.

Natalie stood up tentatively as Brady approached and said, "She'll bring Sarah back in fifteen minutes." When Natalie did not move, he said, "That's all the time I'll need right now."

The bedroom door closed behind them, and Brady pushed her back against it as gently as his trembling hands could manage. He kissed her, his mouth driving deeper as he lifted her skirt and pulled down her panties. He stopped to reach for one of the condoms they'd put in the dresser drawer, and then she felt him against her, hard and firm as he nudged the moist heat between her legs and slid himself inside her.

Natalie clung to him. She met Brady's powerful impetus with her own. The groan that escaped her lips when he sank himself deeper was magnified a thousand times inside her mind as their heated frenzy accelerated, then burst into mutual culmination that left them breathless.

Brady withdrew himself from her. Still holding her close, he pressed his lips against her eyelids, her temple, the curve of her cheek. He brushed her mouth with his as he whispered, "I want you to be safe, Natalie. I need to know nothing will happen to you."

"It won't, as long as we're together."

Brady looked down at her as he drew back. She glimpsed something akin to pain in his eyes as he said, "Did it ever occur to you that your 'security blanket' might not always be as secure as you think it is?"

"Don't talk to me about security blankets, Brady. As a matter of fact," Natalie whispered as she raised her mouth to his, "please, don't talk at all."

TWILIGHT WAS FADING into night when Hadden stood still, silently reviewing the day's events in his mind. The e-mail he had sent to Natalie had been inspired. She wasn't sure whether she could trust what he had said yet, but he would soon convince her otherwise.

Hadden smiled at the providence that had intervened that day on the street when she survived his softly spoken farewell. Providence…because he knew now that the last thing he wanted to say to Natalie was goodbye.

Hadden's smile dimmed. Her most recent choices did not please him. Brady Tomasini functioned adequately as a detective…and perhaps as a man, as far as Natalie was concerned, but his own expertise was such that he would be able to do so much more for her than that simple fellow could.

Natalie was so bright, yet she did not seem to be smart enough to realize that Tomasini was taking full advantage of his present position in her life. That reality might have angered him, if not for the realization that he probably would have done the same thing had the opportunity presented itself to him. Subsequently, he could not help but admire Tomasini for seizing the moment, tenure that was temporary, after all.

He had great plans for Natalie; yet Hadden knew she needed more time. His messages to her would begin to cause doubts in her mind. She would look at the scientific contributions he had made in the lab, at his worth in the future, and she would begin wondering if he had not, indeed, been justified in what he did.

A few more convincing notes, a little more gentle persuasion, and he would arrange for them to meet. His eloquence would win out in the end.

Chapter Twelve

Natalie walked into her apartment and watched as Officer Dillon did a cursory check, clearing one room and then entering the next. She didn't doubt for a minute that it was safe since Sarah had been protecting it throughout the day, but Jeremy Dillon was a nice, quiet young officer who was determined to do his job. He'd had a difficult time of it lately. Divorce from his childhood sweetheart had hit him hard. With no family remaining in the area to hold him, he had moved to the city to start over. A rainy night, an unexpectedly slippery road and brakes that didn't hold had kept him from starting on the job for several months, which had made his transition even more difficult. She supposed the physical trauma he suffered was part of the reason he had been assigned less active duty on her guard detail. At any rate, he was efficient and determined to please, and she liked him.

Natalie waited until Jeremy signaled that the rooms were clear and turned over the watch to Officer McMullen, who waited at the door. She reached into her pocketbook when the door closed, remembering the innocent smile on the face of the young lab assistant who had given her the letter that had been incorrectly addressed to her.

Natalie had recognized the handwriting immediately. Yet for a reason she did not quite comprehend, she did not open it at once. The envelope had pressed against her thigh in the pocket of the oversized lab coat she wore as the horrendous details of the past two weeks returned to haunt her.

Actually, seventeen days had passed since she'd received Hadden Moore's e-mail, yet it felt like a lifetime. Moore's next communication—delivered by regular mail—had arrived only a few days later. The letter, dropped in a mailbox located only a few streets from Natalie's residence, made it clear that Moore was too smart to ever use that café again.

Moore's letters urging that they meet began arriving only days apart after that.

She remembered the cold knot of fear that settled in the pit of her stomach when she found the second note from Moore underneath a stack of papers on her workstation at the lab only a few days later. The note directed boldly that in order to signify she was willing to meet with him, she need only hang a scarf in her bedroom window that faced the street, and he would take care of the rest. A thorough search of the lab building had been a waste of time, as had been a review of the surveillance tapes of the corridors. Moore's manner of access to the building had not been ascertained.

The third note was slipped under the door of her apartment building superintendent. Again, surveillance tapes were no help.

With the fourth note, delivered by overnight mail, Moore's deferential tone urging that they meet started to change. He hinted at a series of incidents that would begin occurring in the city—frightening incidents that would continue until she consented to meet with him.

In the fifth note, terrifyingly discovered in a bag of take-out food Brady and she had ordered, Moore's threats continued.

Natalie's blood ran cold when the first, near fatal incident occurred—when a rising female executive of a Fortune 500 company was almost pushed to her death beneath a subway car by an unseen hand—only to be pulled back to safety at the last moment. The incident was confirmed as Moore's handiwork when the woman found a note in her pocket carefully and succinctly inscribed in Moore's easily identifiable handwriting, reading:

Regards,
HM

With the sixth note, Moore returned to a more reliable source for delivery—the U.S. mail. The note, mailed in Staten Island, warned that her time to make a decision to meet him was growing short. It stated that the next incident would be fatal, and the fault would be hers. When she did not respond, a homeless man was found brutally stabbed only a few blocks from Natalie's residence. In his pocket was a note in Moore's familiar script that read:

I warned you, Natalie.

Brady insisted that the man's death was not her fault; that Moore, a psychopath whose thought processes were too convoluted to understand, was to blame. Yet in her heart, she felt the homeless fellow's blood was on her hands.

Natalie stared at Moore's latest note. It read:

My dearest Natalie,

I regret the steps I have been forced to take in order to convince you how important it is to me that we should meet. We have so much in common and so much to discuss. I know that once I have been able to talk to you and plead my case to you in person, you will understand the motivation for all I have done. I know you will absolve me of blame then. I am confident of it.

Unfortunately, you leave me no alternative but to warn you again of the dire result if you do not accede to my request. I have chosen a public official as my next objective—someone we all are familiar with—to prove my certainty that a meeting between us is essential to both our futures. His death will be on your conscience if you delay, for it surely will not be on mine.

I am aware that thus far, you have turned my letters over to the task force and your intimate friend, Detective Tomasini, but I suggest more caution in the future if we are to meet. I know I can depend on your prudence.

A simple meeting and a few words of discussion are all I ask. I know this is not an easy decision for you to make. I will give you three days before the unsuspecting public official suffers for your indecision.

I await your signal.

HM

Natalie stared at the carefully composed letter. She had no choice. She knew what she must do.

BRADY STRUGGLED to control his ire as he crossed the squad room and approached the conference room where Captain Wilthauer had summoned the squad to meet. He glanced at Stansky as the smaller man walked beside him. Stansky's expression was noncommittal. His partner had not balked at the extra time the meeting was destined to waste or the danger involved in the case. It occurred to Brady that Stansky was the voice of reason in a crazy situation that grew crazier every day. Although Stansky was not personally as heavily invested in the case as Brady was, Stansky was as dedicated to apprehending Moore as Brady was, something that did not escape Brady's notice. That said it all about Stansky's professionalism.

But Stansky's laid-back attitude in the face of his own current annoyance just ticked him off.

It had been more than two weeks of daily morning meetings and intense scrutiny of every detail of the case since Natalie received her first communication from Hadden Moore; yet they were no closer to apprehending the man than they were before.

Natalie remained adamant in her refusal to consent to a safe house, even when Moore's notes began arriving regularly, only days apart. She refused to budge, even after Moore began to make homicidal threats and then carry them out.

Several days had passed since Moore's last communication. Another one was due to arrive soon. Already pounds lighter, Natalie had suffered greatly. He was not sure how much more she could take.

As he neared the conference room, Brady remarked, "The squad room is empty. Wilthauer must have a full house in there. I hope he has something important to add to this case, because we sure don't."

Brady pushed open the door and scanned the congested quarters. His gaze halted abruptly at the sight of Natalie standing beside Captain Wilthauer in the front of the room. She had left for the lab as usual that morning, but she obviously hadn't gone there.

Stansky entered and took an empty seat while Brady pushed the door closed behind him. It occurred to him that Stansky knew what this meeting was all about.

He was beginning to suspect he did, too.

All eyes turned in his direction. The most sober and uncertain was Natalie's gaze. He read the silent plea for understanding in her eyes…and he knew instinctively that he was right.

"I DON'T LIKE THIS. No matter what Captain Wilthauer says, the plan isn't foolproof!"

Brady waited for Natalie's response as they dressed in the silence of the apartment bedroom. He knew the moment Natalie looked at him that further argument was a waste of time. Under other circumstances, he might be pleased at the anticipation of a night out with Natalie, even if they were going to the *opera*. She had dressed carefully for the occasion, with a simple black dress that bared her neck just enough to reveal her delicate bone structure and clung to her slenderness just enough to make his heart jump a beat. With her hair hanging loose against her shoulders in a casual style that framed her face, with a minimum of makeup and wearing only an oversize pin to complement her diamond stud earrings, she looked…beautiful.

But it galled him that she had dressed for Hadden Moore—not for him.

Brady persisted, "This is a mistake, Natalie. Too many things can go wrong."

Natalie turned to face him fully, her face paler than usual as she said, "Do I really have a choice, Brady?"

"Yes, you do. You've had a choice from the beginning. You don't have to put your life in jeopardy. We'll catch Moore. It's just a matter of time."

"A matter of time until you get him…and many people might die while he proves he means what he says." She shook her head, appearing suddenly incredulous. "I don't really know how all this came about. It's like a dream, a nightmare that I can't escape, but if Moore kills even one more person to prove his point, I'll know it's my fault because I could've saved him."

Brady stared at her intently without replying. It had been a nightmare come true, all right, when he walked into that conference room several days earlier and found everyone waiting. He had known the moment he saw the expressions of the men that Captain Wilthauer had made a decision superseding Brady's command of the case. He had argued his point vehemently—the wrongness of accepting a situation planned by the perpetrator of several murders; the countless unforeseen circumstances that could turn the situation to Moore's favor despite all their careful planning; and lastly, but most importantly, the danger to Natalie. Yet when all was said and done, Natalie was determined to take the chance that the trap Wilthauer had devised to apprehend Moore would work.

Natalie hung her scarf in the bedroom window after he left for work the following morning. She removed it before he returned at night in an attempt to make Moore believe neither Brady nor the task force knew she had finally acceded to his plan. Everyone, including himself, however, suspected Moore knew everything that was going on. The only thing they had been unable to ascertain was *how* he knew so much. The fact that a surveillance camera and several officers attached to the task force were on duty around the clock, watching for suspicious vehicles or persons who might attempt to observe Natalie's signal in the window, did not afford him peace of mind or any clues. Nor did the tight security of the operation or a second sweep of the apartment and Natalie's workplace for a listening device that Moore might somehow have planted there. Two days later, Natalie found a note from Hadden Moore concealed between slices of lunch meat in the sandwich she had ordered at the lab. It read:

Dear Natalie,

 I was pleased to see your signal. We may now begin. I know you are a devotee of the opera, as am I. Ask Detective Tomasini to take you to the Met to see *La Traviata* on Saturday. Tell him you need respite from the tension you've been under, and this is the last week *La Traviata* is being performed. I know Verdi is your favorite, Natalie, which will make the request more convincing. He'll find it impossible to refuse you. I'll take care of the rest.

HM

No, he didn't like it at all! Despite the care that had been taken to make it appear that Natalie was following Moore's directions and meeting him on his terms, he could not make himself believe Moore would be foolish enough to believe Natalie would agree to meet him.

Yet the evening was about to go into play.

Brady reached for his jacket and shrugged it on. He saw a hint of moisture in Natalie's eyes as she whispered unexpectedly, "You look handsome, Brady."

"But not handsome enough to make you listen to me."

"Brady, please." Natalie repeated, "I'll be guarded well. You said so yourself. Moore will expect to see the familiar faces of the uniformed officers in my protection detail posted at the Met, but he won't know there are plainclothes detectives stationed all over the theater waiting for him to make his move. He can't possibly escape if he approaches me." She hesitated as she reached for the device lying on the dresser nearby. She frowned, aware that it had been hastily modified to be practically invisible in her small ear as she added, "And if I can insert this thing correctly, I'll know exactly where the task force is at all times."

Brady adjusted his earpiece. His device was more visible, enabling him to communicate with the task force both ways throughout the night. Wilthauer had agreed with him that Moore would easily accept that situation as the norm under the circumstances and that Moore might, in fact, become suspicious otherwise.

Noting that Natalie still struggled with the unfamiliar earpiece, he adjusted it, his fingers lingering against her skin as he said softly, "Captain Wilthauer will start transmitting as soon as we step out onto the street. Moore is crazy if he thinks he can pull this off." He added with a half smile as he ran his fingertips down the column of her throat, "But we already know that, don't we?"

"You'll get him this time. I'm sure of it."

Natalie's forced bravado almost more than he could bear, Brady pulled her into his arms. He pressed her tight against him and whispered against her lips, "You're damned right, we'll get him. I don't intend giving you up to that crazy bastard. That should be your greatest guarantee that I won't let anything happen to you."

He kissed her then, long and hungrily. He felt her shudder when he released her and said, "Okay, if you're determined to do this, let's get started."

SHE DIDN'T KNOW how Moore had known, but *La Traviata* was truly one of her favorite operas.

Natalie clutched Brady's hand as they sat in the crowded theater humming with expectant conversation. Under different circumstances she would be thoroughly enjoying the evening. The Metropolitan Opera House was renowned throughout the world, and the opportunity to experience its splendor again firsthand, especially with Brady beside her, would have made it a night to remember. She feared, however, that this evening would not be one she would enjoy reliving in the future.

She was seated directly in the center of the first row mezzanine, the most handsome man in the theater was holding her hand and the overture was about to begin—yet any enjoyment she might have experienced was negated by the grating sound of Captain Wilthauer's gruff tones in her ear as he directed the activity of plainclothes detectives stationed around the building.

Natalie turned a tentative smile in Brady's direction and

he leaned toward her and kissed her cheek unexpectedly. He appeared thoroughly composed, as if he were enjoying himself, which she knew couldn't be any further from the truth. She realized for the first time that along with his other talents, Brady was the consummate actor, another facet of his expertise that she had not anticipated.

Natalie felt the hush as glittering starburst chandeliers strategically placed to catch the eye ascended dramatically toward the textured gold ceiling of the theater, signaling that the performance was about to begin. Applause echoed from every quarter of the audience as the tuxedo-clad conductor entered the pit. The applause stilled, the audience went silent as the conductor raised his baton, and the first few notes of the overture swelled to life.

Natalie's heartbeat quickened despite herself as strains of the familiar musical masterpiece filled the theater and the tragic story of Violetta and Alfredo prepared to enfold. Captain Wilthauer's voice in her ear cut abruptly into her appreciation and Natalie crashed back to reality. She wasn't there tonight to enjoy the performance. Hadden Moore, an unrepentant murderer, was listening to the same soaring melody with only one thought in mind.

That reality sent chills down her spine.

Natalie forced a smile as she struggled to resist the waves of fear suddenly threatening to inundate her. Brady squeezed her hand and she turned toward him. His concern was obvious as he searched her face, and Natalie was suddenly ashamed. Brady's responsibility in the case touched so many more levels than her own, yet his only thought at that moment was for her. She needed to put an end to the torment that now directed every aspect of their lives, both for themselves and for the many innocents who had suffered because of Moore's ever expanding psychosis.

Natalie squeezed Brady's hand in return, her resolve restored. Brady resumed his pretended absorption in the performance and she did the same, yet the minutes crept by with agonizing slowness.

A sudden, crackling blast of sound in her earpiece caused Natalie to jump with a start. She touched her aching ear spontaneously, noting Brady's similar reaction as she did. Relieved when the crackling stopped, she noticed that Brady still covertly tapped his ear. At her concerned glance, he leaned toward her and whispered, "A temporary glitch. Wilthauer will fix it."

When Brady continued to frown, Natalie leaned toward him and whispered, "My earpiece seems okay now."

The annoyed stirring of patrons seated nearby moved Natalie back in her seat before Brady could reply.

Gratified when the end of the first act was drawing to a close, Natalie was startled by the sound of an unexpected, highly accented English voice in her earpiece that asked, "Do you hear me, Natalie?"

Natalie glanced at Brady, then looked spontaneously around the theater. The voice commented, "Yes, I can see by your reaction that you do." The voice confirmed her greatest fear by adding, "It is I, Hadden Moore."

Barely restraining a gasp, Natalie risked a glance at Brady, but he showed no reaction to the voice she heard as he continued to tap his earpiece covertly. Unable to resist another glance around the theater, Natalie went still as the carefully enunciated tones warned, "You're wasting your time. You can't see me, and Detective Tomasini can't hear me. No one else on the task force placed so strategically in the audience can hear me, either. It isn't a difficult task to jam devices as primitive as those Captain Wilthauer provided. The fact that your earpiece required adjustment to fit your delicate ear enabled me to just as easily modify the wiring so the jamming would not affect you. So you see, Natalie, no one can hear me but you."

Natalie sneaked a terrified glance at Brady to see that he was still tapping his ear covertly. She felt the rise of panic as Moore cautioned, "I know you are stunned to hear my voice and are uncertain how to react, but I urge you not to make a mistake you will regret. You must have realized that I would not place myself in a situation I could not control. Although I have great plans for our discussion, I must remind you that I do not take disappointment lightly."

Moore allowed a few moments for her to absorb his veiled threat as the conclusion of the first act neared. Continuing, he warned, "Listen to me carefully, Natalie. I ask you to keep foremost in your mind that the life of the one you hold most dear may depend on it."

Natalie went rigid and Brady turned toward her. He whispered, "Is something wrong, Natalie?"

The cold knot of fear inside Natalie tightened. She wanted to tell him! She wanted to scream that a maniac was talking in her ear, insinuating he would kill him—Brady—if she didn't do what he said, but her voice froze in her throat.

As if reading her mind, Hadden cautioned, "Don't do it, Natalie. It would be wise for you to remember that I do not tolerate failure."

When Brady frowned at her silence, Natalie managed to whisper, "I'm fine."

Aware that she had no option, Natalie did not move as Moore continued in a voice sharp with command, "Listen carefully and follow my instructions exactly. When the first act ends, tell Detective Tomasini that you need to visit the restroom. He'll accompany you and wait in the hallway while the rest of the task force moves into predefined positions. The ladies' restroom will be crowded. The line will doubtlessly extend into the hallway. You will wait patiently, but once out of Detective Tomasini's sight, you will go directly to the supply closet inside and remove the coat, felt hat, eyeglasses and boots you find there. Don't worry about Officer Black. I'll take care of her. Put them on, making sure to tuck your hair out of sight. You needn't worry that any of the other women there will spare you more than a few moments' thought. Unusual behavior is the norm in this city. You will then pull the brim of the hat down low over your forehead and wait for the fire alarm to sound. With the terrorist threat ever present in the city, the common herd inside will panic. The women will pull on whatever outerwear they are carrying and will run helter-skelter as they try to either save themselves or find their escorts. You will take advantage of the pandemonium by following the crowd out of the restroom and down the staircase to the floors below that allow access to the street."

As if in response to her unspoken question, Hadden warned, "Detective Tomasini will be waiting for you to emerge, but neither he nor any other members of the task force will be looking for a dowdy woman in a plaid coat and fur-trimmed boots. It will take Tomasini a few minutes to realize you've managed to slip away from him, and precious minutes longer until he's able to alert the task force to your disappearance. By that time, you will have followed the frantic rush toward the floor below street level, where you will exit the building unrecognized, turn right, and start toward the parking garage. Keep walking when you enter the garage."

"Natalie…?"

Natalie turned sharply toward Brady. She felt her color draining under his scrutiny and managed, "I'm sorry, Brady. It looks like I'm not as brave as I thought."

"Shhhhh!"

Ignoring the harsh admonition from a seat nearby, Natalie sat motionless, her heart thundering until the curtain fell on the first act.

BRADY SCANNED the crowded upper lobby as the first inter-mission progressed to a social gathering that included laughing patrons milling with drinks in hand and light, more-than-obvious flirtations. He glanced at the line extending beyond the ladies' room door and shook his head. It didn't seem to matter whether it was a local hot spot or a high-class theater like the Met—there always seemed to be a line at the ladies' room door. He unconsciously wondered why no one thought to find a way to combat that problem, but he supposed it was a problem that no one felt necessary to solve.

Brady spotted Detective O'Reilly moving casually in the crowd on the floor below. He caught the man's eye and raised his hand inconspicuously to tap his ear. O'Reilly did the same, indicating that he was having the same trouble with his earpiece. Great. If it had been up to him, he would have called the whole operation to a halt then and there, but he knew what Natalie's answer to that would be.

Brady's agitation stepped up a notch as Natalie moved patiently toward the ladies' room inner sanctum. Officer Rhonda Black, who was dressed as a patron and who had been stationed for quick accessibility to the ladies' room on that floor, had covertly informed him that she'd been summoned downstairs to get replacement listening devices for the team on that level.

It occurred to him that there wasn't a woman on that line who could touch her—not that blonde with the tight red dress and her carefully arranged *casual* hairdo, or that brunette wearing a suit that had obviously cost a week's pay. Hell, with little effort involved, Natalie had it all…and he was crazy about her.

Natalie slipped from sight beyond the restroom door, and Brady tensed. He consoled himself that Wilthauer had checked the building plans cautiously and the restroom had no alternate entrance. Natalie would have to come out the same door she went in. Any threat would have to come from another direction. Still, he'd feel better when Officer Black returned.

A fire alarm sounded, breaking into Brady's thoughts as instant pandemonium began. His earpiece still dead, there was no information forthcoming from central command, but he felt in his gut that the fire alarm was being used as a distraction despite Wilthauer's precautions to the contrary.

Snapping into action, Brady charged into the ladies' room as frantic women rushed past him in an effort to get out. When he did not see Natalie in the outer room, he ignored angry protests and pushed his way into the lavatory area, calling Natalie's name. With angry squeals his only reply, he pounded on the few closed doors remaining, his jaw tightening when the last one opened to reveal an irate, white-haired woman who shoved him aside with an expletive and headed for the exit.

Panicking, Brady emerged into the upper lobby cursing his own stupidity at the realization that Natalie had to have been somewhere in the throng that had pushed past him as he entered the ladies' room. He glanced at O'Reilly as the breathless detective ran up the stairs toward him, noting that Potter was not far behind. O'Reilly was tapping his earpiece, and it was suddenly clear that the jamming of communication between task force personnel was no accident. He glanced at the last stragglers moving rapidly down the staircases, then at the mezzanine balcony that appeared to have emptied. With the breakdown in communication, there was no way to warn other task force members what had happened, no way to know what areas of the building were being covered in the present state of emergency, or if Natalie had possibly been spotted anywhere in the building.

Natalie was gone. He had no idea how she had managed to slip past him.

More important, he had no idea why.

FRANTIC PATRONS thundered down the staircase beside her, but Natalie was hardly aware of the terror surrounding her as the fire alarm blasted, raising the panic level ever higher. She did not bother to stop when her glasses were knocked off in the rush. An older woman beside her faltered on the stairs, but Natalie didn't stop to help. She wished she could tell them all that the alarm was just a strategy mercilessly employed by a madman who would not stop at murder to satisfy his egotistical demands—but she dared not.

Gratified when street level was reached and the crowd raced for the door, Natalie continued on down the stairs to the lower level. She held back a sob, remembering Brady's expression as he had pushed past her into the ladies' room.

When he had pushed right past her…

He hadn't recognized her because he hadn't thought for a moment that she might possibly exit the restroom disguised. He'd had no reason to think she'd try to escape him, and a sense of having betrayed him burned deep inside her. She had glimpsed a few other familiar faces as she had raced down the stairs. In a strange twist of fate, Detective O'Reilly and his partner had been fighting their way up the stairs as she had followed the crowd down, but they hadn't noticed her, either. She knew the panic those detectives felt had no relationship to the ceaseless din of the fire alarm. Rather, it was the realization that the worst was happening, and they had no way to stop it.

The lower-level exit doors came into view and Natalie stopped short at the sight of Officer Dillon directing frantic patrons out of the building. She would have to walk right past him in order to get to the parking garage. If she could signal him somehow—

Natalie halted that thought. If she did, the well-meaning officer would try to stop her and she could not be sure what Moore would do. There had to be a better way.

Turning as a frantic group of young women raced down the stairs, Natalie waited until they were abreast of her, then joined them as they ran toward the door. She turned her head when Dillon glanced her way, but not before she thought she saw a spark of recognition in his eyes. Slipping through the doorway as quickly as she could, she headed toward the parking garage.

Her heart pounding, Natalie stepped out onto the floor of the parking garage and stopped still, suddenly uncertain. She glanced back to see Officer Dillon still directing the last of the stragglers out of the theater.

Hope faded as she walked cautiously forward into the unexpected stillness of the garage. The area was deserted, she reasoned because most patrons would not risk getting their cars out from underneath a building that was possibly threatened.

It occurred to Natalie as she took a few more tentative steps that contrary to original plans for the evening, it was now she, instead of Hadden Moore, who was trapped.

The lights dimmed, and Natalie felt a new panic choke her throat. In the dim light, there were shadows in every corner and movement in every shadow.

Her terror mounted.

She heard footsteps behind her and she turned abruptly to see Officer Dillon approaching. Suddenly frantic when she saw he was alone, she said, "Are you crazy following me by yourself? Get out of here and get help! Moore is down here somewhere. There's no telling what he'll do if he sees you."

Unnerved when Officer Dillon continued his approach, Natalie pleaded, "Please, he'll kill us both!"

Halting a few feet away, Officer Dillon replied with a suddenly familiar, perfectly enunciated English accent that made her blood run cold, "Hadden Moore has never been a problem for me, Natalie."

Shock held Natalie motionless.

No…it couldn't be true.

But it was.

He was…Hadden Moore!

"Surprised?" Natalie stared into the face she had come to know well. She was incredulous as Moore continued, "I would have thought a woman of your intelligence would have realized who I was the moment you saw me at the Exit door—but it was inconceivable to you that the quiet, agreeable Officer Jeremy Dillon could be Hadden Moore, wasn't it? I suppose I can't really blame you. No one else suspected the truth, either."

Natalie backed up as Moore came closer and he said more sharply, "Nothing has changed, you know. The threat still remains if you refuse to accompany me willingly. I have no true desire to hurt you. I was honest when I said I simply want an opportunity to explain my motivations to you. I know you'll understand when I elucidate how much more I have to contribute to scientific research. My work at Manderling Pharmaceuticals is legend. No other researcher ever accomplished more than I did there. A breakthrough in the experiments I was conducting against cancer was imminent when Mattie Winslow entered my life. After her betrayal, I needed to clear my mind of all negative experiences so my thought processes would be free to flow. She needed to be eliminated…for the benefit of mankind."

Moore continued more softly, "I confess that I was angry when I first learned you had discovered the presence of Candoxine in the Winslow liver tissues. I considered you to be another negative experience that I needed to purge from my life, but I was wrong. I now know the reason I failed in my attempt that day on the street. I was meant to recognize my error. I admit that realization came slowly, Natalie. And when it did, I needed to be sure about you. I needed to observe you more closely, to be able to test you in so many ways. I was determined not to repeat the same mistake I made with Mattie Winslow, and I knew I could accomplish that only by getting close enough to you to observe you on a daily basis.

"It amuses me to recall how successfully I placed myself within a hairsbreadth of capture the first time I entered Detective Tomasini's precinct masquerading as a snack machine repairman. The ignoramus actually tripped over me without realizing who I was when he came in. Without his realization, the very vocal Desk Sergeant Santini was particularly helpful with all his talk about the new personnel he was expecting. It was he who inspired my present masquerade and made it so easy to accomplish. I simply removed the personnel paperwork from Sergeant Santini's desk when he stepped away and tucked it into my repair kit to be studied later. It amused me to learn how he complained about misplacing it afterward, bemoaning the delay it caused—a delay that benefited me immensely.

"I perused the paperwork carefully, and Officer Jeremy Dillon proved to be a very good fit for me—a childless fellow who had gone through a recent, bitter divorce…no family…a wish to break contact with the past so he could start anew. We were of similar age and stature, and it wasn't difficult to change the color of my hair and eyes with easily available modern innovations…then surgery to liken my features to his after I disposed of him. Finally, a smashed windshield in a staged car accident which excused any remaining scars from the surgery and discouraged further comparison to the true Officer Dillon's photo, and the staging was complete."

Natalie was stunned into silence at the ease with which Moore dismissed the atrocities he had committed. Her silence caused him to comment, "I am very thorough, Natalie, which is part of the reason for my success in every field of my endeavor. In any case, my arrival at the precinct went exactly as planned. Unfortunately, your police protection had been removed and a team of private detectives had been installed in its place. It became necessary for me to provide an incident that would make Captain Wilthauer reinstate your police protection. Larry Segram was that incident. Yet even I did not anticipate the good fortune of actually being assigned to your protection detail. That was extremely fortuitous." He smiled smugly. "Everything fell so neatly into place then. The point I made of directing you to put a scarf in the window to indicate your agreement to meet me was unnecessary, considering I was privy to the task force plans, but it was a brilliant touch, don't you agree?"

Moore did not wait for Natalie's reply as he continued, "Needless to say, you passed all my tests, Natalie. Your discovery of the Candoxine presence was truly exceptional, proving your intelligence. Further scrutiny revealed that you are unusually intuitive and devoted in your work. With those qualities, I became assured that there was no limit to the heights we could reach together."

Moore added with a deadening glint in his gaze, "I admit to becoming increasingly aware of your beauty—which grows greater upon close scrutiny—but you are not a slave to the mirror, which gratified me. I also found you to be kind and generous in most cases, certainly courageous, and surprisingly moral, although you are not above the pleasures of the flesh. That also pleased me, despite your poor choice of lovers, because I know I will be able to satisfy you far more adequately than the common detective you settled for out of fear and desperation."

Finding her voice, Natalie retorted, "You're wrong about me. There's no way I *settled* for Brady, and there's no way I'll *settle* for you!"

"And you are loyal. I find that quality particularly charming in light of my past experience. In short, you have none of Mattie Winslow's negative characteristics."

Suddenly frowning, Moore said, "But we can discuss all this in detail later. Your detective has doubtlessly informed the task force that you're missing by now. This area will be searched as soon as the fire alarm is verified as false. Fortunately, I had the foresight to park my police car out of view here. No one will stop a uniformed policeman as he pulls away from the building; and by the time that error is discovered, we'll be untraceable."

Hardly aware that she was trembling, Natalie responded, "What makes you think I'll go with you? You know my intention was that you would be apprehended and I would be free of you."

"That is what you choose to make yourself believe, but I observed your growing fascination with my letters. When you held back that one letter, refusing to read it until you were alone—then kept it a secret from your lover until the decision to meet me was irreversible—I knew I had won."

Natalie took another backward step as Moore drew his gun from his holster and said, "I regret having to do this, but I feel I must inform you that I am not adverse to using this primitive weapon if you attempt to call attention to us as we leave. I must also remind you that should you choose to ignore my warning, the blood shed will not only be your own."

Natalie glanced desperately around the deserted garage. Her mind went blank when Moore pressed the cold muzzle of the gun into her back and urged her forward. Walking behind her, he repeated, "I regret this necessity, Natalie. I promise to make it up to you."

Horror filled Natalie's mind as she turned a corner in the garage and saw a police car parked there just as Moore had said. She couldn't let this happen! There had to be a way!

Natalie's heartbeat rose to a roar in her ears when they

reached the car. She looked up as Moore pulled the car door partially open and motioned her inside with his gun hand.

Natalie flushed with a sudden rage.

No, she wouldn't go!

Slamming the car door back against him unexpectedly, Natalie heard Moore's pained cry as the sharp corner of the door struck the muscle in his thigh, knocking his leg out from under him.

Natalie burst into a run without looking back. She ran breathtakingly fast, dodging between the maze of parked cars in a blind attempt to escape. Her throat choking with the sudden fear that she was running in circles and getting no closer to escape, she ducked into the shadows and remained motionless in an attempt to gain perspective.

Panicking when she heard stealthy footsteps growing gradually closer, she darted from her hiding place and started to run again.

The realization that the stealthy footsteps had broken into a run behind her, that they were gaining on her, became a terror that caused her to look back at her pursuer.

She gasped.

Brady!

She stopped running with a sob of relief as Brady reached her side. She did not move when he silenced her with a finger to his lips before pushing her behind him as they faded into the shadows.

Emerging into sight within moments, Moore limped toward them. Waiting until Moore was abreast of them, Brady stepped into view with the command, "Drop your gun, Moore."

His face distorted with fury, Moore was about to raise his gun when Brady knocked his weapon from his hand. Turning in a flash of unexpected movement, Moore struck out wildly, and Brady staggered backward.

Unable to move, Natalie watched as the two men struggled for the gun Brady still held in his hand. A gunshot blast rocked the violent tableau that suddenly went still.

Unable to breathe, Natalie watched as Hadden Moore turned back toward her with a vicious smile that faded as he fell heavily to the ground.

The sound of heavy, running footsteps stopping abruptly beside them…Wilthauer's voice barking sharp commands… uniformed officers encircling them…a detective kneeling beside Hadden Moore's body before standing up again with a negative shake of his head—Natalie was unconscious of it all as Brady's arms closed around her.

Chapter Thirteen

Brady drove cautiously northward on the icy roadway. It was cold outside. It had snowed again the previous week and a high snowbank lined the highway where snowplows had obviously been exceedingly active. Not a flake of the frozen mass appeared to have melted. He supposed that condition would continue for another month at least, considering the difficult winter weather since the season had started.

But it was warm and comfortable in the car. The "elevator music" presently playing on the stereo was a compromise between the classical compositions Natalie favored and the hard rock better suiting his sensibilities, but neither of them was complaining.

Brady glanced at Natalie where she sat silently beside him. They had been driving for a few hours, hoping to get a jump on the traffic. They'd soon be arriving at their destination, and the Candoxine case would be officially closed at last.

Natalie glanced at him. Her eyes looked troubled and his throat tightened. Damn...he loved her so much that it hurt during times like this when he was so close to her, yet was unable to ease her distress. He had half a mind to pull over to the side of the highway and chase that look from her eyes in the best way he knew how.

Natalie flashed a reluctant smile. "Keep your eyes on the road, Brady. We're almost there."

"Reading my mind again, huh?"

"I don't pretend to be a mind reader, but I've seen that look in your eye often enough to know what it means."

"Yeah?" Brady challenged, "What does it mean?"

"Do you really want to know?"

"I asked, didn't I?"

"Okay. You're looking at me as if you'd like to pull onto the shoulder of the road right now and have your way with me."

Brady took a shaky breath. "Sounds good to me."

"Sounds good to me, too, Brady."

Brady shot her a sideways look, and Natalie laughed. "Don't take me literally!"

"Too late."

Natalie flushed and avoided looking at the revealing part of him that told no lies, and his thoughts wandered. The Candoxine case had ended two months earlier with Hadden Moore dead on the floor of the parking garage. He remembered thinking as he held Natalie in his arms that she was safe at last and he'd never let her go, but doubts had slowly edged into his mind.

Natalie was a hero in the media again when news that Hadden Moore was dead broke in the press. TV, newspapers and radio were all filled with discussion of her heroism in agreeing to put her life in jeopardy in order to capture a homicidal maniac. The NYPD received nominal credit, but Natalie was the story of the month as much as she tried to avoid it.

Natalie turned to him even more completely in the aftermath, and their lovemaking was tempestuously fulfilling. She was everything he wanted in a woman and he made no attempt to change their living arrangements, while still keeping his small apartment in expectation of "the inevitable."

He recalled the night when Natalie and he had lain in bed in the afterglow of their lovemaking. Natalie's smooth, naked flesh had been pressed tightly to his and her head had lain against his chest with the scent of her hair intoxicating him even in retrospect when she had asked, "Do you love me, Brady?"

He had looked down at her to see the troubled look in her eyes that he had somehow been expecting. He had responded cautiously, "What kind of a question is that?"

"You're answering a question with a question again—which means you're avoiding the answer."

"Why would you think that?"

Natalie's clear eyes had misted. "What's the matter? Can't you make yourself say the words?"

"What words?"

Momentarily silent, Natalie had responded hoarsely, "I guess that's my answer."

Annoyed that the dim light of the room made it difficult to assess her expression completely, he had whispered, "You know how much I care about you."

"*Love,* Brady. I'm talking about *love.*"

Natalie was right. He had been unable to make himself say the words. Somewhere in the back of his mind was the thought that if he did, she would feel trapped by him…that she'd think he was looking for a long-term relationship that didn't suit her plans for the professional life she had fully earned. He figured the time would eventually come when she would start seeing him for the beer and pizza man that he was. She'd figure out that wasn't good enough for a woman with a future as bright as hers, and it would be over between them. But he didn't want to rush it. Hell, he hadn't even figured out how he'd be able to make it without her yet!

He had responded evasively, "Yeah, so…what about it?"

Natalie had jerked back from him abruptly. The blanket

had fallen away from her, exposing her small, perfect breasts as she said, "All right, forget it."

She had gotten up abruptly. He had watched the sway of her sweet backside as she walked into the bathroom. Within minutes, he heard the shower running.

Suddenly despising himself for having become a coward, he had gotten up and walked resolutely into the shower behind her. She had been wet and shiny, and more beautiful than ever with her hair plastered to her head and her lashes curling with the dampness…and he had been lost.

He had whispered huskily, "What do you want me to say, Natalie? That I love you? That you're a part of my life that I don't want to give up? That you've become the focus of every day for me…because it's true."

He remembered the look on Natalie's face when she'd said almost incredulously, "Really?"

Never one to mince words, he had replied, "I said it, didn't I?"

"So why didn't you say it sooner? Why did you wait for me to ask?"

Natalie brushed the water from her face, waiting for his reply. With no other recourse but to state a truth he had avoided, he said, "Because I love you too much to corner you…and because I didn't want to put you in a position where you'd have to tell me you didn't feel the same way."

Natalie shook her head. "But I said I love you a hundred times."

"Yeah…" He had paused, uncertain if he was ready for the answer when he asked, "But do you love me enough for a lifetime?"

Natalie had gone still, staring at him as the shower pounded down on them. "Is that a proposal?"

Still wary, he had replied, "Only if you want it to be."

"Yes."

"What?"

"Yes. I accept your proposal."

He remembered the sense of disbelief that swept over him as he said, "You mean it?"

"Dammit, Brady, I mean it!"

He remembered what followed then, when they proved to each other how much those words meant and…well, he knew he'd never forget it.

Not ever.

Shortly afterwards Natalie resigned her position at the CDC in Atlanta and accepted the position Dr. Gregory had offered her. Dr. Ruberg was openly pleased, having already designated Natalie as her replacement when she retired.

Stansky was now Natalie's greatest fan. He and Janie had welcomed her into the fold and had warned him to make sure he was good to her. Par for the course.

Chuck Randolph remained his negative self when it came to Brady, but Brady didn't expect anything else from a man who had loved and lost. He amended that thought—from a *stuffed shirt* who had loved and lost. Natalie said Chuck would come around and realize he had made a mistake in judging Brady so harshly. Brady hadn't commented. He had known Natalie wouldn't like to hear that the truth was, he couldn't care less.

Aunt Charlene, the maiden aunt who had raised Natalie, was another matter. Aunt Charlene had scrutinized him from head to toe when they went back to Atlanta to visit, but there was something about the old lady he had instinctively liked. He wasn't sure if it was her outspoken honesty that reminded him of Natalie, or the fact that he had the feeling she had been prepared to dislike him and had discovered she couldn't. Whatever, he had the feeling that he'd never have to wonder what Aunt Charlene was thinking, and when Natalie and he left, he had known they'd be back.

Natalie was wearing his ring now. They were looking for their own place while secretly wishing Dr. Gregory's daughter would never take back the apartment that all three of them had grown accustomed to.

Yes, all three of them. It seemed that Natalie loved Sarah, too.

But it hadn't all come full circle yet.

Natalie interrupted Brady's thoughts as she said quietly, "I've thought it over a thousand times, and I still don't think I'll ever understand Hadden Moore's reasoning."

"Don't even try. Moore's thought processes weren't influenced by sane reasoning."

"He was a brilliant scientist, Brady. He told me that his work at the Manderling lab was legend, and it is. Manderling will probably never find another Ph.D. with his talent."

"Or with his manias."

"We'll never know what he could have accomplished."

"Except the murder of anyone else who stood in his way, you mean?"

Natalie's voice dropped to a whisper. "I know he was psychotic, and I know things couldn't have ended any other way. I'll never forget the way he rationalized the murders he committed. There was a look about him, as if he was almost proud. If it wasn't for you, Brady—" Natalie unconsciously shivered. "He would have killed me just as easily if you hadn't stopped him. I still don't understand how you managed to find me in time."

His voice touched with the self-recriminations that had silently tormented him, Brady responded, "I should've realized earlier that the Officer Dillon we knew was a fake. The mistake I made was in relying too heavily on official reports from Dillon's former law enforcement assignment and medical paperwork Moore probably managed to alter somehow. His evaluations were all extremely favorable and, taking into consideration the official report of the facial trauma he suffered in the car accident that delayed his arrival on the force, the difference in his appearance seemed minimal."

"You can't blame yourself, Brady. Moore was exceptional—a former child prodigy with many talents that went undocumented."

"It takes the average cop years to learn all the criminal justice information he seemed to absorb in a few months from the instructional volumes we found in his apartment. He shouldn't have been able to fool me."

"He fooled everyone, not only you."

"It was my case."

"Don't take that load onto your shoulders. Anyway, you're the one who figured it out in time."

Brady nodded, recalling his panic as he had stood on the mezzanine floor at the Met with the fire alarm blasting and pandemonium lending further confusion to the scene—totally at a loss as to how or why Natalie had slipped past him. He remembered that for a fraction of a second, he was unable to think past the horrifying images that flashed through his mind—until he forced himself to step back and ask himself some questions.

Exactly when had Captain Wilthauer's carefully calculated plan to catch Moore start to fall apart? That answer was simple—with the breakdown in communications between the task force members.

He remembered then that Natalie had said something to him about her earpiece having stabilized while his was still jammed. Protests from the surrounding seats had cut short further conversation between them, and his preoccupation with his earpiece had taken precedence.

It all had begun to add up then. He knew instinctively that Natalie had had no inkling of Moore's plan before they attended the performance. Moore would have needed to make some sort of contact with her so he could threaten her into following his instructions without alerting the task force. Some sort of direction would also have been necessary for her to be able to follow through on Moore's plan, and for her to be alerted in advance that the fire alarm was a diversion. The only time she could have been contacted by him in that way was *during the performance*—and the only possible answer was communication through the earpiece that had been altered to fit her ear.

Officer Dillon had delivered Natalie's altered earpiece to her personally.

Wilthauer had considered the possibility of a fire alarm being used as a diversion. In lieu of disabling them all—a proposition that was both illegal and dangerous—Wilthauer had stationed men within viewing distance of them to make certain they could not be tampered with.

Officer Dillon had been stationed near the fire alarm in the lower level of the building.

Moore would have needed to find a way for Natalie to run directly toward him despite the panic.

Officer Dillon's position was at the lower level exit of the theater.

Officer Dillon.

Everything fell into place, and Brady had raced to the lower level exit of the building where a shaken woman told him that the officer who had been directing the evacuation of the building had gone into the parking garage.

The rest was history, yet Brady could not count the number of times he'd had nightmares about what might have happened if he had arrived at the garage only a few minutes later.

Silent, Brady followed the signs and turned off the highway. Minutes later, he negotiated the curves into the main street of town.

"Brady…?"

Even the faint frown lines squeezed between Natalie's brows could not compromise the pure, honest beauty that turned him inside out with wanting her every time she looked at him.

It was love, all right.

"Brady, I think the building we're looking for is at the end of the street."

Still silent when he finally pulled into a parking space, Brady shut off the engine and turned toward Natalie. He said softly, "Are you ready?"

Waiting until she nodded, he picked up the package on the rear seat, then walked around the car and opened the door to help her out. He took her hand and squeezed it tightly as they walked toward the building.

He remembered the notice forwarded over the wire by an upstate police force advising that skeletal remains had been discovered in the Adirondack wilderness. It hadn't taken the state police long to link that report with the NYPD report on the disappearance of the genuine Officer Dillon. He remembered even more clearly the notification that the findings had been verified, and the charred remains of the former John Doe were officially declared those of Officer Jeremy Dillon.

Brady gripped Natalie's arm as they walked up the stairs toward the building housing Officer Dillon's hometown police department. She glanced up at him with a look so emotional that Brady felt his own throat tighten. Officer Dillon's personal belongings had been retained by the NYPD after they were found in Hadden Moore's apartment. They were released upon official identification of Officer Dillon's remains, but it had seemed somehow a disservice to a young police officer innocently slain by a madman to ship them home by mail.

Natalie and he had agreed to take them back personally. It seemed the least they could do.

Natalie glanced up again at Brady as they approached the desk sergeant. Brady placed the package containing all that remained of Officer Dillon's promising life on the desk, but Natalie realized in that moment that Brady still carried much more. On his broad shoulders he carried the direction of the future they would share, and in his light eyes she read the determination that he would make that future bright—because he loved her.

Despite the solemnity of the moment, Natalie felt blessed. She had found the unlikely man of her dreams.

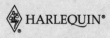

HARLEQUIN®

INTRIGUE®

The mantle of mystery beckons you to enter the…

MISTS OF FERNHAVEN

Remote and shrouded in secrecy—our new ECLIPSE trilogy by three of your favorite Harlequin Intrigue authors will have you shivering with fear and…the delightful, sensually charged atmosphere of the deep forest. Do you dare to enter?

WHEN TWILIGHT COMES
B.J. DANIELS
October 2005

THE EDGE OF ETERNITY
AMANDA STEVENS
November 2005

THE AMULET
JOANNA WAYNE
December 2005

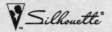

SPECIAL EDITION™

presents

the first book in a heartwarming
new series by

Kristin Hardy

Because there's
no place like home
for the holidays…

WHERE THERE'S SMOKE

(November 2005, SE#1720)

Sloane Hillyard took a very personal interest in her
work inventing fire safety equipment—after all, her
firefighter brother had died in the line of duty. And
when Boston fire captain Nick Trask signed up to
test her inventions, things got even more personal…
their mutual attraction set off alarms. But could
Sloane trust her heart to a man who risked his
life and limb day in and day out?

Available November 2005 at your favorite retail outlet.

Where love comes alive™

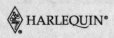